LIGHT IS THE SHADOW

A Women of Greece Novel

ALEX A. KING

Copyright © 2014 by Alex A. King

All rights reserved.

No part of this book may be reproduced in any form or by any electronic or
mechanical means, including information storage and retrieval systems,
without written permission from the author, except for the use of brief
quotations in a book review.

❀ Created with Vellum

AUTHOR'S NOTE

Like Agria, Trikeri is a real marker on a map, but every person I've put on my version of the island is a work of fiction. There is a *taverna* owner who ferries visitors to the mainland, and a resident priest at the monastery. But they are not the people in this story. And for all I know, the miracles reported by people who have seen the icon at the *Monastery of the Virgin Mary* on Trikeri are real.

For my grandmothers, Dorothy and Margarita

And for Bill and Corinne, always

PROLOGUE

Nine-year-old Lucy Shake was sitting on the toilet when the quake happened. A minor ground grumbler that rattled the china and shook pretty much nobody out of their beds.

"Mom?" she hollered.

"It's just a quake," Mom called out from the bedroom. "We live in California. Get used to it."

Get used to it. The '*or move somewhere else*' hung in the hallway separating the two rooms.

Or move somewhere else was on Lucy's mind as she crawled back into the bedroom she shared with Lana, her little sister. She planned to do that—tomorrow.

THE NEXT MORNING SHE PACKED UP HER NINE-YEAR-OLD life. Up to the attic for suitcases, into the garage for boxes. She sneezed her way back down to the bedroom. Mom caught her mid-move.

"Where are you going with those suitcases?"

"I'm running away."

"Anywhere in particular?"

"Where they don't have earthquakes."

"Everywhere has earthquakes."

Not true. *Google* said so. There were all kinds of places in the world where the ground hardly ever shook. And one of them happened to be in Denver where Grandma lived.

When she was done packing, she said to her mother, "Can you drive me to Grandma's place?"

"I thought you were running away."

"I am. But I need a ride."

Mom laughed and steered her back to her room. "First rule of running away: do it when no one's looking. Second rule of running away: find your own way there."

❧ 1 ❧

Lucy - Age 25

I<small>T TAKES A DEAD CAT TO THROW</small> L<small>UCY OUT OF HER RUT.</small>
Not her cat (she doesn't have a cat), but somebody's beloved
pet stretched across the road in a permanent snooze.

The radio is loud. The car windows up. And she's busting
her lungs singing along with Taylor Swift about how she's
never ever getting back together with whoever it is she's
never ever getting back together with.

When she sees the cat, it's too late. Whoever hit the poor
thing is long gone. Nothing left but tire tracks, long stretches
of black rubber that meant to stop but kept on going at the
last moment.

She stops the car, kills Swift's song, gets out.

Looks both ways.

It's a residential street in what city people think of as a
lazy suburb. People who say that have never been here on a

sunny weekend, when every yard is humming with home-owners mowing lawns and fixing what needs fixing.

But on a week day—a Thursday—and late morning, yeah, it's quiet in the Denver neighborhood. Which means the odds of getting hit by a car were thin to begin with.

She picks up the cat, gives its head a rub it will never know about, wraps it in the hoodie she keeps in the trunk. Then she gets back in the car, resuscitating Swift and the engine with one twist of the key.

This isn't her neighborhood. Where she lives is a few miles west, in a similarly quiet (on weekdays) neighborhood. Grandma's house.

She's been living there since ... Since she lost everyone except Grandma.

So what is she doing here?

Lucy parks a block away from where she wants to be, outside a different house to the one she parked in front of yesterday, and the day before, and the day before that. She's running out of hiding places. Well, not really hiding places. More like discreet watching places. Because that's all she's doing—all she has been doing—up until today.

Six months of watching, long fair hair tucked into a ball cap. Not one of those months less painful than its predecessors.

The house she's watching is white with green trim. Perfect lawn. Neat gardens. Roses lining the wide, clean driveway. Triple garage.

Room for three cars, but one is taking a break outside.

Doctor Kellerman's BMW 6 Series. It has the shine of a recently-detailed automobile. Except for the copper smear on its bumper. The stain of the recently, prematurely, deceased cat.

And that's when Lucy realizes she's going to screw things up, for the second time in six months.

✿ 2 ✿

Akili

HE TAKES THE BOAT OUT EARLY, LOOKING FOR FISH AND inner peace.

It's his best friend's old boat. Blue bottom, orange deck and cabin.

The gulf is flat. Crystal. Science says there are waves, but if there are he's not seeing them. Must be underneath, down below the surface. Turmoil, the push and pull of the sea, it's all a metaphor for his life.

That's why he likes being out here. No need to pretend.

He and the sea, they're the same.

Six months since his best friend, former owner of this boat—a man who was a brother to him—died.

If you can call Stavros's murder a death.

His killer confessed, but not until after Akili did his share of shoveling shit on Stavros's fiancée. Everyone thought it was her—and he did, too.

When his grief was fresh it made sense. Now ... not so much. Kiki never had murder in her.

He hasn't gone to her for forgiveness. And she would forgive him—she's that kind of good. But forgiveness is for the deserving.

What has he done to earn forgiveness from the world?

Catch fish and throw them back again, because he doesn't have it in him to kill them. But a few fish don't make up for his sins.

"You did the world a favor," Stavros says. He's sitting atop the tiny cabin, legs dangling. Squinting at the sun. Mid-summer tan. Except he died in spring, before the first swim of summer.

Stavros isn't there. He never is. But that doesn't stop his mouth moving, his words pouring out.

Akili reels his line in. Nothing on its hook. Good. Saves him the trouble of disconnecting the fish and setting it free.

He turns the boat back toward Agria. He's had enough for one day—of Stavros and the sea.

THE GATE SQUEALS ON HIM, TELLS HIS FATHER HE'S HOME. The kitchen door does the same when he slaps it open. Even the house is on his father's side.

It's not even his father's house—it's his. Mama left it to Akili when she died, and before her it belonged to his grandparents. But his father was already here, and there was no squeezing him out, into the street or into a home.

Akili is doing time, and his father is the prison.

"Is that you, Akili?" Rough voice, years of *retsina* and cigarettes.

Who else would it be? No one comes; not since Mama died three years ago.

"It's me."

"What is for lunch?"

Not fish, Akili thinks. He yanks the refrigerator open, pours a tall glass of chilled water. "I don't know."

A grunt from the living room, then his father rolls into the kitchen in his wheelchair.

Look at that old bastard. He's sixty going on a thousand, if Akili's counting the crevices on his face accurately. Akili looks and looks, but there's nothing of his old man in him. Small blessing. His father's in a sleeveless T-shirt that used to be white. Now it's a sick shade of yellow, like the old man's teeth. No black armband in sight. Where is the sign of his grief? Nowhere, that's where. He spent a week wearing the black band for his dead wife, then he cast it aside.

It's on the list of sins Akili will never forgive him for.

"Where have you been, eh?"

Akili chugs down the water. Pours a second glass. Knocks that halfway back before saying, "On the boat."

"On the boat, on the boat," his father says in a mean voice. "Always on the boat. What about your job, eh?"

"What about it?"

"How will we live if you do not go to work?"

Never mind that the old man is raking in a sweet pension, government-paid.

Akili snatches a clean apron off the kitchen counter. "On my way."

"What about lunch? What will I eat?"

"You have two hands. Cook something."

This is a life sentence. Until death do they part—his father's or his.

❧ 3 ❧

Fotini

Two women meet in a trendy Denver coffee shop, but neither orders a drink.

"You need to do something about that dog of yours, before it hurts someone."

Oh, that how is how she wants to play, eh?

"That dog is my granddaughter, and she's not normally aggressive. But you did kill her sister."

That knife twist hurts the woman, she can tell. Good.

Fotini isn't aggressive either, but she had two granddaughters and now she has one, thanks to the woman sitting in front of her. It's all she can do not to wring her neck and smile as her life fades away.

Sixty-seven-years-old and she has lost so many people. Her first and only love, her daughter, her son-in-law, and six month ago, Lana, her youngest granddaughter.

"I didn't ... I—"

"Do you know what I have discovered?"

Doctor Kellerman fidgets with the car keys in her hand. The younger woman is in her late forties. She has a bad marriage, no children, and lipstick on her top teeth. The first two Fotini knows because she excels at research. The third ... Eh, the woman is sitting across from her and her vision is not so bad that she doesn't know matte lipstick on teeth when she sees it.

"What?"

"My Lana wasn't the first patient you lost through negligence. Your medical career is littered with bodies. And I know why they still allow you to practice medicine—although all this practice does not seem to be helping you."

Arms folded. Not as effective as a shield or clanking armor, but still defensive.

"I guess you're about to tell me."

"You have family on the state medical board. More than one member of your family. And my Lana, she had no family on that board."

"I didn't—"

"Maybe you did, maybe you didn't. But for you they looked away because you are blood." She leans forward. "And I understand. I would do the same for family."

For Lucy—not her family in Greece. They can rot.

"What are you going to do with this knowledge?"

"Nothing. It's public knowledge, if you know how to look. I should tell people so they can take their health somewhere else, so the families who have lost their loved ones thanks to your *care* can take that beautiful house." If that is care—who needs it? "But I'm a selfish old woman. Lucy is all I have left. So I'm going to do nothing."

"What do you want? What's the catch?"

Ah yes, the catch. Always one of those in situations like these. And really there needs to be, because that's what the corrupt know. Show them fairness and they do not recognize its face.

"Drop the charges. Drop the restraining order against my granddaughter."

"I ... How did you know? I haven't filed it yet."

Not too bright, this one. "I have my sources."

Her source is herself, her knowledge of human behavior, and every book, movie, television show ever. People who hurl paint-filled buckets, who carve words into cars, win restraining orders. Ask *PETA*.

"What about your granddaughter? I don't want any more trouble."

"Lucy won't be a problem."

That's a promise she's not sure how to keep. Lucy is Lucy. She marches to a rhythm only she hears.

What is she going to do with her girl?

Time, she thought, would heal them both. It has before, in a temporary sort of way. Some wounds go too deep, shred the soul too much for the edges to be stitched together seamlessly. She has some seams, yes, but they are thready, rough, almost as if they have been cut with pinking sheers.

She has to get Lucy away from here for a while. Remove her from the scene of all her sadness. Change the background and maybe Lucy will change, too.

Not to her old self—never that. There is no returning to life's original blueprint, no matter how much a person wishes for it.

❧ 4 ❧

Lucy

JAIL'S GETTING TO BE A HABIT.

Is twice a habit? She's not sure. Three definitely is, but she's not there yet.

"Back again, Lucy?"

That's Officer Pike. He and Lucy were in school together, about a million years ago. Barely friends back then, but they're getting to know each other now, thanks to Lucy's life of minor crime. He's rounder than he used to be, and she's thinner.

"You know it."

"What'd you do this time?"

"Called a murderer a murderer."

"So the usual?"

"Maybe I wrote it on her car this time."

"Paint?"

"Rock."

"I'll remember that next time I'm playing Rock, Paper, Paint-job," the officer says. "Anyway, you can go. Go on, git."

Is he kidding? The expression on his face says no. "Really?"

"Kellerman's not pressing charges."

"Why not?"

"Don't know. We forgot to interrogate her."

"Ha-ha," Lucy says weakly.

THIS PLACE MAKES HER CRAZY. DARK PANEL WALLS. BIG, bleak bookshelves filled with those leather-covered books that don't invite a reader to, well, read. What good is a book that doesn't want to be read? Heavy desk made of one of the harder, darker woods. Looks like it would fall through a lesser floor. There's a leather couch she's supposed to be on, but she prefers the chair. It makes her feel closer to sane.

"Lucy, Lucy, Lucy."

She breathes deep. As always, the room carries a hint of spice not strong enough to identify, and behind it, the sweetness of the cookies in the cow-shaped jar on the desk. The jar is this office's lone tribute to kitsch.

"I know."

"What do you know?"

"I did the wrong thing."

"Is that what you think?"

She laughs, but it's half-hearted. "No. I was just telling you what you want to hear."

"I thought so," the tiny woman says. "Why don't you tell me what this is really about?"

The psychologist—not her psychologist—is skimming seventy, but her face is stuck in its late-fifties. Good genes or the olive oil she swears is the world's best moisturizer? But she doesn't wash her hair with oil, does she? That's still in a time warp, too. Dark, barely touched by gray. It's short now, cropped at the neck, but for years she wore it long.

"That bitch ran over a cat, and she didn't have the decency to stop."

The therapist looks at her. Hard. It's the don't-spin-me-bullshit look she's come to know and—can she call it love?

"It's true! Ask the vet. I took the cat there afterward. But it was too late."

"About the cat, I believe you. But we both know the cat was a catalyst, not the problem itself."

That's the problem with psychologists. They've got a way of knowing what makes people spin and whir.

And this one has a double helping of knowledge when it comes to Lucy. She's watching Lucy, and Lucy is starting to squirm. She's not a fan of scrutiny—not when it's aimed at her.

"She got away with murder—again. It's not right."

"Is that how you still see it, as a murder?"

What other way is there of seeing it? The view doesn't change if she tilts the facts a different way. "She killed my sister. She killed that cat. End of story."

"She misdiagnosed your sister. It was negligent, yes, but the medical board—"

"Screw the medical board. They were wrong!"

"—said it was an accident. It could have happened to any doctor."

"And the cat, was that an accident, too?"

"You do not even know if she hit that cat."

"There was fur and blood on Kellerman's bumper! Jesus, do you even hear yourself? Why are you defending her?"

"Lucy," the psychologist says gently. "This is not about the cat and we both know it. Today you are lucky, because that woman is not going to press charges. Another person would, but she feels like she owes you something."

Lucy rubs her forehead. Here comes the headache. "This office makes me feel crazy."

"You need to get away from all of this. Go someplace where the world around you is not a constant reminder of Lana."

"Like where, Grandma?"

"Cabo. Hawaii. Does it matter? Find the sun and let it heal you."

"I can't go anywhere. I have to say here."

"For what, Lucy? For what?"

"You." The smile she makes comes out sad. "Me."

"You lost a sister and I lost a granddaughter." She leans forward, takes Lucy's hand. "If I call Lana's death a murder I will go mad, do you understand?"

"No. If you call it anything less, you're just lying to yourself."

"Then let me lie to myself. Please."

LUCY DOES A LOT OF THINKING—AT WORK, MOSTLY. Mixing drinks comes easy to her. One of those things she can do in her sleep.

Twenty-five-year-old college graduate, working in a bar. All that time (and money) wasted if she doesn't do something with her degree soon, but she likes working in this dive.

Shitty money, questionable company; what's not to love?

Grandma told her to go on a vacation, but where's she going to go? Vacations were something she did with Lana. Yeah, Lana was younger, but she was the planner, the decider. That's how they ended up in South Beach one summer,

Hawaii the next. If it was up to Lucy she'd have buried them in snow or Disney characters.

What would Lana do?

Or rather—where would Lana go?

Someplace warm. Lots of sun. Beaches.

"Hey, Grandma," she says the next morning (who is she kidding—it's almost midday). "You know that vacation you wanted me to take? Come with me."

"Come with you where?"

"I don't know yet. But it'll be awesome if we go together. Double the fun."

"And if I don't go?"

Lucy crosses her arms. "You don't go, I won't go."

"Lucy—"

"Kidding. I'll go, but I'll hate it. I'll email you constantly, complaining about everything. The shitty beach. The crappy five-star service. The ugly men."

"Do I have a choice?"

"No."

Grandma laughs. "Buy a ticket and I'll go with you."

5

Akili

BUSY NIGHT AT THE PIZZERIA. PEOPLE COME FROM ALL over for the pizza he hand-tosses and flips into shallow tins. Some of them are skeptics: Pizza where they're from—or where they've been—is the best, they say.

In the end, they walk away from the pizzeria's tables, strung along the promenade in a neat red-and-white line, as believers.

Akili's Pizza is king.

He doesn't feel like a king. He feels like a man doing what it takes not to drown.

That's what men do. They face one day, then the next day, until they run out of days. No complaining. If they have regrets they stuff them deep down. If life isn't fair ... that is life.

The pizzeria is his. Never been anything he wanted to do more than cook.

Now he's got gold and red snakes up and down his arms from the ovens. That ink he got when he was in the army is ruined. But he likes the way they look now—lived in, unique. They're one-of-a-kind.

"Akili," Patra says. She came with the place when he bought it. Back in those days it was a mediocre souvlaki joint. What made it special was Akili and his pizza. He kept Patra and the other servers, ditched the *souvlaki* grills for pizza ovens.

GREEKS INVENTED PIZZA. JUST ASK THEM AND THEY WILL tell you. It came from the Greek word *pita*. Flatbread with delicious toppings. Then one day, Italy threw some mozzarella on top and called it theirs.

PATRA SLAPS HER ORDERS ON THE COUNTER. WIGGLES HER ass she carries away the pizza he just dumped on the counter. A *souvlaki* pizza. Lamb *souvlaki* chunks on a *tzatziki* sauce base. Feta, tomato, olives, onions.

Two Greek experiences in one dish.

Patra wants him. No secret—she tells everyone.

He doesn't want her. No secret about that, either. He tells everyone by ignoring her advances, rinsing off her innuendoes before he replies with clean words.

She only wants what she can't have.

"Fuck her," Stavros would say. "Free is free."

Free isn't free. Not when the woman is a Patra. Sex with her would cost him more than he wants to pay.

She's attractive enough, but the kind of attractive that's plain under all the makeup. Plain can rapidly become beautiful if personalities click, but there are moments when Patra's personality knocks her down to ugly.

A moment later, Patra swishes back into the pizzeria, face like thunder.

What now?

Hands on hips, she says, "He doesn't want to pay."

"Who?"

He follows her to the big glass window with Akili's Pizza painted across its face. The artist even drew a figure of that mythical Akili and his busted heel.

"Him!"

She points to a guy sitting at one of the waterfront tables. There's a woman across from him, glancing anxiously at the pizzeria. Not locals, and not on a date. Looks like a couple of tourists, judging by their outfits and the sunburn.

"Okay. I'll take care of it."

"Good. Make them pay." As though she's the one who balances the pizzeria's books.

He pulls off his apron, crosses the busy street.

Night time is fun time on the promenade. Along the concrete lip that butts up to the gulf, tables stretch from one sealed end to the other. It's closed to everything but foot traffic in the early evening. Across the street, all the businesses have strung colored lights. People walk back and forth, watching life, watching each other, talking. This is what Agria and other small beachside villages like to do with their nights.

"*Yia sou*," he says to the couple.

The man looks haunted, the woman tearful. A string of words fall out of their mouths, but his English is limited to whatever he didn't forget after he left high school. Which is basically none of it.

"American?"

"Canadian," they say.

He could call Kiki (God, he wouldn't want to), but she

hates him. Who else does he know who speaks English? He digs for his cell phone, punches some numbers. Asks for the American woman's number. Fifteen seconds later she's answering the phone.

"This is Vivi."

He explains who he is, what he needs.

She laughs. "Okay, pass the phone over." He gives his phone to the puzzled-looking Canadian guy. A minute later Vivi's telling him the guy got pick-pocketed between their hotel room and the pizzeria.

"Keep my number just in case," she says. "I'm happy to help anytime."

"Can you tell them dinner is paid for?"

"Sure," she says.

After another brief exchange with Vivi, the man relaxes. His wife, girlfriend, whatever, bursts into tears. Akili grabs a napkin off the tray passing by, carried by one of his servers. He gives it to the woman to dry her tears.

"Good night," he says in what little English he remembers.

Patra follows him back to the pizzeria, tail swishing. "What if they're lying?"

"What does it matter? If they are, they have to live with themselves. All I see is hungry people. That's one thing I can fix. Box up another one for them. They can eat it for breakfast."

HE TAKES A PIZZA HOME. LAST THING HE WANTS AFTER cooking them all evening. His father will eat it, though. He'll complain, but he'll complain while he's stuffing it into his mouth.

The gate whines.

A moment later: "Is that you, Akili?"

"No, it's the *baboula*."

(The Greek boogeyman.)

"Very clever. My son thinks he is a comedian."

"Did you eat?"

"How could I eat? There was no food."

Akili stalks over to the refrigerator, yanks open the door and reveals the old man's lie. Cold meat, leftover lentil soup, feta and a good chunk of *kaseri* cheese. And on the counter a loaf of bread that wasn't fresh today, but still has enough life in it to keep a man from starvation.

But his father won't take care of himself. He expects Akili to serve him the way his wife served him from the day he left his mother's kitchen.

The old man shrugs in his wheelchair. "What?"

"You don't see all that food?"

"How do you expect me to fix that food?"

"Cut some cheese and meat and a piece of bread. So easy every Greek child could do it."

"So every Greek child is in a wheelchair, too, eh?" He pulls a yellow paper packet out of his pocket, rolls a cigarette with ease and skill. The cigarette is even from end to end—perfect. He strikes a match on the kitchen table, lights up.

No safety matches here.

"You want to smoke, take it outside," Akili says.

"Why should I? I live here."

Yeah, because Akili's too guilty to toss the old bastard out.

"My house, my rules."

His father takes a long drag of the cigarette. A long plume of smoke wafts out of the corner of his mouth. "I shit on your rules."

Two men, both of them rocks. "Good. That would make a change from your pants."

The old man's cackling follows him down the hall.

DAWN IS JUST ANOTHER PRETTY FACE. BEHIND THAT pretty face there's the same-old day ahead of him. No one else out on the dock but other fishermen—professional and amateur. He says his good mornings, then pushes his boat out to sea.

"Nice boat," Stavros says. "Used to have one just like it." His laugh digs another spoonful of dirt out of Akili's soul. At this rate there will be nothing of him left by the time the Boutos family holds the one-year memorial service for their son.

The boat belonged to Stavros. He left it to Akili. There was no saying "No" to a dead man, so he took the boat.

No pretending to fish today. He points the boat towards the islands of Trikeri and Prasouda. On Prasouda there is nothing, just an old monastery he likes to watch from the water. Trikeri is inhabited, but its citizens are few. Not even a hundred full-time residents. There is a tiny market, a couple of *tavernas*, and the Monastery of *Panayia*—the Virgin Mary.

Somedays he docks at Trikeri, delivers olive oil and whatever else Stelios, the proprietor and bartender of the shoreside *taverna* and inn needs.

But most of the time he drifts, his gaze focused on Prasouda and its crumbling skeleton, wondering how long it takes the human body to melt down to its bones.

❧ 6 ❧

Lucy

WHERE WOULD LANA GO?

Lucy consults the oracle: Lana's diaries.

Yeah, yeah, it's an invasion of privacy, but Lana's gone and her diaries are here. When Lucy reads them, it's almost as though her sister is in the other room. Anyway, before The End she told Lucy it was okay if she read the diaries—she wanted her to.

For the first three months she couldn't bring herself to crack open the leather covers and flip the crisp pages, but one day she started and couldn't stop. While she's reading, Lana is still alive, in another room.

Today Lucy avoids their teenage years, when Mom and Dad were killed. She was there, she remembers the grief she and Lana and Grandma shared. What she's searching for is Lana's travel bucket list, the places her younger sister wanted to see before—

Before she died.

When she finds the list, the whole world is on it. But there's one place at the top of the list, a red heart carved beside one country: Greece.

Their grandparents' birthplace, the country her grandmother fled—alone and pregnant.

The country Grandma hates.

Lana wanted to see their place of origin, and now, suddenly, Lucy does, too.

LUCY KILLS THE MUSIC. HALF THE JOINT BOOS, BUT THE boos turn to cheers when Lucy jumps up on the bar. Probably they're hoping *Shenanigans* is turning into a strip club, or going *Coyote Ugly*.

Yeah, no. Not tonight.

"Any of you losers ever been to Greece?"

"I went to Mykonos. Tits and dicks everywhere," one of the regulars calls out.

Nope, not taking Grandma to Mykonos. "Bet you loved it," she says.

"Paradise, baby!"

"Anyone else?"

Nobody.

"You going to Greece?" Betsy wants to know. Most nights it's her and Betsy behind the bar alone, mixing drinks and dodging catcalls. Betsy's her in twenty years—if she doesn't do something else with her life soon.

Not that Betsy's a bad person—she's great. It's just that she's got a look in her eyes that says she's seen it all—and everything and everyone there is to see is shit.

"Maybe," Lucy says. "Yes."

"Worse places you could go on a vacation. Hot Greek billionaires ..."

No. No hot Greek billionaires. Ask Google.

Greece has three billionaires. They're old. Only way they'll ever be hot now is if they're cremated.

"... Greek food. Beaches." Betsy sighs. "Want company?"

"Grandma's coming with me."

"Anyone else and I'd say buzzkill, but your grandma is one cool lady."

Grandma is cool, but Greece is on her no-go list. She never says why, only that she'll go back to Greece when the country hands itself over to Turkey.

So, basically never.

But it's at the top of Lana's list, which means it just took the express elevator to the top of Lucy's list, too.

"Does Greece have earthquakes?"

Betsy shrugs. "If you find a hot Greek guy, I bet it does."

What to do?

Greece straddles two plates. Northern Greece on the Eurasian Plate, Southern Greece on the Aegean Sea Plate. The African plate is constantly shoving its fingers up the Aegean Sea Plate's skirt.

Makes for some serious friction.

GOOGLE'S GOT A LOT TO SAY ABOUT GREECE AND ALL ITS earthquakes.

Mostly things like "Hate earthquakes? Don't go to Greece," and "Terrified of earthquakes? Don't go to Greece," and "Remember that part in that terrible *2012* movie (the one with John Cusack) where the ground in Los Angeles tore apart? Know where that could happen? Greece."

Very reassuring, Google.

They tell people to avoid *WebMD*, but where are the cautionary tales about the Lucys of the world, poring over every tiny natural disaster?

Nowhere, that's where. Lucy Googled that, too.

Before she loses her nerve—and before the Internet dishes up yet another tale of earthquake horror—Lucy buys two tickets to Greece, departure date, a month from today. That gives Grandma time to shuffle her patients. And it gives Lucy time to talk herself into going—earthquakes or no earthquakes.

What are the odds of a Big One while they're there, anyway?

No way is she Googling that. She's got the feeling the Internet knows.

7

Fotini

"No."

There is nothing else to say.

"But why?"

"Oh, Lucy, which part of 'No' did you not understand? The N or the O? It's a very simple word—dogs understand it. Cats, too, but you know how cats are."

"Grandma, please. This was your idea."

She shakes her head. "Greece was not my idea."

"But a vacation was."

"Do you know how many countries there are in the world? One hundred and ninety-six. America does not count Taiwan, but I do because I do not blame them for not wanting to be a part of China. So pick one and we will go there."

"I already did."

She holds up one hand. "Do you know what this is?"

"Your hand?"

"Very good. Talk to it."

In Greece it's an insult. She'd tell Lucy that, but she wants to steer the conversation into safer waters.

GREECE. NOW THERE IS ONE OLD BITCH SHE CAN NEVER forget.

Fifty years since she jumped aboard the first ship she could find, and still she and Greece are attached by an umbilical cord that drips memories into her mind. So many nights she wakes up with a desperate feeling of longing, as though Greece is a long lost mother.

When she is awake ... eh, it is different. Awake, she remembers precisely the shape of the hands that pushed her onto the ship.

She will never go back.

Ever.

꧁ 8 ꧂

Lucy

GREECE SEPARATES THEM INTO DIFFERENT LINES.
Grandma's a Greek citizen and Lucy's one of those untrust-
worthy foreigners with very nice money.

What brings you to Greece?" the immigration official
asks, his English buffed to a high sheen. He watches a lot of
British movies. Something about the way he clips his words
before they roll off his tongue.

"Vacation."

"Are you carrying anything illegal in your bottom?"

Lucy blinks. She's heard Greeks are blunt, but this is
crazy. "Like what?"

He points to a sign—a non-smoking sign.

"Drugs. Meats, fruits, vegetables. Exotic animals.
Weapons."

The only weapon she ever carries is the multitool Dad

gave her years ago. Now it's in the luggage she checked back at LAX.

She considers the sign's message. "Cigarettes?"

He frowns. "Why would anyone put cigarettes in their bottom?"

Why would anyone put anything up there? She gives him what she hopes is a confident smile. "Does airline food count?"

"No. It is not contraband."

"Funny, it tasted like it."

He throws her a weird look, like he's in pain and she's the reason why. Flips open the passport. Takes a long look at the snapshot. The photo shows her five years ago, brunette and more tanned. Now she's back to her natural glossy blonde, and her skin says vampire more than it says melanoma.

His tough shell cracks when he takes in her last name.

"Shake. Your last name is Shake?" Captain Obvious asks. "Shake your groovy thing, yes?"

"Not so much."

"Do your milkshakes bring some of the boys to your yard?"

Ha-ha. "Very funny."

"I know. That is what everybody tells me. Your first time in Greece?"

"Yes." She keeps her mouth closed until it's clear he's never going to quit staring. "My grandmother insisted we take a vacation. I chose Greece."

"Your grandmother? Where is she?"

Lucy leans sideways, points to where Grandma is standing in a different line, looking pissed off at the entire world, Lucy in particular.

"She didn't want to come, but I twisted her arm."

Immigration Guy is aghast. "You twisted her arm? What kind of monster are you that you abuse your grandmother?"

Oh, God. "Not literally—figuratively. It's a saying. It means I had to convince her coming here was a good idea."

He snorted. "Greece is the best place on earth. All civilization comes from here, yes? Except men kissing. That is a vicious rumor spread by the Turks to defame the Greek people."

Before she can answer, he slams a stamp onto her passport, thrusts it at her face and moves on. "Are you carrying anything illegal in your bottoms?" he asks the elderly couple behind her.

The old woman leans over to her husband. "He's asking about your colonoscopy, dear."

"Is that a dangerous animal?" Immigration Guy asks. "A parrot maybe. Ah, I know, it is the from the Greek word *kolos*." He stands, slaps his butt.

Lucy shoots them a sympathetic look as she dodges their duty free bags. They're carrying enough tobacco and booze for a portable speakeasy.

———

THE WHEELS ON THE BUS FROM ATHENS TO VOLOS GO round and round, but they're not happy about it. The road is hot, the bus crowded, and the bus driver has one lead foot.

She's stuck next to an old woman who might be dead. It's been two hours since the woman dropped her crochet into her lap, head slumping over her chest. Lucy's been alternating between snatching glances of Greece out the window and watching the woman's chest. But with the way this bus is moving, it's hard to say if the woman's breathing or jolting as the tires hit pothole numero whatever.

She cranes her neck, looks at Grandma across the aisle. The bus is too full, and they were the last ones aboard, so it was sit apart or wait.

"I think she's dead."

"Pinch her nose," Grandma says.

"I can't pinch her nose."

"Why not? If she is dead she will never know or care. If she is alive, she will be grateful she's sitting next to such a caring young woman."

Lucy is pretty sure that's not how things will go. The living have a way of not appreciating nose pinches. They're too busy trying to sleep.

Five hours. One bus. A full load.

The math isn't pretty. But somehow the bus rolls into Volos without dying or killing them.

Volos looks like a city.

Very astute, Lucy. Come all this way and a city looks like a city? That the best you can do?

It's ... it's all so concrete. It seems like the cities in Greece should be greener and more exotic. But a city is a city, it seems. People like to stack themselves on top of each other the same way, no matter which continent they're on.

The signs are different, though. Dustier, dirtier, one hundred-percent less intelligible—to her, at least.

Soon the bus shudders to a stop outside a terminal where the signs are in Greek and—blissfully—English. They swap the bus for another bus, this time a local vehicle that chugs toward—hopefully—the ferry terminal.

THERE'S NO FERRY THIS LATE IN THE DAY. THE BOAT TO and from the Sporades islands has already done its to and from-ing for the day.

So they get on a local bus that rattles its bones along the coast.

It's a handful of minutes until they leave the city behind. Now they're rolling east with the gulf at their side.

There's no name for this shade of sea. Azure? Cerulean? Emerald? None of them fit. It's a cross between blue and green, but it's been blended by a mystical hand to make something completely new. To their left is a bank of hills, marred only by the huge factory hulking in a dimple at their base. Its two arms cross over the road to form twin jetties for arriving and departing rust buckets, with cyrillic names tattooed on their flanks.

She flips open the travel guide she brought for the trip. It's filled with polite, useful phrases and colorful descriptions.

"Cement plant. That one is the biggest in Europe."

Grandma's reading her mind.

A minute later, the hills flatten into tree-covered land, with the occasional rise reminding people that Greece's terrain is anything but static.

Earthquakes. Greece gets more than its fair share.

It better not have one while she's here, or she's running for the nearest plane.

Not that she has a phobia or anything. It's just that earthquakes are a big, fat, unpredictable unknown. Living in California for all those years made her twitchy. People won't shut up about the "big one" that's coming "any day now, when we least expect it." Sometimes she thinks the doomsayers are itching for the San Andreas fault to buck the west coast into the sea, just so they can say they told us so.

GREEKS KNOW EARTHQUAKES. THEY GOT SMART YEARS BACK and started preparing for the one hundred and eighty quakes that shake them every year. All new construction is earthquake-proof. That's the law.

Now Greece is unsinkable.

Kind of like the Titanic.

THE TREES DON'T VANISH COMPLETELY. THEY SLIP IN between the buildings, leaving glimpses of green that evoke a feeling of mystery.

"What's this place?"

Grandma is tensing up. She could be a bow with those stiff shoulders.

"Agria," Grandma says. "This is where I grew up."

"Here? Cool." Because it is cool. The seaside village emits an air of contentment, as if it's completely satisfied with its lot in life. "Did you go to that church?"

It's big, it's white, it's wearing a big cross on its domed hat. No mistaking it for anything but a church.

"Too many times to count. That is Saint George's."

After the church, it's *taverna* after *taverna*. On the bus side of the street there's concrete sidewalk, wide enough to fit tables and chairs for drinkers and diners.

"You see that dock?" Grandma points.

Yeah, Lucy sees the dock. It's a long concrete finger.

"At night the *tavernas* cover it with tables and chairs. It gets very busy down here in summer and spring. The nightlife is all here."

Lucy's going crazy trying to drink it all in. The sea is tugging on her sleeve, demanding to be seen, but this village was Grandma's stomping ground, way back when.

Grandma isn't a woman who talks about her time in Greece—ever. When prompted, she normally brushes off the whole country like a childhood disease she was lucky to survive. It's almost voyeuristic, being here.

"Has it changed much?"

"I doubt it," Grandma says. "Places like this never change in the important ways."

"But does it look different?"

"A little."

See? Very forthcoming, her grandmother. Very mysterious.

Not about anything else—normally she has the transparency of a window. But about Greece? Gargantuan mystery.

A mystery Lucy intends to solve while they're here.

As the bus crosses another invisible border, leaving Agria behind, Grandma's knots unravel. She reels off the names of the towns as they pass through, until Lucy's hands are overflowing with figurative map pins.

Mount Pelion is the reason for this peninsula they're skimming. When it was formed, it assumed the fetal position, and it's been that way ever since, with its non-prehensile tail curled around this pool of sea.

Yeah, Lucy did a lot of Googling before they left. This is what she knows about their ultimate destination:

Palio Trikeri. Old Trikeri. As opposed to the nearby mainland town of Trikeri. Population: not many.

Two hotels, if you can call them that. One is a group of fancy new villas. The other is two rooms joined at one seam. The Internet said one of the *tavernas* also rents its two rooms, but business is booming and they're both full.

No cars on the island. By donkey, by foot, or by boat—those are the transportation options. A boat moves between the island and the mainland, steered by the bartender at one of the island's two *tavernas*. It's that or wait for the ferry that passes by twice daily; once on its way to Sporades, once on its way back to Volos.

To get there you call the *taverna* and ask for Stelios.

When they get to the tiny village of Alogoporos, that's exactly what they do.

❧ 9 ❧

Fotini

At first the man is a speck on a boat. As the motor pushes the vessel closer, the man evolves into a larger speck.

Very observant of her—no?

It's hard to think. Greece is dipping its spoon in her head, stirring. Being here, it's like walking back into an abusive relationship. At least she managed to steer Lucy away from booking a room in Agria.

Trikeri is a good compromise. It is still Greece, yes, but not her Greece. The air is saltier than she remembers, with a hint of something sweet. Fruit, perhaps? Oranges, or maybe grapes.

The boat cozies up to the deck. Its captain is her age, with maybe a few years shaved off. He is lean, skin the color of tarnished gold. It's a good face he has: worn, but not worn out, with lines that show he is a man who knows how to laugh

—and enjoys it. Hair more dark than gray. A mustache that says he does not spend too much time in front of the mirror.

Somebody needs to attack that thing with scissors.

The idea of it pushes a laugh out of her, so the man's first words to her are: "What is so funny? Tell me so I can laugh, too."

Lucy looks at her, brows raised.

She waves her hand at the two of them. "Nothing. It is good to be on vacation, that is all."

The Greek man jumps down onto the dock. Fit. Athletic. "You are *Kyria* Fotini and Lucy, yes? Fotini from the word *fos*, which means light. And Lucy, from *lucius*, which also means light, if you speak Latin."

"You speak Latin?" she asks the bartender and boat's captain.

"Only enough to impress beautiful women. Are you impressed?"

"No."

Doesn't put a dent in his confidence and enthusiasm; he keeps on beaming.

"*Kyria*?" Lucy asks.

"That means *mrs*," Grandma says. "Just Fotini," she tells him. "I am not married."

"A widow?"

"An impatient woman who has been traveling for too long. If you do not take us to Trikeri soon, I will make your wife a widow."

He laughs, hefts their bags into his boat. "I am Stelios, and there is no wife." One by one, he helps them aboard, then he fires up the motor. A hint of exhaust throws a blanket over the briny air and its mystery sweetness. "And that," he says, nodding to the island, "is Trikeri."

"How long are you in Greece?"

"Two weeks."

She looks at Lucy, who is too busy hanging over the bow to be interested in this conversation. Her granddaughter's like a little girl again. What a dear thing she was—and still is. Lucy and Lana, both of them brimming with enthusiasm. Lana was a touch more sedate, but together they attacked life with the force of a pressure washer.

Thinking Lana's name makes her heart hurt.

That Kellerman woman complains that she cannot sleep at night, but she has no sympathy for the doctor. Let her lose sleep. Lost sleep is nothing compared to a lost grandchild.

Stelios says, "Not long."

"Long enough."

"For what?"

"I did not realize we were paying for an interrogation."

"You paid for the boat ride. The interrogation is free." Beneath that mustache he's smiling.

"Are you flirting with me?"

"No. If I was flirting you would know it." He nods to the approaching island. "So what do you think of my island?"

"It's an island."

"The best island in Greece."

The laugh sneaks up on her from nowhere. She wasn't in a laughing mood, yet here she is doing it again.

"That we will see," she tells him.

"Trust me," he says. "By the end of two weeks, you will never want to leave."

That will never happen.

YES, SHE SAID THAT ABOUT COMING TO GREECE, TOO.

But Lucy played the Lana card and showed her the diary

her youngest granddaughter kept, with Greece at the top of her bucket list as the place she wanted most to see.

She hates Greece, yes, but she loves Lucy with all her heart. And she still loves Lana with that same fierce devotion, so how could she say no?

For her girls she would sacrifice anything, including herself.

🌾 10 🌾

Fotini

STELIOS HAS THEIR ROOM KEY. "THE OWNER DOES NOT LIVE on Trikeri, so he leaves the keys with me."

One room in a two-room inn is theirs, but what a room it is. Two queen-sized beds, a small kitchen, polished marble floors, and a view worth hundreds of times what they paid for this place. It smells not like a hotel room but a home, with its wood-burning fireplace, and windows and shutters set to the open position.

"I opened the windows when you called." The Greek man sets down their bags, turns to leave. "If you need anything you know where to find me, eh?"

"Do you live above your *taverna*?" Lucy asks. She's busy hunting through her luggage for something. A moment later her search ends when she clips the multitool Michael gave her when she was younger. Their father gave one to each of his daughters. Just in case.

"No. I live in the *taverna*, but I sleep in my house."

He gives them a wink and leaves.

"He likes you," Lucy says, that grin she's wearing entirely too big for her face.

"He likes me. Ha! He is a lonely old man, that is all."

"Uh-huh."

WANT TO AVOID JET LAG? SAY NO TO SLEEPING BEFORE nighttime—local, that is.

Too bad that bed is doing everything it can to seduce her.

Sleep with me, it's saying. *Look at these sheets. Soft—yet crisp—cotton. This pillow? Down from the finest geese.*

Not that there's such a thing as a fine goose; they're born bad-tempered.

She convenes with the hag in the bathroom mirror, convinces her to slap on some moisturizer and lip balm and maybe a touch of eyeliner.

"Hungry?" she asks Lucy, who has allowed the other bed to have its way with her.

Lucy opens one eye. "Must sleep. Otherwise will turn into ogre."

"I will bring you something back, okay?"

Her granddaughter shoves her head under the pillow. "Okay."

She ventures out alone.

It's a short jaunt from their room to the shore-side *taverna*. The path is a jigsaw of flat stones, winding its way to the *taverna*'s front door. There it splits and runs in two opposing directions, terminating somewhere beyond her line of sight.

The way is lined with a mixture of olive trees and low, flowering shrubs. Someone has taken the time to stab solar lights into the ground, but this early in the evening, they're dark. The sun isn't quite done with Greece for today.

The entire front of the *taverna* opens onto a deep, wide porch, that she's thinking has never been full. Several tables are set up with blue tablecloths, their accompanying chairs painted a clean white. The *taverna* itself is a neatly stacked pile of stones, painted a similarly pristine shade of white.

Stelios is behind the bar, head bowed over a paperback book.

"*Yia sou*," she says, stepping up onto the porch.

That book vanishes at speed slightly slower than light.

"*Kyria* Fotini."

"Just Fotini. And not ever Fotoula," she says, referencing a popular nickname for girls and women who share her name.

"Not even when you were a girl?"

"Not even then."

"What did they call you?"

"Does this interrogation come with a drink?"

He laughs and reaches for a glass. "Name it and you will have it."

What to drink? His bar has the basics and a few unfamiliar faces.

"Do you have a bottle of *Mavrodaphne*?"

Mavrodaphne. Black laurel. It's a Greek dessert wine. Very sweet, very dark. With a sting that creeps up on you.

"*Mavrodaphne* I have. But if you drink it, you must eat."

As if she can eat. "What were you reading?"

"I have *baklava*, made by *Kyria* Maria. And she also brought some *moussaka* this morning, if you do not want something sweet."

Very deft, the way he sidesteps her question.

"Who is *Kyria* Maria?"

He waves a dismissive hand. "She is an old crone who brings food for the *taverna*. Very good cook. Much better than me." He glances past her shoulder, mutters, "Here comes trouble."

Trouble looks suspiciously like a priest. This one is in a black cassock, tall black hat perched on his head. Long, tidy beard, Greek Orthodox style. He's young, maybe in his late thirties or early forties.

Further down the path, out of sight, there's a screech. "*Ay-yi-yi!*"

He waves. "*Kalispera, Kyria* Maria!"

It is a good evening, and it's a funny one when the priest slides onto the barstool next to her and says, "God is telling me to drink."

"Did you give *Kyria* Maria a fright again?" Stelios asks.

"Old Greek women and their superstitions," he says cheerfully.

Stelios uncorks the wine, pours a long stretch of the dark liquid into a glass. This he slides in front of her. Then he twists the top off a *retsina* bottle and shoots it to the priest.

"I have not heard that one," she says.

"It is bad luck to see a priest walking around the streets," Stelios supplies.

Huh. Who knew? "Sometimes it seems like Greeks make up superstitions as they go."

The men laugh. Big belly-slapping guffaws. "You are right," the priest says. "Every day it is something new to be afraid of, a new sign to interpret."

Oh, she can beat that. "I live in a country where they believe if the groundhog sees his shadow there will be six more weeks of winter."

"His shadow?"

"Yes."

"That is ridiculous," Stelios says.

"Only slightly more ridiculous than believing a walking priest is bad luck."

The two men nod solemnly. "People, we are ridiculous creatures," the bartender says. "We believe in imaginary things all the time."

"God is real." The priest knocks back half the *retsina* bottle before setting it back on the coaster. But it's not a big bottle—beer-sized. "I know because He talks to me all the time. He has never set my bushes on fire, but the other night He was in my bathtub."

"Interesting." The poor man is obviously suffering from some kind of delusions. Not surprising, if he drinks this much.

"Our island is one of the few places God works His miracles. Many miraculous things have happened here."

"What things?"

"Miracles."

Okay ... "What miracles?"

"It is a miracle the good Father's liver still works," Stelios says.

"See! A miracle!" The priest holds up his empty bottle. "Another, friend."

"Father Yiannis lives at the Monastery of the Virgin Mary. It sits on the top of the island, like a big cherry."

The priest is nodding. "That is where people come to pray to the icon of the Virgin Mary—the source of the miracles."

"I think I will take that *baklava* and a piece of *moussaka*," she says. "All this conversation is making me hungry. And do not skimp on the wine."

She needs it for this crowd.

✿ 11 ✿

Lucy

SHE SLEEPS HARD. IT'S ONE OF THOSE WONDERFUL dreamless nights, without ambulances and funerals and her family coming back as zombies.

Makes a nice change.

At home she's all jeans and shirts, but this is Greece in August. Dress weather. She pulls a stretchy blue dress over her head, shimmies it over her hips, douses her face with sunscreen, then she's gone.

Grandma's at the *taverna*. Still in the same clothes she was in last night.

She looks at Stelios. Surely she didn't—

"I couldn't sleep," Grandma says. "So Stelios and the crazy priest kept me company."

Riiiight.

"He is very crazy," Stelios confirms. "Coffee?"

"Normally I'd tell you to shoot it straight into my arm,

44

but I feel great, so a cup is fine. How is Greece so far?" she asks Grandma.

"Awful. I hate it."

Stelios almost drops the coffee. "You hate Greece? It is paradise."

"To you it is paradise. To me it is hell."

"What did Greece do to you?" he asks.

"It made her who she is," Lucy says.

AT THE END OF THE DOCK IS A MAN TENDING TO HIS BOAT. The boat is an unfortunate mixture of blue and orange, but the man ...

Yum.

Tall. Dark. Handsome. He ticks all of Lucy's boxes—and a few extras. Skin the shade of a dark honey. He's built like throwing a woman over his shoulder is no problem. Very caveman, very sexy.

"Greek men are trouble," Grandma says, following Lucy's gaze to its resting place. "What is that if it is not trouble?"

"He's just a guy with a boat."

"Trouble."

"Is this a psychologist thing?"

"No. I can see with two regular eyes that he is trouble. All the psychology would tell me is how he is trouble, and there are some things I don't want to know."

If all trouble looked like that, women would get into it even more often than they already do. Unconsciously, she bites her bottom lip.

"I see that look," Grandma says. "No. No trouble for you. I brought you here to keep you out of trouble."

"I wasn't in trouble."

"You were about to be." She drifts away for a moment.

45

When she comes back, it's with a new opinion. "Come on." Grandma nods to the man with the boat. "Let's go and climb something old." She gets moving down the dock, Lucy's hand in hers.

"I thought you didn't want me to get into trouble."

Her mouth gets moving at a speed that would get her a ticket back home. When she's done, she turns around, beckons to Lucy.

"Come, he is going to take us to Prasouda."

"What's Prasouda?"

"It's an island. A very small island. The only thing there is an old monastery and some trees. I like old things. They remind me of me."

Grandma holds out her hand to boat guy. He helps her aboard, then he reaches for Lucy's hand.

Nice hands. Big. Strong. He and his hands are bronze from the sun. But his arms are a mess of scars old and fresh. They're twisted up his arm like gold vines.

She's staring, isn't she?

"Sorry," she says, then takes a running leap onto the boat.

Grandma tells the man something, and for a second he almost smiles.

"Hey, old lady, what did you tell him?"

"You want to know? You better learn some Greek, eh?"

Good sense of humor, her grandmother. Anyone peering through the window into their lives would never know what they'd been through if all they caught was an eyeful of the family's matriarch. Only if their gaze slipped sideways would they see Lucy's new, perpetual wilt.

And they'd wonder what kind of train slammed into this family.

12

Fotini

Fotini isn't a woman who changes her mind for no reason.

Two weeks until they go home.

Wait—minus a day.

Does it matter if Lucy has herself a vacation romance? No. As long as she is careful and does not have a vacation baby or catch a vacation venereal disease.

"If you look at his penis and see spots, do not touch it."

"Grandma!"

"I am serious. Spots, sores, lumps. All bad."

"Jesus," Lucy says, staring up at the sky, hands on hips. "I'm not listening. La-la-la."

"Fine. But do not complain to me when you need antibiotics. Did you bring condoms?"

"If you keep talking, I'll set myself on fire. Seriously. Enough. He's hot, but he's not that hot."

Yes, he is. Greece makes some beautiful men, and this is most definitely one of them. American men are nice, yes, but European men have their own, unique edge. There's a fire in them, an innate confidence, a charm that has the ability to strip off a woman's underwear. Not until he is gone does she realize her underwear is missing and her butt is cold.

There was a time when she had a cold butt. But her Greek man did not leave of his own free will.

❧ 13 ❧

Lucy

NICE MONASTERY. IT'S A NEATLY STACKED HEAP OF PALE stones with faded domes. Around the island, the water is opalescent, changing colors with every new tilt of her head.

"It is Byzantine," Grandma says. "Very old. The Monastery of *Zoodochos Pigi*. Life-giving Spring. That is what Akili says. And there is a reef here, surrounding the island."

That explains the shifting colors.

She leans past Grandma to get a better look at Mr Tasty. "Hi, Akili." She sticks out her hand. "Lucy."

"Lucy," he repeats. But does he take her hand?

Negative. Okay, so he's busy steering the boat closer to shore, but still. Looks like English isn't exactly his thing. That's okay, she's just window shopping. And he's a very nice window. Spectacular view.

She tries not to think about Grandma and her spotted dick.

"Are we going ashore?"

Grandma says something to Akili. He shoots off a rapid reply.

"It is not a good tide for the boat. There is a risk of damaging the boat on the reef."

Oh well, at least the view is great.

"I wonder why they built it here? I wonder why they left? Why do we abandon our things so easily?" she muses.

Grandma wraps one arm around her waist. "Everything is temporary, Lucy. Some things just take longer to die."

❧ 14 ❧

Akili

HE'S NOT A TAXI SERVICE OR A TOUR GUIDE, YET HERE HE IS playing both.

Every day he brings the boat out, hoping for change.

Now here it is, his change.

Not exactly what he had in mind. He was shooting for something of the closer-to-home kind. Hoped maybe his father would discover a wealthy relative and vanish. Hoped his best friend's murder was one of those mistaken identity scenarios.

No dice. What he gets is the blonde and her grandmother. The grandmother asks about Prasouda, next thing he knows he's volunteering to show them around.

Too bad this tide's not cooperating. A meter or two in the wrong direction and this boat is going to lose its bottom. Bye bye, boat. They'll be swimming back to Trikeri, and he'll be catching the bus back to Agria.

ALEX A. KING

Doesn't matter—she's worth it. The blonde woman, that is.

She's watching the island, and he's watching her from behind his dark sunglasses. She's wearing a shiny, happy coating, a playfulness that doesn't tell her whole story. He glimpses the darkness in an unguarded moment, when her back is turned to her grandmother.

Bravery not for herself, but for her grandmother's sake.

What injures a young woman that way?

A broken love affair?

He recognizes something in her, something he's seen in his own mirror.

15

Lucy

WHEN GRANDMA SLEEPS, IT'S FOR A WHOLE DAY. SHE'S rubbing sleep out of her eyes just as Lucy's raring to go.

"Going to the beach, Grandma. See you there."

Two minutes later she's on shore, towel at her feet, staring at the row of boats beached on the pebbles, their butts hanging in the water.

Guess this must be a boat parking lot.

When she hears the tick of a boat motor, she swings around.

Look who's back. It's Mr Tasty—AKA Akili.

"Nice boat," she calls out. "Did you paint it yourself? Because those colors really work well together. Bold choices."

Not a word from the hot guy. He smiles, finishes docking his boat, then he's onto dry land.

They reach the *taverna* at the same time. He steps back to let her enter first. Nice of him.

"Help me please, Stelios," she says. "I need coffee, and you're my only hope."

"I have heard that before," he tells her and she laughs.

"You and everyone else."

She scoots further down the bar so Akili can take care of his business with the bartender. They chat for a moment, then Stelios nods to Lucy. "I will make that coffee to go, yes? Akili is taking you back to the island, if you want to go."

"To Prasouda?"

Akili nods.

"What about Grandma?"

"What about her?" Stelios asks. "I will take care of her. Go."

She goes—but not without her coffee.

Priorities, she has them.

"I LIKE IT OUT HERE. CAN I STAY? THAT'S PROBABLY A NO. I mean who wants to stay on a tiny boat on the sea forever? It's avoidance—I know it is. I'm avoiding dead people, mostly. If I stay here, no one else dies. Unless you decide to jump overboard or something."

Not a word from the Greek man—not even a Greek syllable.

"Are you one of those tortured hero guys? Because you look slightly tortured. Not all over. Just ... in your eyes. They'll tell the truth even when your mouth is bullshitting about how great life is. Very Byronic."

There's something refreshing about talking to a guy who doesn't talk back. Not that she doesn't love guys. She does. It's just that she's met more than her fair share of guys who want to steer her life their way. This one's not steering her anywhere. He's busy coiling a fishing line onto a plastic yellow reel.

"I'll take that as a no, because it looks like you manage to dress yourself just fine." No color clashes there. He's in long shorts and a T-shirt that—if it's meant to be a disguise—is a lousy one. The man is put together like a wall, one solid brick at a time. If he fell on her, she'd be crushed. Good guy to know if you're in a fight, though. Not that she's planning to fight anyone.

Still, that's the thing about fights. Like shit, sometimes they happen.

Take the Kellerman thing. She wasn't planning to deface her car, but something snapped when she found the cat and traced it back to the doctor's wheels.

And the Kellerman encounter before that ... Lucy's grief was fresh that day, the day the medical board decided Kellerman wasn't culpable. Nobody wanted to take responsibility for a twenty-two-year-old woman's death from breast cancer. Kellerman snatched away Lana's treatment choices by blaming her overactive imagination.

The red paint was nothing, it washed off. Meanwhile, it rains and rains and Lana never comes back.

Akili is staring down at the sea. So she looks, too. No way does she want to miss out on seeing something awesome.

There's something about the water. It's shivering.

Not awesome. Not awesome at all.

Water shivers like that for two reasons: Tyrannosaurus Rex (see: Jurassic Park) and earthquakes. And these days the planet's dinosaur population is floundering.

Suddenly, the boat lurches. There's a huge cracking sound, followed by what sounds like Freddy Kruger's nails trying to claw through the boat's hull. The water pushes on through the hole, makes itself at home on the wrong side—the inside —of the boat.

Akili drops the fishing line, grabs her arm, dragging her toward the cabin. But neither of them is going anywhere— fast. That fishing line has curled itself around them and now it's conspiring with the sea to turn them into food for whatever lives in the sea around here.

Sharks?

She keeps the curse words tied up in her head. Doesn't freak out, which is surprising, because she really wants to freak the hell out. If ever there was a time for freaking out, this is it.

But no, she's going to drown the cool, calm, dignified way. *The way Lana died.*

"This isn't so bad," she says, as the water inches up their legs. "I'll see my sister again. I hope. Unless she went up and I'm destined to shoot downstairs. Which seems probable, especially after the rock thing. And my parents. They're dead, too. So really I've got more people waiting there than here. What about you?"

Nothing from Akili.

He's busy trying to untangle the fishing line.

❦ 16 ❦

Akili

THEY'RE DROWNING, AND WHAT DOES SHE WANT TO do? Talk.

What is it with women and conversation?

They can't even die in peace.

His father would say there are two good ways to shut a woman up, and one of them involves food.

When he was a kid and the old man got to talking like that, dumb kid that he was, he assumed he meant the second way was a good beating. He saw his father give his mother a hard wallop too many times. And as he got older, he realized that's not what his old man meant at all; his mother was anything but silent after the bastard struck her.

Now his father's the quieter one since last time he beat his wife, but that's what happens when your son gets tired of watching you pick on someone smaller, gets big enough to show a man what happens when you take on someone your own size.

Although at sixteen, he had five inches on his father, and a lot more muscle. On top of that he had twenty kilos of fat, but bigger is bigger when it comes to dealing with bullies.

Anyway, his father didn't do as much talking after that. Mostly shit his pants a couple of times a day and demanded constant attention. So maybe Akili didn't do Mama any favors.

What can he say? He loved the woman and did all his stupid teenaged ass knew how to do. If he'd been a man he'd have done things differently.

He'd have killed him.

By the time he'd punched a hole in his father's life, he'd already figured out that second thing his old man was talking about. And he was already busy silencing as many girls as he could.

Which wasn't that many.

Stavros was the one the girls liked. All of them except the Andreou girls, which was a problem for Stavros because he was meant to marry the youngest one. Anyway, there were plenty of others. Stavros was drowning in girls and women by the time they hit puberty.

His leftovers filtered down to Akili, but Akili was only interested in the ones who were in it for him. A few weeks into his mandatory stint in the army, the fat was gone, the muscle had multiplied, and more women looked at him than away.

He tells the American woman all of this, but she looks him square in the eyes, trying to make sense of his words.

If she figures it out, maybe she'll let him know.

"Stay still," he says, holding up one hand to reinforce his meaning. Then he bobs below the surface, looking for their problem.

Damn fishing line. It's still wrapped around them both and winding up someplace he can't see. No pocket knife in his pocket. It's gone.

Back up for a swallow of air.

Down again.

He bites into the line, but it's very stubborn, very Greek. There's no cutting it with teeth. With eyes closed, he tries again, grinding it between his molars.

Nothing.

The boating is sinking fast, and them with it.

He doesn't mind dying. Maybe he'll see Stavros again, haunt the seas side by side. But the woman? She's young, and for her life is supposed to be beautiful.

The bottom of the sea clears. Stavros is there, beckoning. "*Ela*," he mouths. *Come*.

What kind of friend wants him to die?

Maybe one who knows him too well.

Up for another breath. This time he's forced to lean his head all the way back to pull in anything other than sea water.

As he sinks, he sees the woman is gone.

❧ 17 ❧

Lucy

THE THING ABOUT DEATH IS THAT IT REALLY PISSES HER off. It almost never happens to people you hate, only the ones you love. Three. That's how many times she's had death splashed in her face. Mom, Dad, and Lana.

Grandma's tally is even higher, though she doesn't speak about it much.

Well, never.

So, no way is she going to drown out at sea and add another notch on Grandma's death o' meter. Not when she's carrying her keys, and with them the small multitool Dad always insisted she keep handy. Smart man.

Akili's doing his share to try to save them, but he's running out of chances. She's been trying to stay still, trying not to exacerbate the problem, but in real life no one saves a woman except the woman herself.

And if she can save him, too, that's syrup on the *baklava*, isn't it?

If she were Klingon, she'd say today is a good day to die. But she's human, which means dying on any day is a really sucky idea.

So she sinks.

Not much, just enough to raise her knee and jerk the fishing line to where she can grab it. Above the surface, her hand flips the stainless steel scissors open.

Snip, snip, snip. She kicks her legs and the line slowly drifts away. Now she can reach Akili, who's gone up for another swallow—maybe his last—of air. He jerks as she grabs his arm, tugs. But he plays along, lifting his ankles so she can reach the line.

Her oxygen is running out and her lungs know it. They're inches away from blasting her mouth open. Betrayed by her own body—just what she needs.

Another series of snips before the line floats off to wherever fishing lines go when it's lost at sea. Probably going to wrap itself around a poor bird.

But they're free, and she's dragging Akili up to the surface, the neck of his shirt twisted in her hand.

Her mouth opens, her lungs claw at the air. They're greedy and they want it all—right here, right now. Akili's having the same problem, panting and gasping.

For several moments they bob on the surface, watching the boat go Titanic.

"I hope that was insured," she says. "But if it's not, you can cut down a tree and make another one—right?"

No answer.

"Can you swim?" Nothing. "Because I can swim. And I can drag you to that island if I have to, but it would be so much easier if you could swim." She nods at the island with its solid land and mimes swimming.

No, there aren't mimes swimming—she mimes swimming.

Big difference.

Turns out Akili can swim, and better than her. He's faster, but he slows himself down to keep pace.

It's not long before he's hoisting himself up onto Prasouda's rocky shore. His arms and back go Rambo or Rocky or one of those super-strong guys. Whatever. Watching his muscles move that way is making her a combination of relieved and interested. He reaches out, scoops her out of the water, caveman-style.

Then he sets her on her feet, grabs her shoulders. Turn her this way and that.

"I'm okay," she says. "You okay?"

He nods. "Okay."

That's the one English word he knows? Oh well, could be worse.

She turns back to the sea. Watches what's left of Akili's boat sink.

"Maybe it's just me," she says, "but I think you need a new boat, and we need a ride off this island."

Earlier there were boats sprinkled around the area, but they've all moved on. This could be *Lost*, minus the polar bears, the smoke monster, and one of the worst series endings in television history.

So here they are with nothing but this old monastery, a bunch of olive trees, and all the fish they can catch without a fishing rod or line.

She should have paid more attention to those shows about tickling trout.

Hand shielding her eyes (bye-bye, sunglasses; the gulf ate them) she considers their situation and decides there's nothing to be done. They can sit and wait or stand and wait.

"Earthquakes," she says, pulling her dress over her head. "I hate them. We used to live in SoCal—Southern California —when I was a kid. Funny—" She glances sideways; he's staring out to sea. "I still say 'we,' when I'm the only part of that 'we' left. So let me start over—I used to live in California, where the ground is always shaking. California's sitting on a great big fault line, and nobody ever shuts up about how the earth is going to punch the whole state off its face someday, but do they move? Nope. But we moved—at least Lana and I did, after our parents died. We were in high school when it happened. Drunk driver catapulted through a red light and used my parents' car as brakes. They died instantly, but he—the drunk guy—took about about a week to go. Which is good, because he suffered. A lot, apparently."

Her shoulders are starting to tense up as though they're paper wadded in a fist. She squeezes water out of her dress's soft cotton, trying not to care she's standing here in her red bikini. He's looking at her, isn't he? Checking out the places the bikini barely covers. The sea's not so interesting now.

"If that sounds harsh, too bad. People who've never lost anyone that way have the luxury of talking about forgiveness and how it's the right thing to do. But I won't forgive him, and I won't forgive Dr Kellerman, either. I can't talk about her right now, because it's all too fresh, and if I cry you'll think it's because we're stranded on this island—which is pretty damn beautiful, by the way."

Akili doesn't say a word. He sits there frozen, watching her unspool her words. She should feel awkward, but she doesn't. He's a good-looking man, but she's used to dealing with hot guys on a nightly basis. They lean on the bar, watch her work, and all too often they tack their sexual wish list onto their drink orders. She says no to most of them, but sometimes—not often—she says yes.

"I know not being able to forgive them makes me a terrible person, but I can live with that. I am living with that."

If she can call it living.

✢ 18 ✢

Akili

THERE ARE WORSE THINGS THAN BEING STRANDED ON AN
island with a beautiful woman.

Too bad she's not his.

But he can enjoy her—and is—from a comfortable
distance. That lean body, the gentle curves. Her perfect ass.
The thick, blonde hair that's lightening as the sun dries it out.
Those dark, soft eyes. There's an awareness in them he
doesn't often see, an intelligence, as though she sees the
world for what it is beneath its pretty surface.

He sees it, too. He knows the hefty price a person pays to
gain that knowledge.

Who has she lost?

"My best friend was murdered," he tells her. "Shot. By his
mother-in-law. Six months ago it happened, but I see him
every day on the boat. It was his boat. He left it to me so I
took it. Can't say 'no' to a dead man."

She looks at him. No smile, but there's a lot of interest, as though she genuinely wants to know what he's saying.

"Stavros—my friend—his family was a second family to me." He laughs, tries not to taint the sound with bitterness. "I say that, but my family wasn't a family. There was my mother and there was him—the man who calls himself my father. My mother was a good woman, but he wedged himself between us and kept us distant. But Stavros's family never showed me anything but kindness."

Words pour out of him, praise for the Boutos family, sadness that Stavros's death meant he lost both a friend and a family. The American woman doesn't speak, but she's the best company he has known in a long time.

He watches Lucy stretch and flex, twist her body into delicious shapes so her limbs don't fall asleep. Yeah, he wants to throw her down, fuck her on this deserted island. He's been broken since Stavros died, disinterested in women and the problems they bring. Biased, he knows; that's what happened when his best friend's mother-in-law killed Stavros. Thing about murder is that it's a splash of ink, staining the world and all its contents. It changes everything. It changed him.

But Lucy, she's a window. Through her, he's seeing a light he hasn't seen for months.

He's contemplating making a move when he sees it: the boat. Lucy sees it, too. They get up slowly, balancing on the rocks.

Lucy waves, a big, wide, two-armed gesture. The boat's occupants return her wave.

Spell broken.

What can he do? He waves, too.

❦ 19 ❧

Lucy

THEIR SAVIORS ARE GERMAN. NOT ONLY DO THEY SPEAK English, but they're staying on Trikeri, in one of the rooms above Stelios's *taverna*.

"Thank you, thank you," she says, as the boat turns toward Trikeri.

They're a husband and wife duo, both of them tall and thin and relaxed.

"You're welcome," the woman says. "You're lucky you didn't go down with the boat."

"We almost did." She recounts the events, throwing in actions for Akili's amusement. The Germans don't speak Greek beyond the polite basics, so soon they're all telling tales through the art of charades.

Most of them seem to involve livestock.

GRANDMA IS ON THE BEACH WHEN THEY LAND, JUST HER and a deck chair and a romance novel. One of those books with a cover that's mostly big dress and several acres of manly chest. She lowers the book to inspect them as they jump from deck to dock.

"I remember him on a different boat," Grandma calls out. "What happened to the old one?"

"Good news." She glances back, needs to make sure Akili isn't a dream. He's not. There he is, shirtless and tan. "We found a genie and he granted us one wish. Bad news: Akili wished for a bigger boat."

"Really?"

Sun must be getting to Grandma—sun or Stelios. "No, not really. You need to get that your gullibility meter checked. Pretty sure it's got pink eye or cataracts."

"What do you expect? It's old." She nods to the Germans, who are on their way back out to sea. "What happened?"

"Earthquake. Boat sank. We almost drowned. Have I mentioned how much I hate earthquakes?"

"Once or twice." Grandma nods to Akili who is standing hands on hips, looking at the sea. "I see he saved you."

Oh, that figures. "I saved us, Grandma. I saved us."

"Really?"

With a sweep of her hand she says, "Ask him."

A string of Greek words hangs itself up between Grandma and Akili. "He says you did the rescuing, but he helped."

Akili busts out laughing. It's infectious. The laugh spreads from Akili to Lucy. It's a relief to be alive.

"Come on," she tells Akili. "Let's drink." She performs a brief charade of a happy drinker knocking back a bottle. Less Marcel Marceau, more Robin Williams.

He stands there staring at her, blinking.

"Grandma, tell him we almost died together, so it's totally appropriate for us to share a drink."

Grandma reels off another string of Greek words. Akili doesn't have much to say. His reply is a shrug chased with an "Okay."

There it is again, his one English word.

It's a start.

TWENTY CHAIRS. FIVE TABLES ALONG THE PEBBLED BEACH. A half dozen more on the porch. The bartender with a face that's at least twenty-five percent mustache. Stelios is leaning on the bar, reading a paperback novel again. *Tavernas* don't get any Greeker than this, she's guessing.

"What are you drinking?" she asks Akili. He nods to Stelios. Holds up two fingers. Says, "*Retsina*."

"What's *retsina*?" She's seen a lot of drinks cross the bar, but never that one.

No comment from either man. That can't be good.

RETSINA COMES, DELIVERED IN WHAT LOOK LIKE CLEAR BEER bottles. Some kind of wine? It's the color of first morning urine, and it smells like a Christmas tree.

"Pine?"

"Pine resin," Stelios says. He goes back to his bar and his book, but part of his attention is latched onto Grandma on the pebbled beach.

Interesting, she thinks, and kind of adorable.

Akili nods to her bottle, lifts his own, takes a long swallow.

"No glass? Because where I come from wine usually comes in a glass."

Unless she's already buzzed. A few times she and Betsy

have shunned social graces and sucked wine straight from the bottle, after the bar closed for the night.

Yes, she always catches a cab home when they do. No way would she ever inflict her parents' fate on someone else's family.

What would Grandma do? Get a glass, probably.

The Greek god sitting across from her is leaning back in his chair, that pale smirk daring her to go where she's never gone before—at least not with a bottle of *retsina*.

Oh well, when in Greece, on a tiny island with fewer than fifty year-round locals, and with a seriously hot guy after a fun day of dancing on death's front lawn ...

She wraps her mouth around the bottle's opening, takes a long pull.

The retsina goes down. But is it a smooth ride?

Uh, no.

It punches her in the mouth, in the back of the throat, fists swinging all the way down to her stomach. Even her gastric juices are no match for *retsina*. Her gut immediately start howling about the intruder and issues an eviction notice.

The only thing stopping her from spraying Akili and the table is sheer determination. The bile rises and she swallows it back down.

Stelios looks up from his book. "Good?"

There's a long pause while she wrestles her body for control. "Have you ever licked a car's tail pipe when the engine is running?" He looks at her. "It's exactly like that."

He chuckles and goes back to his book, obviously amused with her comparison.

She looks at the bottle in her hand. If ever there was a wine that needed to breathe, it's this one. "I need a glass. Can I have one, please?"

"Put retsina in one of my glasses, the glass will melt."

"Cool story," she says.

"I just made it up."

She scoots around the bar, grabs one of the long-stemmed glasses dangling from the rack. Back at the table she pours the bottle of Satan's saliva into her new conquest.

It's not so bad after that, in the same way a truck stop bathroom on the backroads of Montana isn't so bad if you're dying to pee. The wine is wet, cold, and laced with alcohol.

But then so is rubbing alcohol if you stick it in the refrigerator.

"I drank rubbing alcohol once," she tells Akili. "I was fifteen and impressionable, and the hand pouring the drinks was attached to the hottest guy in school. It wasn't so bad mixed with apple juice. This—" She nods to the glass in her hand. "—is so much worse than that. Next time we almost drown, I'm choosing the drinks."

❧ 20 ❧

Akili

"HOW IS THE PIZZA BUSINESS?" STELIOS ASKS HIM.

Deadpan: "Busy. You know how that is."

Stelios's face splits in two. "Heh-heh. I have all the business I can handle. Any more and I would not have time to read."

"What are you reading?"

"A romance novel."

"A romance novel?"

"Good news, Akili: your hearing is excellent."

"You're reading a romance novel?"

"Why not? Love is not only for the women. I am very romantic."

Akili turns back to the American woman sitting across from him. She's looking at the wine glass like it contains a predator.

"You should come to my pizzeria. My *retsina* is better."

Stelios grunts behind the bar.

"And my pizza is the best. Everyone says so. They come from all over to eat at *Akili's Pizza*. The recipes, I learned some of them from my mother. Her cooking was good, but her pizza was the best. Even better than mine. She had a kind of magic and baked a little of it into every crust."

Yeah, he knows he's spoken more words to this women than he's spoken in total since Stavros died. But there's something freeing about talking to someone who doesn't understand him. Who knows? Maybe he'd feel the same way if they could communicate in the same language.

"What do you like on your pizza? I'm going to guess." He leans back in his seat, hands behind his head. "It's a game I play sometimes, guessing what customers want. Not the ones who sit outside and eat, but the ones who come into my shop. I watch them looking over the menu, and that's when I play the game.

"When it comes to pizza, women are more adventurous with toppings. Men, we like things simple. Meat, cheese, maybe some onions. But women are more complicated. They are more likely to build a pizza, not choose from the specials. You ..." She's watching him with those dark eyes. They're almost out of place with her blonde hair. "... are a little more complicated. I get more English and German customers than American. The few Americans that come in like salami and ham and pineapple, and sometimes bacon. Unless they're from New York, where a pizza can be just cheese. New york pizza I understand. But those Chicago pizzas? Make a bucket with the dough and pour everything inside. That's not pizza —it's *soupa*. I bet you like ham and pineapple—the Hawaiian pizza. With peppers. Red peppers."

"She does not understand a word you are saying, friend," Stelios says.

Like he doesn't know that. "That's the whole idea."

The bartender chuckles. "You have mistaken her for a psychologist and a priest. She is neither. She is a woman. And women have a way of understanding what you're saying, even when the words coming out of your mouth are *skata*. If you keep talking to her, she will see into your soul and, if you are not lucky, shit in your heart."

"Did you learn that in your romance novels?"

"Where else? I am at the part where it is obvious these two cannot be together. I would cry, but here you are. And a man does not cry in front of another man."

"I have to go," Akili tells Lucy. To Stelios: "Can you take me to the mainland?"

"Two more pages until the end of the chapter, then I will take you."

Akili knocks back what's left in the bottle. She's watching him with a mixture of disbelief and awe. "You get used to it," he promises. She shrugs, knocks back what's in the glass.

The woman's got guts, he'll give her that. Useful if you're drowning, too. And beautiful. That's the part he's trying not to fixate on, but what can he do? He's a man. Even if his head's telling him not to look, his dick didn't get the news.

A man's brain isn't in his pants, but most of the time his eyes are.

"I have to go. Work. You and your *yiayia*, you should come to Agria and try my pizza."

She'll never come. Not when she doesn't understand a word he's saying.

She looks at him, direct, question in her eyes. "Agria?"

He nods. Points to himself. Draws a house in the air with two fingers. She points at him and he nods again.

She holds up on finger, says something he doesn't understand. Then bolts outside like she's on fire.

"She's telling you to sit and stay, like a dog."

"She said like a dog?"

"No, I improvised that part to amuse myself."

"Your tip is growing smaller by the second, friend."

Stelios laughs. "This is Trikeri—who tips? Tips are for you mainlanders in tourist towns."

21

Lucy

GRANDMA IS STILL BURIED IN HER BOOK. DOESN'T LOOKS like she's planning on moving—ever. Too bad, because she needs her to move, like, now.

Lucy plants herself in front of the chair, hands on her hips. "Want to hear something interesting?"

"If you want to tell me, then I want to hear it."

"Akili is from Agria."

Does she look up from the book? No. "Oh? How do you know?"

"He told me." Now Grandma looks up her, not exactly buying the story. "He drew a house in the air with his fingers."

"Very resourceful."

"And he said something about pizza. Ask him."

"Ask him what, my love?"

"About Agria and the pizza."

"Can't it wait? I am reading."

Lucy looks at the cover again. "Where *did* you get that?"

"Stelios. He said they were his mother's."

Yeah, right. "Ten bucks says they're his. He's reading one as we speak."

"Really? What a surprise that man is." Grandma sets aside the book; a reluctant move, but at least she does it. "Okay, I will go and talk to Akili."

🎋 22 🎋

Fotini

AGRIA: THE CLOSET THAT HOLDS ALL HER SKELETONS.

Lucy holds her hands out, digs her heels in the pebbles, pulls her out of the chair. It's one of those things they have always done. Even before Lucy could walk, when she was learning to stand without tipping over, she would hold out her tiny hands to help. That girl, when she was small she was fierce, determined. She would pull Fotini off the couch, out of a chair, up off the floor, then she would clap her hands and laugh.

Today she still does the same thing.

Since they got to Greece some of her ferocity has returned.

Good. A woman needs determination, otherwise she floats through life pushed and pulled by stronger, bossier currents.

She knows; how she knows. There was a time—her time

in Greece—where she was a leaf on the ocean. If she had stayed, she would have drowned like any other leaf and become part of the ocean herself.

It is not always good to be just another drop.

Together they traipse across the pebbled shore up to the *taverna*'s porch. The boy—Akili—is reading the label on a bottle of *retsina*. He looks up at her when she walks in.

No. His eyes go to Lucy first, then they come back to the her. Who can blame him? She is old, but Lucy is young and so beautiful. By the time she is thirty she will be magnificent.

There are two ways for a woman to become magnificent, to transcend the temporary state of beauty. Be a good, kind person, or become powerful. Not in a business sense, but as the person people go to when they seek wisdom and truth. Lucy ... Lucy could be both. She is already kind, whether she realizes it or not. The whole mess with that Doctor Kellerman, those were unusual circumstances. That woman had it coming.

"My granddaughter says you know Agria."

He tilts his head down once in assent. "I have lived there my whole life. I have a pizzeria."

"Ah, that is why she mentioned pizza."

"How do you know Agria?"

She pulls out the chair, sits across from him. Lucy is behind her, a shadow ignoring the sun's limited reach. "I am from Agria. Many, many years ago now. I have not been back since I left."

"Do you have family there?" Akili asks.

With luck, no. But she doesn't say it. Doesn't want to sound cold.

She's not cold—she's honest.

"There was some, but that was a long time ago. Who knows where the winds have scattered them now?"

Stelios laughs on the far side of the bar. He has abandoned

his book for their conversation. "Where else would they be? Greeks are not seeds. We do not let the wind take us anywhere. We are trees." He holds up his fist. "We dig our roots deep down and stay, no matter how difficult life gets. That is why I am here." Palms up, he shrugs. "Business is terrible, but I stay. I am a tree who likes to read."

She turns around, looks up at Lucy. Lucy gives her a told-you-so look. So the man likes romance novels. Interesting. It is not every day she meets a man who likes romance in his books.

Akili says, "I invited Lucy—both of you—to Agria for pizza. Maybe you should come. See what has changed, see what is the same."

"Maybe," she says.

When he looks at her, he looks into her. He leans forward, resting his tanned forearms on the table. "It can be just pizza. No trip to the past."

Ah, she thinks. This is a man who knows what it is like to have *baboulas—the* bogeyman—lurking in his past. She recognizes the shadows weighing down his shoulders.

"Ready?" Stelios says, slapping his book on the bar.

Akili shoves his chair back, stands. "Let's go." To her he says, "*Akili's Pizza*. It's on the *paralia*, you cannot miss it. There's a big picture of the famous Akili on the window. Lucy saved my life, the least I can do is buy you dinner."

"It's a very kind invite. We accept."

He nods to Lucy. "Aren't you going to ask Lucy?"

Hearing her name, Lucy's glance ping-pongs from one to the other.

"Lucy loves pizza. She will not say no."

"See you both soon, I hope."

Then he and Stelios head out to find the boat Stelios keeps for ferrying himself and others to the nearest chunk of mainland.

Two good-looking men. Both of them Greek, both of them trouble. But there are worse things than trouble.

"He is still trouble," she says to her granddaughter. "But maybe the kind of trouble a woman should get into at least once. Or the kind of trouble a woman should let get into her."

Lucy rolls her eyes. "Oh God."

Sometimes she still sees the little girl in Lucy. Sometimes she sees the woman she will become.

She scoots behind the bar, opens the refrigerator and pulls out two bottles of *Amstel Light* and gives one to her granddaughter.

"Let us have a drink, then we will go and talk to God and see what He has to say."

❧ 23 ❧

Lucy

WHEN LUCY WAS THREE MONTHS OLD, HER PARENTS HAD A brief argument.

(This is hearsay, of course.)

Mom wanted her baptized in the Greek church, and Dad didn't want her baptized or christened, or anything in any church.

"Let her decide for herself when she's older," he said. "I don't want to be one of those parents who shoves religion at my child."

"That's all very well, but what until then? Who will protect her soul? If she is unbaptized, the devil could snatch her soul in the school yard."

"The devil does that?"

"The Greek devil does," her mother said.

"Really?"

"Oh yes. *Diavolos* is even more terrible than the American devil."

"Aren't they the same guy?"

"Who knows? All I know is that Lucy needs protection, just in case."

So Lucy was plunged into the local Greek Orthodox Church's font naked, pre-rubbed with a mixture of olive oil and holy water. The latter provided by the church, the former by her godparents.

And when she went to school, it was with the blue and black medallion pinned to the inside of her clothes, to ward away the evil eye.

Greeks have to be doubly alert for trouble. They're in high demand. Not only does the devil want them, but the evil eye is everywhere, hunting for attractive, successful people and adorable babies who haven't been spat on recently.

LUCY'S NOT BIG ON CHURCH. SHE GOES WHEN IT'S required (weddings, funerals, and Easter, when she goes with Grandma, because Greeks make Easter beautiful with all their candles and flowers), but she brings along a fence to sit on. It's not that she doesn't believe. But it's not that she doesn't, either.

The universe hasn't convinced her one way or another yet, so she's hedging her bets. God—if He exists—hasn't shown her much leniency in life. He's taken more than He's given.

But she's alive and she's got Grandma, so who knows?

Still, a beautiful church is a beautiful church—and the Monastery of the Virgin Mary is beautiful, in a wild, untamed way. The setup is courtyard style, its exterior walls surrounded by an orange grove that stretches its fingers almost to the sea. The road leading to the church is dirt—like most roads on the island—until a small, stone path wanders out to greet travelers.

When they reach the doors, the universe gives them a sign.

A cardboard sign.

"It's a sign," Lucy says, lips twitching.

Grandma swipes the back of her head. "Very clever. And because you are so clever, I will let you tell me what it says."

Not a chance. It's Greek penned in a spidery hand. She knows the letters, but strung together they're meaningless.

"Gone Fishing?"

"Close," Grandma says. "But not even close. The monastery is only open certain days to the public. The sign tells us—well, not you—which days those are." Grandma turns on her heel, headed back the way they came.

"Which days?" Lucy calls out.

"Where is *Google* when you need it, eh?" She's chuckling as she says it.

"Which days?"

"Not today."

Very funny. This is what she gets for shunning the Greek language. Mom tried to sweet-talk both daughters into taking Greek classes, but to a couple of American kids there was no future in a second language the way there was in ballet and piano.

Those ballet skills come in really handy when she's trying to read Greek signs. And Lana, the piano really helped her, didn't it?

Yeah, Greece is paradise, but the heat is putting her in a snit.

There she goes blaming the country, blaming the heat, when she's the problem. She carefully packed that snit in her carry-on luggage and forgot to declare it at Customs. Probably, it's illegal to bring a bad mood into Greece. The people seem that kind of laid-back. Even Akili handled almost-drowning with a disturbing amount of calm.

Who walks away from death without a blip in their pulse?

Robots, that's who. Sociopaths. Aliens of the outer space kind, maybe.

But not people.

A quick jog brings her abreast with her grandmother. "What's the deal with Akili, do you think?"

"Who knows? But he carries burdens, and they are heavy. Poor man. I wonder if maybe he would not have minded dying out on the sea?"

Lucy double takes. A death wish—really? "I don't understand anyone who commits suicide. I mean, I get that it happens, but I don't *get* it."

"My love, too many people who have sat in my office wanted death—or believed they wanted it. Sometimes I do not think they realize how permanent that arrangement is. Others understand the permanence and embrace it. Both types of people break my heart; they carry so much pain. Sometimes I see myself in them, not as I am now, but as a girl."

Lucy slides her arm through Grandma's. "You never talk about Greece much. Or your family. And mine, too, I suppose."

"Some memories do not deserved to be remembered. And if they are, it should only be as a cautionary tale. My father—your great-grandfather—was not a good man."

Not easy asking a question and holding her breath at the same time. This is the most Grandma has ever said about Greece, or her family, in one conversation. It's a moment fragile and precious.

"What about your mother?"

"She was a Greek wife in a time when Greek wives had no

voice. To speak was to invite bigger problems than she needed. She was a mouse, married to a lion."

"Like Scar in *The Lion King*?"

A small chuckle. "Scar was a pussycat compared to my father. Come, let us forget him. He is long gone, buried who cares where? There is not even enough anger left in me to want to piss on his grave."

They wander back to their room, a slower trip down than up. The sun is reaching for its topmost rungs. Before long it'll be climbing down the other side. It's siesta time in Greece. That block of hours reserved for sleep and other languid pursuits.

Grandma kicks off her walking shoes, settles onto her bed book in hand, the couple on the cover still clinched. "I was thinking that maybe tomorrow we will go to the mainland. I have a friend in Platanidia. She is a grandmother now, like me. Maybe even a great-grandmother. And in the evening, we will go and see a man about some pizza, eh?"

Her pulse starts to skip, thinking about seeing Akili again.

It'll be fun. She can't understand him, he can't understand her. Perfect.

"Sounds great."

Not great at all. Grandma's expression says so.

🕸 24 🕸

Fotini

WHAT WERE THEY THINKING, SHE AND SARAH, NOT making sure the girls could speak Greek? The opportunity to know another language is a gift. It keeps the brain sharp and opens doors to other worlds.

To know one tongue is to be limited.

Yes, her granddaughter has that travel book with its polite phrases, but life is not lived with words polished and printed so that anyone can use them without offense, or anything to separate them from the next person with the same travel book.

Oh well, it is too late now. What's done is done.

Or what's not done is not done, in this case.

Lucy lets out a sigh as she falls onto the crisp sheets. "Logically I know it's the same summer we have back home, but it's like this heat carries a giant hose so it can suck the life out of you."

"We are on the coast, yes, but it is a dry heat. And also we are on vacation. There is nothing we are expected to do except relax."

"Is that what it is?" Lucy asks. "Then I accept."

There's a small *poof!* as her granddaughter punches her pillow into a more comfortable shape.

Fotini stays on her back, hands resting against the book tented on her stomach.

Agria. Oh, it was just another village in a country filled with villages. Beautiful, yes, but is there a Greek village not worthy of a photographer's snapping eye? Even the ugly places in Greece have their own wild charm. Or they used to. Now, who knows? That cement plant outside Volos huffs and puffs in the gulf's face. There is no beauty in a manmade construct when that construct is designed for biting into the land.

Agria will have grown. It is inevitable, especially now that it's a suburb of Volos. It used to be its own entity, but the city gobbled it up in 2011.

She wants to laugh.

Bet that went over well, especially with the older generation—her generation. People in Agria are proud. To them, their village is paradise, a civilized getaway from the city. But now they are just another one of the city's limbs.

What would her father think if he was still alive? She can almost picture his tantrum and subsequent heart attack.

Eh, who knows? Maybe the old bastard is still alive. The worst people have a way of clinging to life, long after the world is sick of hating them.

A cold front moves across her chest.

Here she is, an old woman, and still he has that power over her. She cannot follow her own professional advice and leave her family to rot in the past.

A grown woman afraid of monsters. What a waste of energy.

They will go to Agria, she and Lucy, and they will eat Akili's pizza. But that is all. She won't ask about old friends, about family, about people who might still remember her name. Not her married name, but the one that was hers before she married—

Before she married.

So many years, so many memories stuffed between the bookends of her life, and still she cannot think her husband's name without the bottom falling out of her life.

"Can't sleep, Grandma?"

She turns her head, smiles at her granddaughter. "No. I am too used to living the American way."

"Not me," Lucy says. "I fully embrace this siesta thing. We should have that back home. Mandatory nap times. Can you imagine?"

Fotini laughs. Yes, she can imagine. Every company in the country would—as they say—shit themselves. "Sleep. I think I will go for a cold drink, maybe sit in the shade and read."

"Have fun," Lucy mumbles. "And don't do anything I wouldn't do."

SHE SLAPS THE BOOK ON THE COUNTER. "WHAT ELSE HAVE you got for me?"

Stelios chuckles. He reaches below the bar, drags out a huge shopping bag stuffed with books, dumps them all on the polished wood. "You want a book, I have books."

Romance novels, all of them. English language, too.

"Why English?"

"Because I dream of meeting a beautiful English-speaking

woman. And if I read these books I will know how to woo her, yes?"

"Or maybe you just like romance novels."

He grins, nods. "Or maybe I just like romantic stories."

"I like romantic stories, too. The endings are always happy and they are full of hope. Which one do you recommend?"

"Eh ... Let me look. These are not all I have." He starts digging through the pile, sorting them into stacks on the bar. The books are in varying states of decomposition, read by a hundred pairs of eyes.

"Where do you get them?"

"Sometimes people leave them behind. But most of them I get from *eBay*. They sell big lots of them, you know. Ten, twenty, or more at a time. And for almost nothing but the cost of shipping."

"*Ebay*!" She laughs. "You have Internet here?"

"No. Of course not. We barely have electricity. For Internet I go to the mainland."

What a surprise he is. Face like a rock, body like an aging god, mind like a box of soft-centered chocolates.

"I do not want to go to Agria," she says carefully. "But tomorrow, I must go."

He doesn't look up from his books. "Why go if you do not want to go?"

"Do you have grandchildren?"

"No. I never married."

"Why not?"

"I never found the right woman. Only many of the wrong women. Although at the time I was young and stupid and I thought they were right."

There's no stopping her smile. "You are all the same, Greek men."

"Ha! Show me another Greek man who reads romance novels and I will shake his hand."

But she can't can she? She can't even point to an American man who reads them. If they do it's in private, not at a bar when anyone can see them.

"So which one is best, have you decided?"

He taps on a book. On the cover are a man and woman permanently locked a painful-looking pose. A human arm cannot do that without snapping. The background is a castle, and the threat to the couple's happiness seems to be a very angry horse. "I like this one. The man is a rake, but by the end he is transformed."

"Aren't they always?"

"Yes. But if the book is good, then you believe in that transformation." He nods at the book she's inspecting. "You want a *frappe* to go with that?"

"Of course!"

There's a sparkle in his eye. "Make me one, too, eh?"

"You wish, old man."

The smile he gives her is a broad one. He sweeps the books back into their bag, stows them in their hiding place under the bar. Then he gets to work filling a shaker with coffee, sugar, ice cubes, and cold water."

"You remember how I like it?"

He taps his head. "My memory is like a razor. I forget nothing. Of course when you only have a few customers ...."

When the iced coffee is done and poured into a tall glass, he goes back to leaning on his bar. "Why did you ask if I have grandchildren?"

She drags on the straw before answering. The caffeine gets to work shaking the drowsiness from her bones. "If you have children and grandchildren you do anything for them. I do not want to go to Agria, but I will go because of Lucy."

"Why does Lucy want to go to Agria?"

"Akili."

"Ah."

"What do you know of him?"

He shrugs. "Very little. I did not know him until a few months ago. Now he comes in maybe once a week for a *frappe*, always alone, always with his boat, and he brings me olive oil and occasionally other supplies. But now I suppose he will not be back—at least not with that boat. Who knows if he will buy another one?"

"Why wouldn't he?"

"He inherited the boat when his best friend was killed a few months ago. Very terrible story. His friend married a girl in secret, and her mother murdered him."

"How awful!"

"Yes. Very bad business. I think maybe his friend was the only true friend he had. They were friends since they were small boys. Today was the first time I have ever seen him smile."

"With Lucy."

"Yes, with Lucy."

"She has that effect on people. Or she used to. I have lost a daughter, a son-in-law, and a few months ago I lost my other granddaughter—Lucy's sister."

"How are you coping?"

How is she coping?

Is she coping?

She must be if she is here, but it is daily struggle. All she has in the world now is Lucy, and she wants to hug the girl to her and keep her safe forever. But that's not good for Lucy.

"I do what I have to. And what I have to do—" She waves the book at him. "—is read."

He grins at her. "Go, read your book, drink your *frappe*. And when you are ready, I will be here with more books and more *frappe*."

"Okay, okay, I'm going. Can you take us to the mainland tomorrow?"

"Let me know what time and we will go. But I want to hear all about Lucy and Akili. All the details."

Yes, he is a surprise. Maybe a good one.

❧ 25 ❧

Akili

UNTIL SIX MONTHS AGO, HE PUSHED THIS GATE OPEN EVERY day of his life, as far back as his memory goes. These days when he pushes it open, he feels like an intruder. Doesn't matter than *Kyria* and *Kyrios* Boutos treat him like a second son, guilt still slides its long blade between his ribs and twists.

The Boutos house is typical for Agria. L-shaped, flat-roofed, white. Not too different from his own house.

Kyria Boutos is in the yard, sweeping invisible dirt. That's how it is here—everybody sweeps. When they are done sweeping, everything gets the hose.

When she sees him, she ushers him to sit in the yard with her. She rushes inside, and when she comes back out, it's with coffee and the *koulouraki* she knows he loves. Then she sits in her usual chair.

(*Koulouraki* is a not-too-sweet Greek cookie. It's usually a twisted or looped shape.)

Helena Boutos looks well. Better than she has since Stavros's death. She's regaining lost weight, taking pride in her appearance again.

Elbows on knees, he rubs his forehead. "I lost the boat today."

"Stavros's boat?"

"Yes."

Silence.

One thing Stavros left him, now it's gone. Lost isn't an accurate word—he knows where it is: at the bottom of the gulf, or thereabouts.

"How did it happen?"

He unravels the whole story, right down to the happy ending where a couple of Germans rescued them from Prasouda.

Helena rocks back in her seat, hands in the air. Reminds him of Kermit the Frog. "Akili, you met a girl!"

He lost her dead son's boat and she's excited he met a girl? Greek mothers ....

"This is wonderful," she continues. "A girl! At last!"

"I've only met her twice."

"Yes, but you will marry her. What else can you do with a woman who rescues you?"

"What about the boat?"

She scoffs. "I hated that boat. It was ugly. Who paints a boat orange and blue? It looks much better on the bottom of the sea, I guarantee it." A laugh wrings itself out of her chest. "So ugly. I do not know what he was thinking."

"It was ugly," he admits, then sets about changing the topic.

Small talk? She won't do it. Not when there's blood in the water. And as far as a Greek mother is concerned, a single woman is the equivalent of a bleeding fish. Helena Boutos wants Lucy's entire life story.

Too bad he doesn't know it.

He buys *Kyria* Boutos off with a description and a promise to deliver more details when he's got them. Then she hugs him the way she always has, except now there's a slightly desperate edge. He understands, and he lets her have this moment. He is not Stavros, but like this, she can pretend he is. She kisses him on both cheeks and smiles up at him.

"Akili, before you go ...."

"Yes, *Kyria* Boutos?"

"Do you have any positions open at the pizzeria?"

"What kind of position?"

"Anything. Waiting tables, food preparation. Dishes."

"You looking for work?"

"No. But Drina ..."

Drina. Stavros's widow. The Romani girl. "Would she want to work for me?"

"She is too proud to say she needs work, but I know she would welcome the opportunity, especially from you."

Especially from him, Stavros's best friend.

"How is she?"

"Her husband is dead, her mother is in prison. But she gets up every day and looks for work that is not picking fruit."

"She's living here now?"

"No. With her father still. Kristos and I, we keep asking her to move in here, but she is proud."

Too proud, or maybe she just has a father she loves too much to leave.

Got no idea what that's like, does he?

HAWAIIAN, HE THINKS. THESE TWO TOURISTS WILL ORDER Hawaiian pizza. Ham, cheese, pineapple. Maybe that's not what they like, but it's what they'll order. They're on vacation in a warm place, and Hawaiian pizza is—in their minds—synonymous with warm vacation spots. Their matching shorts, shirts, and belt bags say so.

He spins the dough, loosening the gluten chains so it can stretch. When it's done, he slaps it into the oiled tray. Some places use stone, but Akili's Pizza does a thin, light crust. For that, the tins are better.

Sure enough, they order the Hawaiian.

Thanasi leans against the counter between orders. "What happened to your boat?"

Good kid. Fresh out of high school, but he's a hard worker. He does a little of this, a little of that where the pizzeria needs it. Tonight he's bussing tables. It's a fast night, a lot of turnover. People eating and moving on.

"Did something happen to your boat?" Patra shimmies up to the counter, arranges herself in the alluring position.

He's not allured. "It sank."

"What happened?" she asks.

"Earthquake banged the bottom against the rocks near Prasouda. No more boat."

Thanasi's eyes widen. Now that he thinks about it, the kid's got Lucy's coloring. Fair hair, dark eyes. "Whoa, you were on it at the time?"

He looks at the newest ticket. *Souvlaki* pizza—no olives. "Yes."

"How did you get back?" he asks.

"I swam."

"Really?"

"No." Akili laughs. "I caught the bus after the bartender on Trikeri gave me a ride to the mainland."

Thanasi slaps his shoulder. "You are one lucky man. You could have drowned out there."

"I almost did, thanks to the fishing line, but I had a savvy passenger on board. She saved both our behinds."

Patra's eyes narrow. He's not even hers and she's jealous. "She?"

"Just some woman—a tourist—from Trikeri."

"Who goes to Trikeri? Nobody."

"Some people go," Thanasi says. "Otherwise why would they have hotels and a ferry from Volos?"

Patra ignores him. "How did she save you?"

Akili looks up. "I'm not paying you two for the conversation. Want to talk? Go talk the customers into eating more pizza."

But he's smiling as he says it, isn't he?

Makes a change.

"I lost the boat today. It sank."

Nothing but a grunt from the old man.

When he got home, he threw open the windows and doors, let the fresh air in. Then he rolled his father outside into the night. He plated a slice of pizza, gave it to the old man, then took a seat on the opposite side of the iron table.

Now here he is, trying to be a decent guy, make some conversation. The old man's got to be lonely, rotting in his chair.

"I'm thinking about buying another one."

"What for?"

He leans back in the chair, hands behind his head, takes in those stars. Is Lucy seeing them, too? He wonders what she makes of Greece's skies.

"I like the sea."

"Obviously the sea does not like you or your boat would not have sunk."

Virgin Mary, the old man is a sour bastard. "Wasn't the sea, it was the ground. Earthquake."

"What do you expect? We live in Greece. All Greece does is shake, shake, shake. You want steady ground, go somewhere else."

"Wasn't complaining. Just making conversation."

Grunt. "Where will you get the money for another boat?"

"I have the money."

"Oh, you do, do you? How much money do you have?"

"Enough for a small boat." More money than he'll ever let his father know about.

"Maybe you should put me in a home with that money."

"This is your home."

"It's not a home. It's two men under one roof. I am a cripple and you are an idiot."

Old news. He's always been an idiot in his father's eyes—has been since long before the old man was disabled.

"You want to go to church Sunday?"

"No, I don't want to go to church Sunday. What for?"

"Socialize," Akili says. "Get right with God."

"Get right with God," he mocks. "Socialize. Why would I do that? God knows what I am and I know what He is. Socialize ... bah! My friends are dead or busy. Why would they care about me?"

Good point. His father never had friends—just men down at the *kafeneio* who liked to yell about politics. After his father's accident—

(Ha. Accident.)

—none of them cared enough about his sudden absence to come calling at the front gate. There was never a Stavros in his life.

"Don't go to church then. I don't care."

"Of course you don't care. Why would you care? You're waiting until I die, then you will throw a party."

Akili brings out a second slice of pizza, drops it on the old man's plate. "I'm going to bed."

"Always you are running somewhere. Run, run, little boy. Life will still catch you."

When he flops on the bed, his pulse is galloping. That old bastard boils his blood. No matter how good or bad the day is, his father's always here with a shovel of shit to heap on him.

Akili closes his eyes. When he does, she's there. The American woman. Lucy. He's watching her take that virgin swallow of *retsina*. Feeling the fear when he came up for air and she was gone. Seeing her in that red bikini, waiting on a boat to drift by so they could get back to Trikeri.

He remembers her every move, every curve. That tiny birthmark at the base of her spine.

His cock remembers her, too. It would do anything to bend her over this bed and slam her hard enough to almost break her.

Not that he wants to break her, but his cock would like a shot at it. The man part of his brain just wants her in the same room so they can talk. Him at him, her at him. Two different conversations, but so what?

It doesn't matter when the person feels good.

26

Lucy

LUCY'S UP BEFORE THE SUN. IN FACT SHE'S HEADED TO THE beach, waiting on it to arrive, for a change. Usually she keeps the sun waiting and wondering if today's the today she'll get up and shine.

The *taverna* is closed but its doors are open. That's invitation and loophole enough for Lucy. She glances up at the ceiling, speculating whether the rooms upstairs are both still occupied.

Doesn't matter, she moves quietly anyway, making coffee in the thinning darkness.

Before the percolator's done she hears feet tramping down the stairs.

"Coffee?" The question comes from the German man who saved them from their temporary exile on Prasouda. He's a beanpole, with a reddish-blond mustache that hangs like Spanish moss.

"Coming right up," she says. "Two?"

"Two," he tells her. "My wife will sleep until she smells coffee. Then like magic, she will jump out of bed the way Claudia Schiffer used to jump out of David Copperfield's box."

She laughs. "Sounds like me. Coffee is the best reason to get up in the morning."

"I try to sleep in the mornings, but I never can. Too many years of getting up early for work."

"You're retired now?"

He pulls out one of the four barstools, sits. "Since last month."

"How is it—retirement? My Grandmother's keeps talking about retirement, but she likes working too much to quit." Or is she stuffing the gaps in her life with other people's problems?

"We are in Greece, how can we complain?" He chuckles. It's a big, belly-shaking sound, which is funny, because he's a skinny guy. "We come to Greece every summer. A different place every time. Eventually we'll see the whole country."

She pours coffee into three mugs, puts two on a tray with sugar and cream from the bar's refrigerator. "Any favorites?"

"Delphi. It would be a shame to die without seeing Delphi, or without dancing on a tour bus."

"You danced on a bus? How?"

"We were traveling to Thessaloniki. The Greek passengers put on some music and began to dance in the aisle. So we did too."

Lucy laughs. Dancing on a Greek bus sounds fraught with peril. She's experienced firsthand how Greek bus drivers handle roads.

"I think I'll pass."

He pours cream into his coffee, takes a sip. Makes a satisfied sound. "Don't pass on things because they seem crazy.

You will lead a very boring life if you do. The crazy moments stick with you. They're what you will remember at the finish line." He lifts the tray. "Live, love, eat strange food. Get coffee from a pretty girl who has broken into a bar."

"The door was open, I didn't break in."

"It is still a good story, yeah? Something to take home and remember. My wife says thank you."

Then he vanishes up the stairs.

She carries her own cup outside—milk, too much sugar—and sits on the smooth pebbles a billion or so years worth of tides carried here.

The sun is coming. Won't it be surprised to see her here?

She is, that's for sure.

⸻

SLOWLY, PEOPLE TRICKLE INTO THE BEACHSIDE *TAVERNA*. People being Stelios and Grandma. Yes, from different directions.

"You made coffee?" Stelios calls out.

"I made coffee."

"You want a job?"

"You can't afford me."

He laughs. "I cannot afford me, either. But here I am. You two want breakfast?"

"Let me guess," Grandma says. "If we say yes, you will ask us to make you breakfast, too."

He winks at Lucy. "Already she knows me too well."

"She's a psychologist. She knows everybody too well. Especially me."

"A psychologist, eh? Go ahead, analyze me."

Grandma snorts. She sips her coffee, raises her eyebrows. "I think you are a man who wants to make us breakfast—and soon, before we die from starvation."

"It could happen" Lucy says. Back of her hand pressed to her forehead, she says, "I already feel faint. I ... need ... bacon and eggs."

"What do you want bacon for? You are already a ham," Grandma says.

Above their heads, the floor starts squeaking.

"Newlyweds?" Grandma eyes are twinkling.

"Oldlyweds," Lucy tells her.

"Sex is life," Stelios says casually. "No bacon, but I have *spanakopita*."

"Who made it?"

Both palms up. "*Kyria* Maria. Who else?"

Grandma shrugs. "Okay, we will eat her spanakopita. But if we get sick ..."

"If you get sick, who will I talk to about romance novels? No one. You will not get sick from *Kyria* Maria's food."

He disappears into the tiny galley kitchen, leaving the two women to listen to the ceiling's complaints.

"Someone has a lot of energy," Grandma says. "I wish I had that much energy."

Grandma's got plenty of energy. Lucy was the one struggling to keep up with her yesterday on that walk to the monastery. Okay, so she'd had a traumatic morning, what with the near-drowning, but still, Grandma was the powerhouse.

"I wish I had someone to have that much energy with."

"I hear you," Grandma says. They look at each other, laugh. It's always funny when her grandmother uses trendy lingo. "It's been too long."

"La-la-la. I don't want to know."

Hoisting herself up onto one of the barstools, Grandma sighs. "Neither do I. What about you?"

That's Grandma the therapist talking, not Grandma the grandmother.

Lucy hopes.

"Not since Lana got sick."

Grandma looks at her. No judgement, just—okay, lots of judgment.

"What? It's not that bad. I meet guys, but there's almost never any spark."

"Spark I understand. The strongest spark I ever knew was with your grandfather. I think spark is for the very young. Young people are chunks of flint, and they make sparks with almost everyone they bump into. Sometimes—like with your grandfather—those sparks ignite and become a flame. But more often they just fade, and if you are lucky you do not get a disease."

Lucy holds her breath. Granddad is another one of those mysteries. All she knows is a name and that Grandma was pregnant with Mom when she fled to the United States.

"What was he like?"

"Your grandfather?" Lucy nods. "Handsome. Very kind. He only had good things to say about people. He wanted to be a doctor, but his family would not allow it."

"How did you meet?"

"Who remembers? It was another life." Her attention shifts to the open door between the bar and kitchen. "Where is that Stelios?"

That's some professional-grade avoidance.

"Good food takes time," he bellows from the kitchen. Then he appears—*abracadabra*—balancing three plates. He slides all three onto the bar. Two plates covered with generous slabs of *spanakopita*—spinach and feta pie—and a third with two slices of roughly cut toast and a puddle of olive oil.

"What's that?" Lucy nods at plate number three.

"What does it look like?" Stelios asks.

"Toast and olive oil."

"Good news: you are not blind." He winks at Grandma,

tears a chunk off his toast, dipping it in the oil. "This is good oil. It is made by an American woman. Can you believe it?"

Grandma raises an eyebrow. "American olive oil?"

"No, the oil is Greek, the woman is American." He chews for a moment, swallows. "Funny coincidence, she lives in Agria." He nods to Lucy. "Your friend Akili brings me her oil."

Not her friend. Not her anything, really.

Okay, so he crept into her dreams last night, replacing the usual nameless, faceless guy in her sexual shenanigans. But that's only natural, isn't it? They almost drowned together. A shared traumatic experience has a way of binding people together. Look at 9/11. Every American was a New Yorker that day.

"Nice sunburn," Stelios says, his mouth full.

Good thing Lucy looks good in red, because her skin matches her bikini. Today she's wearing it under her dress for support, because if she puts on a bra she'll cry.

"Oh, you like it? I got it in Greece."

"No!"

"Yes! And it was free."

"I cannot believe it."

"True story," she says, shoveling another load of pie into her mouth.

"Sunburn is like Chinese food," he says. "It does not last long."

They eat breakfast, talk, but it's Grandma and Stelios who keep the conversation afloat. Lucy is content to drift into the background so her wheels can silently turn. Today they're going to the mainland, her grandmother's Greece. What are they going to find? Will being there loosen Grandma's tongue or tighten her lips? She's already won a couple of puzzle pieces since they arrived, but Grandma's past is an enormous puzzle; a busy landscape where there are more unfolding flowers than sky.

When they're done, Lucy clears away what's left of breakfast (nothing), leaving her grandmother and Stelios to talk. It feels good to move around the kitchen, washing dishes, being useful, while the chatter keeps her a distant sort of company.

Maybe she should do this back home, open a Greek style *taverna* in a town nobody's ever heard of except the people who live there.

It's a nice dream. Placid, comforting.

Stelios pokes his head around the open doorway. "Are you going to clean my kitchen all day?"

She grins. "Not if I can help it."

"Then come on. Your grandmother is ready to go to the boat."

It's the same smallish motorboat from the day before yesterday. Has it only been two days? Seems longer. Time moves differently on vacation. Or maybe the warping of time is Greece's way.

She wipes her hands, folds the towel, grabs her bag.

"Perfect. Let's get this boat on the water."

THERE'S ALREADY A FAMILIARITY TO THIS PLACE, A FEELING that she's either been here before, or been here forever. What's it going to be like in two weeks when they leave?

Stelios's boat churns the green water into a foam that dissipates almost immediately. On top of his head is a ball cap. Not very Greek.

"Aren't you supposed to be wearing one of those Greek fishing hats?"

He laughs under his mustache. "Those are for old men

and men in movies about Greece. I like this hat. More shade."

Makes sense.

They're not the only ones on the sea. Greece is up and moving, getting the day started before the sun pulls out its daggers. Small fishing boats hold divers pulling on wetsuits.

Now Lucy's got another question. Here she's full of them. "What are they doing?"

"Diving for sponges. Sponges used to be big business here. It is still business, but not so big. Today it is more profitable to buy them cheap from other countries, but Greek sponges —from this area in particular—are very good quality."

She flips through the pages of the travel guide. Doesn't say a word about sponges. "I had no idea."

"In the old days, it was dangerous work. These days ... not too much. But in the beginning, they would send a man down naked, carrying a rock. When he found a sponge, he would cut the sponge loose and put it in a special net, and the men on the boat would pull him back up. Today, they have fancy diving equipment and wetsuits. This is Greek progress."

Ten minutes later, he's inching the boat up to the dock at Alogoporos.

"Call me when you want to come back, eh? I can be here in ten minutes."

"What if you're asleep?" Grandma asks.

"I will wait up. A good book will help, yes?"

27

Fotini

SHE LIKES STELIOS. HE'S GOOD COMPANY. APART FROM
family, it has been a while since she had such good company.
Attractive too, if you enjoy a man whose edges are rough and
salty, like a chip.

It's almost two hours by bus up to Agria, but they're stopping sooner in Platanidia to visit with the Triantafillou family.

She and the family's matriarch are old friends; there was a
time when Irini was her only friend.

The bus has two doors, one front, one back. Passengers
get on the back of the bus, pay the conductor who sits in a
small booth, then when their stop comes, they leave through
the front door.

Do it the other way and the conductor will beat you with
dirty looks. He may not say anything, but try getting on his
bus again.

The bus chugs its way north-west. Look at Lucy; she is

like a little girl with her face pressed to the window. Her breath has made a small, damp circle on the window. Every so often she turns around just long enough to say, "Does it still look the same? What's changed?"

Everything has changed.

But mostly her.

There are more trees, more houses, more businesses. And more traffic. Greece is older, and so is she.

Below her ribcage, a thousand mosquitoes buzz, buzz. Not butterflies. Butterflies mean you are anticipating something exciting and good. Mosquitos ... eh, who is glad to have a mosquito anywhere near them?

Nobody, that is who.

Platanidia is almost the same. She recognizes its face and she discovers her feet still know the way. It is a quarter mile—whatever that is in the metric system—along the beach.

Her friend's house is where it has always been, only now there is a bigger house squatting nearby. Both houses are white stucco, but the smaller house is one neat layer that is more yard than house. It's crammed full of potted plants, in red pots and painted cans. Gardenias, jasmine, geraniums, and a small orange tree that is too young to grow fruit. As is often the way here, a cactus frames one side of the front door, its mirror a laurel shrub. The shrub isn't just decoration; its leaves are better known as bay leaves. Very good for cooking. The cactus is to chase away bad luck; pricks to keep the pricks away.

"*Kalos orisate*, Fotini! Come, come, let me look at you."

It is her old friend welcoming them. Behind the black widow's clothes, behind the years on her face and body, the girl she knew is still in there.

Where is your black, Fotini?

Her guilt has a big, loud mouth, even after fifty years.

Kiss, kiss. One on each cheek, the Greek way. Then they stand apart, holding hands.

"How are you, my friend?"

"Old." Irini laughs. "How did that happen? I was young only yesterday."

"It must be a trick," Fotini says.

"That is what I think, too. Somewhere in time, we are still young and beautiful."

"In a cave, held prisoner by *striglas.*" Lucy's gaze is bouncing from woman to woman. "This is my granddaughter, Lucy," she says, pulling Lucy forward.

Her old friend clutches her chest with one dramatic hand. "*Panayia mou*, she looks like—"

"I know. And so did her mother—my daughter."

"Did?"

"Sarah passed some time ago."

Irini squeezes the hand she's still holding. "Oh, my friend. Come. You are lucky, today my granddaughter and great-granddaughter are here. My Irini is a psychologist, also! She has no husband, but she has a good job, so that is something."

She ushers them into the house, where a lovely young woman is kneeling on the kitchen floor, her hands holding a baby steady as the tot lurches forward on unsteady feet. It is a marvelous game—the baby's giggles say so.

The woman looks up, smiles. "*Yia sou.* I'm Irini and this is my angel."

CONFUSED? GREEK NAMES CONFUSE EVERYONE—EVEN Greeks.

Here's how it works.

The firstborn grandson gets his father's father's name.

The firstborn granddaughter gets her father's mother's name. The secondborn children get their mother's parents' names.

After that, you are lucky. Run out of grandparents and the name you get is yours.

The bigger the family, the more complicated things get. Six cousins with the same name? Tack their parent's name onto the end.

If Lucy was Greek, with five cousins sharing her name, they'd call her Lucy *Thea* Sarah. *Thea* being the Greek word for aunt.

Things are changing in bigger places than this, parents are pinning new names to their children, but here ... tradition matters. Otherwise you do not love your parents and choose to cut out their hearts and feed them to Romani dogs.

THE WALLS ARE THE BRIGHT VERSION OF TURQUOISE, THE floors white and grey flecked marble, the art an even mix between political and religious; it's a home with more love than decorating taste.

"*Po-po*," Irini the elder says. "Why have you got the baby on the floor again? Pick her up."

"Greeks don't believe in letting a baby crawl all over the floor," Fotini tells Lucy.

"Why not?"

Irini's granddaughter scoops up her baby, sits back on her haunches. "Who knows? *Yiayia* says it because her mother said it, and her mother said it, and so on." Her English is close to perfect and only lightly accented. "One of them did it, so they all do it. Like sheep."

"But not you," Lucy says.

Irini laughs. "Not me. I am the rebel of the family. I even

made this—" She holds up her daughter, blows a raspberry on her cheek. "—without a husband. Scandalous."

There's a tightness around her eyes as she says it, as if maybe the husband part was not intentional—or perhaps painful.

Two generations apart, yet she and this young woman seem like they might have more than psychology in common.

During Fotini's time in Greece, guests didn't sit in the kitchen unless they were good friends or family. Most Greek homes in those days kept a room for visitors, one where all the family's finery was on display. Anything precious was kept in that room. Good tablecloths, delicate china, ornate frames with their photos, and trinkets received as gifts. Company would wait there quietly for the hostess to bring her hospitality into the room on a fancy tray: coffee, water, and something sweet. The sweets varied. Sometimes you would get cake or Greece's version of cookies (usually honey-drenched or powdered sugar-smothered), or preserved fruit, dished up on a tiny crystal plate with a polished spoon.

But here and now, she's happy to be in this kitchen. She's grown beyond the stuffy room and its false advertising. A kitchen is the beating heart of a home—unless you're the kind of person who lives on takeout.

Irini the elder chats as she bustles about her kitchen, shaking *frappes* and dishing diamond-shaped, nut-filled *baklava* onto plates.

"Yes, you made that without a husband," her old friend says, switching back to Greek, "but she is so beautiful that we do not mind too much. But if you make another one without a husband, your parents will kill you dead."

Fotini catches the wilt of Irini the younger's smile, but she recovers quickly, fastening its edges into place with invisible tape.

"What about you, Fotini, do you have great-grandchildren?" her old friend wants to know.

It's not really her question to answer. Lucy's business is Lucy's business. But yes, she'd like to have great-grandchildren before she dies.

"Not yet. Someday, perhaps."

Irini the elder nods at Lucy. "That one does not have a husband?"

"Not yet. She's still young."

"Young is the best time to catch one."

Lucy's gaze is bouncing between women. She hates to alienate her girl this way, but her old friend's English is the equivalent of one of those rust buckets that hauls cement out to sea.

But she'll be fine. Irini's granddaughter is speaking to her, and Lucy's attention is shifting from the two old woman to the young woman and her child.

❧ 28 ❧

Lucy

IT'S THE STUFF OF NIGHTMARES, BEING TRAPPED IN A SPACE where every spoken word is foreign. It's as though someone has yanked the plug connecting her to the rest of the world.

Woman in a bubble—that's how it feels.

She looks at the younger woman and her baby. The baby is adorable. Chubby cheeks, sweet face, toothy smile. Her mother is runway-ready. She's not model tall, but she's one of those rare people who gets fashion right. Her hair is pulled up into a perfect ponytail, no escapee hairs in sight. She's in one of those maxi-dresses that skims the tops of her slender, tanned feet. She wears white the way Lucy never can; for her it's an open invitation for messes to step right up and make themselves at home.

Irini's watching the two grandmothers, shaking her head. When she speaks it's to Lucy and it's—blissfully—English again.

"Put two old women together and the conversation inevitably turns toward marriage—who is getting married, who isn't married, and why."

"Figures," Lucy says. "Could be worse—they could be lining up husbands for us."

Irini grins. It's a wide, white, friendly expanse of gleaming teeth. "Give them time and they will do that, too."

"Have they tried yet?" She nods to the adorable baby, who is currently gnawing on one of the table's metal legs.

"Oh, yes. They brought single men from several towns to dinner, one at a time. After the first few, I pretended to have *Dissociative Identity Disorder*. After that, my family stopped inviting them."

"Multiple personalities? I'll have to remember that, just in case."

"I hate to use my job against them, but sometimes you have to—how you say—pull out the big guns. One of my personalities was a little boy with a mouth like a sewer. Another was a dog. I put my dinner on the floor and bit my date's leg."

Lucy laughs. "Desperate times."

"Yes. What about you? What do you do when you are not visiting our country?"

The floor drops out of her gut. What she should be doing is applying for jobs in the financial sector. Instead, she's slinging drinks in the bar, basically using her degree as a coaster.

"Waiting, I guess."

"For what?"

"Waiting to figure out what I'm waiting for."

"I understand. In my own way, I am waiting, too."

"What for?"

"A miracle, the same as most people." She laughs, but it's

aimed at herself. "What a thing it is to be a psychologist who cannot unravel her own life."

"I've always heard that a huge chunk of the people who take psych are taking it to figure themselves out."

Her laugh settles into a smile. "Now that I believe. But I also love what I do. People are interesting. Life is interesting."

Lucy thinks life is interesting right up until you lose most of your family, then it turns into a major bitch. But she doesn't say it, because analysis isn't what she needs. A necromancer, that's what she needs. Someone to raise the dead and make them breathe again.

Grandma's attention swings their way, reminding her of a lighthouse's benevolent beam. "Are you two plotting world domination?"

Lucy exchanges glances with Irini.

"Of course we are," Irini says. "We are Greek, no? World domination is in our blood."

WELL, IT USED TO BE. JUST ASK ALEXANDER.

The Great, of course—who else?

And his father, Phillip II (the alleged originator of *divide and conquer*), who started that whole ball rolling.

Since then, Greece has spent less time grabbing land, more time slamming its front door on unwelcome conquerers. The Ottoman Empire, the Italians, the Nazis.

The Scientologists.

GRANDMA'S UNCHARACTERISTICALLY QUIET.

Which is actually becoming a characteristic since they arrived in Greece.

Around them, the bus rattles and hums. It's gathering passengers with every stop, and losing none. Someone opens a window, but the stink of chickens persists. Could be because there's an old woman further up, clutching a sackful of live chickens, the neck of the sack tied around their feet with string.

That's got to be violating some kind of code.

Not a Greek code, obviously.

She grabs Grandma's hand, tries smoothing it out like it's paper, but her grandmother has herself tied up in knots.

"We won't stay long," Lucy says.

"We will not stay long," Grandma affirms.

Good. It's decided: they're not staying long.

❦ 29 ❦

Fotini

THE BUS IS LIKE A GREAT, BLUE WHALE, SPEWING THEM onto the sidewalk. As they land, a passing man presses his finger to his nose, blows snot onto the street.

It's not personal; it's allergies.

"Okay, we can go now," Lucy says, dodging the man and his mess.

Dear Lucy, she's so accustomed to American-style civilization. Not that people don't blow land oysters there, too, but not usually on the pristine streets of Denver.

"If only that was the worst thing Greece has to offer. Let's not look for a meat market, okay? Otherwise you'll go vegetarian, guaranteed."

"How bad?"

"Bad. They hang the meat from hooks in the window. Not chunks of meat, but the whole animals."

"The whole thing? Seriously?"

She shrugs, glancing up and down the promenade, looking for trouble as though it's been sitting on the shore, waiting for her to show up. But there's no one she knows, no one who knows her. A small blessing. "Sometimes it is just half the carcass. But they leave them to hang, no air conditioning, and the door open."

"What about—"

"Flies? Extra protein."

The laugh bursts out of her granddaughter. "Very funny. You almost had me there."

She threads her arm through Lucy's. "I wish I was joking, but I am not that good a comedian."

THE STREET SHUTS DOWN FOR THE NIGHT—JUST THE traffic part. Where there were cars there's a growing number of people.

"They've been doing this every night during the warm months, ever since I can remember. Maybe they have always done it—who knows? They close the ends of the street so people can walk, talk, socialize before and after a late dinner. The main meal of the day is lunchtime, so dinner—if they have it—is very late and light. The tourists, of course, they come to eat a full dinner."

She and Lucy have been whiling away the evening sipping coffee shore-side at a *kafeneio*—a coffee shop. Lucy's gaze has been dancing between the sea and the street, but not Fotini's. As soon as they sat she turned her back on Agria—a big sign of disrespect in this country. This village should be glad she's giving it that much.

Now the streets are closed, they're on the move with the rest of the burgeoning crowd.

"I wonder how Stelios is enjoying his evening?" Lucy shoots a sly glance at her, sideways.

"Oh, I am sure he is lost in one of his love stories. Probably he is wishing he had long hair like Fabio, so he can flick it over his shoulder."

Lucy laughs. It's contagious. Who wouldn't laugh at the idea of Stelios flicking a mane of glossy hair? What a pairing it would be, that hair, that mustache.

"He likes you."

"He likes everybody."

"Maybe. But he likes you more."

"Lucy, my love, I am too old for vacation romances. You, on the other hand, are the perfect age." She stops abruptly in the street, turning to face a storefront with the Trojan War's most famous hero painted on the glass. "There is your Akili, making pizza."

"Not mine," Lucy says, but she's gone in a swirl of skirts and perfume—something light that reminds Fotini of Jordan almonds.

And now she wants Jordan almonds. They hand them out at weddings all over Greece, *koufeta* wrapped in tulle and tied with ribbons. Always the almonds are divvied up into uneven numbers, to symbolize the sharing married couples do.

At her wedding there was no *koufeta*, but there was an abundance of love—all that two young people could make.

❧ 30 ❧

Akili

EIGHT PM AND AGRIA'S PROMENADE IS ALREADY HARD AT work entertaining people. They're hiking back and forth, from St George's to the barricades on the far side of the Very Super Market.

The market—which is anything but super—is on life-support these days. *Kyrios* Yiannis, the market's original owner, retired to Mykonos with his best friend, and left his shop to Effie Makri, Agria's local celebrity. She spends more time in Athens being famous than she does here, so the running of the store is now in her mother's hands. And her mother isn't business-minded.

Kyria Dora is more of a people person.

She's a woman with big plans for the market. Stand still long enough to listen and she'll tell you. Plans include a coffee-cup reading service—for tourists, for locals, for anyone with ten euros to spare.

Akili doesn't believe in secret coffee cup messages and their diviners. The future keeps itself a secret for a reason: it hasn't decided what it wants to do with us, yet. It's making life up as it goes along, fiddling with this, tweaking that. Stavros wasn't meant to die, but fate got bored that day and decided to shake up a bunch of lives. His mother was supposed to marry a good man, but life threw her a different dish.

When he glances out the window for what feels like the millionth time that evening, he sees Lucy standing there, smiling at the heel painted on glass. He presses the dough into its tray, sauces it up, scatters cheese on top. And by the time he gets to the ham he realizes he's smiling, too.

Did she come alone?

It's horrible, but he hopes so.

But he also hopes not. At least through her grandmother they can communicate, and *Kyria* Fotini is a good woman—interesting, smart. His mother would have liked her.

The answer to his question walks through the door: Lucy's grandmother peers in at him. "I wanted to make sure we had the right place."

He nods to the warrior on the window. "It's the right place."

She smiles. "We know that now."

Lucy follows her in. She's wearing that big smile, a faint blush, and some kind of dress that would look great on his bedroom floor.

That smile of hers falters, as if she just tapped a direct line to his thoughts.

He looks down at the pizza, then jerks his head at the board. "Anything you want, it's yours."

Not just talking about the pizza, is he?

PATRA'S GOT A LOOK IN HER EYES, SAYS SHE WANTS STAB something, like the woman who just left.

"Why are you giving away more free meals?"

"Owner's prerogative."

"What's so special about her?"

"She saved my life," he says. "And more importantly, hers."

"What's so special about her?" she repeats.

He looks across the street, where Lucy's pulling out a chair for her grandmother.

"I don't know yet."

But he wants to find out.

🥀 31 🥀

Fotini

GREEK VOICES EVERYWHERE, MINGLING WITH SNIPPETS OF English, German, and something she thinks could be Dutch. The table next to them is overflowing with Americans: four adults and a half dozen kids between them.

"Americans?" she asks.

Looks of relief soften their faces. "Yes. You?"

"I've been in Colorado longer than I've been out of it."

Small talk piles into the gap between tables. Everyone is jumping on this small taste of home—including her.

Across the street, Akili is leaving his pizzeria. Looks like he palmed the pizza-making onto the good-looking boy who fetched their drinks earlier.

Is he coming for Lucy?

The straight line he's cutting across the street says *yes*. And sure enough, moments later he's crouching between her and Lucy.

"Can Lucy come for a walk before dinner?"

Lucy raises an eyebrow. "What did he say?"

"He wants you to go for a walk with him."

Lucy jumps up. "Sounds good." Then her face falls. "Are you going to be okay?"

"Of course I'm okay. I am surrounded by people and conversation."

Wrapped in all this noise and light, she can pretend this is not Agria. It is some other village on some other coast, not the place where she was ... can she call it raised?

Nobody raised them. Their mother was too busy holding herself together, trying to survive the moments until the next beating. And their father ... ha! That man was not a father.

He started when they were small. At first she and her brother were an inconvenience and a threat. His wife's attention was no longer exclusively his. These two children he put in her were competitors for time and resources.

Later, his children were the enemy. They saw him coming and they would cry. And his wife, she would run to soothe them, leaving him cold, unfed, with no one to bear the brunt of his most recent shitty day.

Bah! All that man had was shitty days. Not once did he come home with a smile. A good day was when he walked in the door indifferent. He didn't notice them and they did their best not to notice him.

The bad days were when he dragged the bad weather inside behind him, wearing a storm on his face. He'd rant and rail, and eventually the fists would fly, usually in Mama's direction, but often in theirs.

Those were times when nobody advocated for children. A child with bruises was a child who had done something to win a beating. Oh, the times they went to school wearing patches the color of a ripe plum and the teachers said nothing.

Then there were the dangerous days, when he was attentive, polite. He asked Mama questions and she responded with the same politeness. When he'd squeezed all he could out of her, he'd turn to his children and slowly wring them dry, until ...

Until one of them gave him an answer he did not like. Which happens all the time when you are a child. On those days the beatings were few, but the torture was fierce.

Only a monster forces a child to sleep outside in the cold, locks a child in a dark closet where the boogeymen live.

But she cannot tell Lucy all this. The girl only knows her grandmother as a strong woman, one who raised a daughter alone, then two granddaughters when their and father were gone. She doesn't want Lucy to see her as a victim, but as a woman who fought Greece and won.

Greece is not a country that likes to let other people win. History is littered with foreign losers.

Fotini watches the crowd for familiar faces, but it's been so long ... Everyone she knew is old or dead or gone in some other way. She wouldn't know their faces if they were in front of her.

Of course she also prayed to God and the Greek gods last night that no one would recognize her. She made all kinds of promises she will never keep; who has time to wash containers before they throw them in the recycling bin?

She laughs at something the Americans say. Very funny people, and their children are adorable. The little ones at that age where every movement is theater—big, dramatic, designed to garner maximum attention.

And she gives it to them.

Childhood is meant to be a time of learning the world has goodness in it.

32

Lucy

AGRIA IS A WONDER. WHY WOULD GRANDMA WANT TO leave this place?

Granted, she's seeing it on a late summer night when the village is at its best, and at night, too, when there's a thousand lights strung between the water and the *tavernas,* when the air is alive and fizzing with a mixture of tinny *bouzouki* music and Euro pop.

And she's seeing it at a time when her obligations are zero.

Have a good time, that's what this trip is about. Enjoy Greece for herself and for Lana. There's no work hanging overhead, no Doctor Kellerman hit-and-running another cat or patient.

She turns to the man beside her, the Greek god in a T-shirt and jeans that look like they're having a great time hugging his ass.

"Know why we're here?" she asks Akili. "In Greece, I mean. Not in Agria."

He glances at her, before steering her past an oncoming high-heeled boulder.

"Of course you don't." Deep breath. It makes her chest sting. "This woman, she killed a cat and didn't stop to help it or pick it up or anything. She left it in the road to die and be eaten by ... I don't know. Whatever eats dead things on the road when you live in the suburbs. Birds maybe?

"So I went to her house with the cat to ask why she'd do that, why she'd just leave it there. Who does that?

"I guess you're wondering how I know it was her. Blood. On the front of her car. Splashed over the headlight and bumper. And a small cat-sized dent. It was definitely her, and she didn't deny it when I knocked on her door."

Akili's hand touches the small of her back, navigates her around a chatting group clogging up the street. They're interfering with the flow of foot traffic, but who cares? Nobody, that's who. Everybody here seems relaxed, happy.

Even the knots in her shoulders are untying.

Happy, though? Not yet. Happiness is a forever-away thing at the moment, but she's hopeful.

"Yeah, she didn't deny it. Do you know what she did?"

Silence from the man beside her, but he wants to know. Those gentle, brown eyes say so.

"She burst into tears, right there in her doorway. Said she was sorry, that the cat just sort of leaped out. Kind of like the way Lana—that's my sister—just sort of leaped into her office and said, 'Hey, I've got this lump. Can you take a look?' "

The beautiful tableau starts to blur. She's tearing up, isn't she? Hell.

"Only she didn't take a look. Not a good one, at least. More of a squeeze and a few words about how it was a cyst and Lana was young and worrying about nothing."

That warm, comforting hand is on her back again, steering her toward a large white building on the land side of the promenade. She can't make out what it is, not with her eyes drowning in a gray soup of mascara, eyeliner, and tears.

The back of her hand wipes some of the mess away.

Church. He's taking her to church?

No—not all the way. As far as the shallow steps. He sits her down, then drops into place beside her.

"Sorry." More tears, more wiping. Akili does that guy thing where he reaches back, grabs the collar of his T-shirt, and pulls it over his head.

When she's not crying it's a hypnotizing and sexy move.

Stupid crying.

Akili hands her the shirt.

Great guy. She doesn't want to pay him back by ruining his clothes. "Thanks, but I can't wipe my face on your shirt."

He takes the shirt, tilts her chin up so he's getting a good look at her worst angle—the crying angle. Then he dabs at her eyes, wipes gently beneath them. The white shirt comes away looking like it just got dragged across the front row of a One Direction/Justin Bieber concert after both acts canceled.

Fabulous. First she cries on him, then she paints his shirt with sadness.

So much for waterproof mascara. Should come with a caveat: waterproof unless there's water.

Done restoring her face back to its original state (sort-of), he pulls the shirt back on. He says something. Could be anything.

"My sister wasn't worrying about nothing." Lucy picks up where she left off, at the climax of her tragedy. "The lump got bigger before she looked for a second opinion. By then it was too late. She died. And Doctor Kellerman carried on like nothing had happened." There's a fist clogging her throat, and behind it a million tears. Somehow, she manages to squeeze the rest of her words out. "The medical board basically shrugged and said these things happen. And I get it, death happens. To all of us, eventually. But Lana was only twenty-two.

"That stupid cow wouldn't take responsibility. For my sister, for the cat, for anything."

She looks at his shirt. Too bad he put it back on. The view is nice underneath. Very nice. Almost intimidating in its hardness.

"So maybe I threw a bucket of red paint on her outside her office and called her a killer. And then after the cat, I wrote 'murderer' on her car. With a sharp rock. It's wrong, but how else will people know what she is?"

🕸 33 🕸

Akili

WHAT'S HE GOING TO DO, LET HER DROWN IN HER SADNESS?

He couldn't dry Mama's tears, but with this woman he can at least try.

She quits talking for looking—looking at him and the shirt he's wearing. Crying or not, there's an interested spark in her eye.

He says, "I used to be fat. Stavros—my best friend—was the total opposite—skinny. Nobody teased me in school, though. Kids here aren't like that. Adults, yes. Every time I saw an aunt or neighbor they'd comment about my weight. That's how people are here. Blunt. They say it like it is. Unless they're gossiping, then they're either whispering behind your back or spinning bullshit to your face. But about things like weight, they're not afraid to speak up. Not the kids, though. I didn't even care I was overweight, until I realized girls gravitated towards guys like Stavros.

"The army fixed that. It evened us out. Stavros bulked up and I trimmed down. Want to hear something funny? I'm still the same weight. Replaced fat for muscle."

Random chatter. About nothing.

What else to do? Bits of him break when a woman cries. Remnants of his childhood, he figures. Mama lost hours of her life to crying. Hours when she should have been laughing and living.

Anger bubbles in his gut as he thinks about that old bastard and the way he made her live.

He's done his best not to make women cry. His goodbyes have soft landings. Akili isn't a guy who lets them hope for more than he's got to give—which isn't much.

Yeah, not going to bring a woman permanently into his life. Not while the old man's still around. His father's had his shot at breaking women. He's not getting another.

He glances at Lucy. She's watching his mouth move.

What happened to you? he wonders. And can I fix it?

KYRIA FOTINI STARES AT HIS CHEST. "WHAT HAPPENED TO your shirt?

"Your granddaughter."

"You made her cry?"

"She made herself cry. I just happened to be there with my shirt."

"Lucky."

"Very lucky." He pushes Lucy's chair in as she sits. "What happened to her? Was it a man?"

The older woman's gaze flicks to her granddaughter, then, satisfied that she's not still falling apart, snap back to him.

"No, not a man. She lost her sister recently—my other

granddaughter. And before that she lost both parents, including my daughter. We cling to together, each believing the other is a lifeboat. We are both the boat and the person drowning."

❧ 34 ❧

Fotini

TEN MINUTES AFTER THE BUS SLOUCHES INTO ALOGOPOROS, its wheezing door ushering them onto the esplanade, Stelios's boat cozies up to the dock.

Under his mustache there's a broad smile. He reaches out, helps them both aboard. His reward is a pizza, courtesy of *Akili's Pizza*.

"Do not say I never give you anything," she tells him.

He laughs. "You are a generous woman, Fotini. How was the mainland?"

"Terrible. But I think tomorrow I will take Lucy to Volos. I mind it less than Agria."

Lights and stars paint pictures on the water around the sparsely populated edge of Trikeri. From the boat, the shimmering patterns look like magic.

Fotini curls her arm around Lucy, giving or getting comfort.

Lucy

THE FERRY TO VOLOS ARRIVES MID-MORNING, ON ITS WAY back from the Sporades archipelago. The archipelago sits on the far side of the peninsula's tail, where it's at the mercy of the Aegean Sea. The Aegean is an offshoot of the Mediterranean, named after a Greek town, or an Amazon queen, or Theseus's suicidal dad. Nobody knows for sure—they just pick an answer they like and defend it loudly.

Twice a day the ferry stops, to and from the islands.

Not an ordinary ferry but what's known as a *Flying Dolphin*—or hydrofoil. Which means the big vessel zips along like a speed boat, because most of its hull cuts through air, not water.

Now more than ever, Greece values its tourism industry. Visitors don't come alone, they bring money—money they're willing leave behind, for the cost of a little sunshine and some dancing.

Greece—and Greeks—need money.

But Greece can be reasonable: Riding the ferry costs just a few euros apiece.

―――

TODAY VOLOS IS THE ATTRACTION. NOTHING SPECIAL, JUST wandering around one of Greece's bigger cities.

(Grandma can handle Volos, she said. It's Agria she can't stomach.)

Ha. Nothing special. Of course it's special—they're in Greece.

A few minutes later, they're stepping off the Dolphin, onto the dock in Volos. A much more elaborate construction than the concrete slab in Trikeri.

In the very-nearish distance, there's a row of *tavernas* with water-side tables, a more sophisticated replica of Agria's setup.

Not as charming though, is it?

And this long, concrete stretch of promenade is absent one *Akili's Pizza*. But it does hold the *University of Thessaly*'s waterfront campus, a lush park, a dark gray stone church, and —the travel guide says—the *Athanasakio Archaeological Museum*.

All that without having to cut inland.

Obviously not a tsunami zone, or whatever the Greek equivalent is.

Lucy pulls her head out of the travel guide's pages. "What do Greeks call a tsunami?"

"Tsunami."

Huh. She never would have guessed. "So they have tsunamis here?"

"In Volos?"

Lucy nods.

"Not in two hundred years," Grandma says, tugging at the neckline of her scooped shirt. "Maybe longer. My God, it is going to be hot today."

"But they can still happen, right?"

"Of course. That's always a risk on the coast, and Greece and her waters are very unstable."

"So why build everything so close to the water? Why not build higher and further inland?"

"Why do they build everything close to the water in America? Why build a city below sea level? People flock to the water because it was—and still is—vital. For fishing, for shipping, for travel. Maybe not so much for travel now, but many people still like to travel by ship and boat. You cannot live a happy life if you are scared to take risks. Building on the coast is a risk, yes, but the rewards are generous."

"Until there's a massive quake and giant waves wash it all away. Trust me, I know tsunamis. I experienced a teeny tiny one just the other day, and look how that turned out. The boat went Poseidon."

Grandma laughs. "Lucy, my love, stop worrying so much. Bad things will happen whether you worry about them or not, and so will good things. Why fixate?"

"It's a sort of talisman."

"How so?"

Lucy shoves the guide into her crossbody bag. "If I worry then I can hold bad things at bay."

"If you worry, then you give those things a key to your front door and invite them in."

Makes sense. She'd live it if she didn't have a death grip on her worries. They're comfortable now, a part of her, like an old T-shirt she can't bring herself to toss away. She pulls them on every day, wears them under her smile.

"I'll try, but I'm not making any promises. I need one of those *frappe* things. How about you?"

"Great idea," Grandma says. "Glad I thought of it."

They stop at a *kafeneio*. Lucy orders two *frappes*, employing the power of sign language, pointing, and smiling like a simpleton.

But the coffee shop's staff are used to people like her. And guess what? They speak English. So when she says thank you, they understand.

"So many people here speak English now." Grandma grabs both chilled, foamy coffees, hands one to Lucy. "They teach it in school, and many of the children take extra English classes outside school hours."

"Useful."

"English is the language of business in much of the world. And Greece is wooing everyone it can to bring their business here. Not just tourists, but big companies. This country needs the money. It's leaking euros all over the place."

IF YOU KEEP UP WITH THE NEWS YOU KNOW GREECE IS hemorrhaging money. What we see now is the perfect storm that has been brewing for decades.

Greece is easygoing, laid-back. A relaxed culture.

They're not so good at things like collecting taxes. Greeks are good at—how you say—sidestepping taxes owed.

(In the US we call this evasion.)

In the 2000s, the country poured big money into defense. You cannot stay at a quiet sort of war with Turkey armed only with centuries of grudges and excellent cheese.

Not to mention (although it is being mentioned now), Greece used to adore its bureaucrats. It collected them and put them in little offices, where they shifted pieces of paper and took home good paychecks. And when their paper-shuffling years were over, at the ripe age of fifty-something, they went home with fat pensions.

To pay for this, Greece borrowed a lot of money, and the very nice people at places such as *Goldman Sachs* and *JPMorgan Chase* were happy to—

"Oh, look over there! Is that a … a … No. Never mind. We were mistaken. Greece is in massive debt? No! You are imagining things. What debt?" *Hand swish.* "These are not the debts you are looking for."

"What do you mean Greece is broke? No they're not! Okay, so Greece is cash-strapped now, but they've promised us their future leaders will line our pockets with gold. We don't know how—but they will. They said so."

Also, maybe Greece fudged the details a bit. For decades.

Until the new government in 2010 admitted that maybe, could be, the previous administration could have possibly, potentially made a little booboo in their deficit reporting. Just a little one.

How much?

Mumble, mumble: "Maybe a few dozen billion dollars."

THE MUSEUM'S NOT FAR AND THE WALK IS NICE.

With every tilt of her head, something new comes into focus. Tourists, mostly. People like them, wandering along like they're going somewhere, but not in any hurry. The gulf accompanies them, staying to the right where it belongs. This whole stretch of Volos is concrete, all the way to the water's edge—no cars, foot traffic only. Ships huff into port. Giant freighters that haul cement from the plant wedged between Volos and Agria shrink as they pull further out to sea.

Charming building, the museum. A single layer painted sunshine yellow with white trim. Ionic-style columns decorate the front entrance. Looks like they snapped a chunk off the Parthenon, glued it to the structure's face.

The museum's pamphlets expand on the travel guide's info. The entire collection is local. Everything comes from the Thessaly area, even the bodies. On the grounds there's a beautiful garden and reconstructions of Neolithic houses from nearby ruins.

By the time they're done peeking through history's narrow window, the sun is clawing up to the day's cruelest summit. They move inland, to cooler climes.

Also known as shops.

Lana was the shopper of the family, not Lucy. She would have loved these cramped, colorful stores with their inexpensive clothes. *Made in Europe* trumps *Made in China*, when it comes to the quality of apparel.

Her lungs pause, heart holds its breath. Eyes fill up with hot, damp grit.

Stupid brain, it wanders back to the museum, with its pits of parched bones. It's very *Photoshop*, the way her mind paints a Lana layer over those ancient remains, curling her younger sister into a permanent fetal position.

Lucy stops on the sidewalk, makes an instant obstacle of herself. People crash into her back, toppling her into the path of a slow-moving bus.

Adrenalin kicks her ass, but her superpowers don't leap to her rescue. Thanks for nothing, *That's Incredible*.

The heaving, panting vehicle stops inches from her face.

But only because there's a Bus Stop sign (Greek and English) jutting out of the sidewalk, and behind it, dozens of people milling around, waiting to go somewhere.

"Lucy, my God!" Grandma hauls her off the ground, inspects her for injuries. "Are you all right?"

"I'm awesome. Never been better."

"What happened?"

"Lana happened, Grandma. Lana happened."

Death takes a person, leaves a void in their place. That emptiness is more dense than osmium.

Grandma brushes the hair from Lucy's face, tucks it back behind her ears the way she did when Lucy was small. "I know. But we are still here, so don't throw yourself into traffic, okay?"

THEY DO VOLOS UNTIL THE MIXTURE OF RELENTLESS HEAT and the city's mild pollution chases them into a bookstore. It's more like a magazine shop with a few spinning racks of English and Greek paperbacks.

Grandma cuts a direct path to the books. No prizes for guessing what she's after—and for who. Lucy can't resist teasing her a tiny bit.

She peers over Grandma's shoulder. "Romance novels?"

"Your deductive abilities are astounding."

"And you call me a smart ass? They for you or Stelios?"

"Of course they are for me. But I will leave them for Stelios when I am finished." Grandma turns around, dumps a pile into her arms. "Take these to the counter. I want to pick out some more."

"You're going to read all these?" The stack is already ten books high.

"He doesn't get to the mainland too often, and all the books he gets on eBay are old. These are new, modern."

Yeah, they're for Stelios.

She peers at the top book on the pile. Nice dress the heroine is wearing—frothy and yellow. The hero is headless, but his breeches are about to pop. "This one is about an Earl who's a rake. Doesn't sound modern."

"I meant written by modern writers today—not thirty

years ago. All of his are ancient, held together with dust and who knows what else?" She holds up a title with a leather-clad vampire on the cover. "And we will throw in a little twist, yes?"

Uh sure, whatever. Stelios doesn't look like a guy who digs vampires, but then he doesn't look like a closet romance reader, either.

"If you say so."

Grandma laughs. "I say so."

❧ 36 ❧

Akili

NICE BOAT. SWEET CURVES. POWERFUL ENGINE FOR WHEN he's not drifting.

The boat dealer isn't so sweet. He's a shark in man's clothing.

"How much?"

"I am almost giving it away. Any less and I would be giving you a boat *and* money." He coughs up a number.

Not bad, but Akili doesn't show it. Instead he puts on an expression like the guy's killing him.

"I saw a better price—"

"What was the price?"

Akili tells him.

Now the other guy looks like he's battling longterm constipation. "That will be a hardship. Times are tough, my friend. Nobody wants to pay fair prices for a boat. And it is a very nice boat. Not big, but how big a boat does one man need to be happy? Do you have a family?"

"No."

"Then you can afford this small boat, I am sure."

"It's nice, but not that nice." But it is that nice, and they both know it. One way or another, Akili's buying this boat. He wants it to be on his terms, that's all. "Okay, I'll buy this boat, but from the other guy."

"Okay, okay. I will give you the boat for that price, but only because you look like a good man."

"Great. When can you have it in the water?"

The sigh is something straight out of the old Greek tragedies. "Maybe tomorrow."

"Maybe this afternoon?"

"It is already afternoon."

Akili smiles. "I know."

Gasoline prices have gone beyond crazy; now they're insulting.

But like the salesman said, no wife, no kids, means he can afford the boat.

Not that he's a bottomless money pit. But he's been careful. House was paid for years ago by his grandparents. Business is profitable.

At a time when the country's pockets are disintegrating, he's a lucky man.

"Nice boat," Stavros says.

So his best friend's ghost didn't go down with his vessel.

"You're not supposed to be here."

"Now you talk to me?"

"Nothing better to do."

"Liar. You're going somewhere fast." He snaps his fingers. "To see that girl?"

To see that girl.

Akili's splitting the water in two to get there, something the new boat does easily. Trikeri is zooming toward him.

"About time," Stavros says. He's reaching over the side of the boat, spray shooting through his hand.

"I don't believe in ghosts."

"Me either. Not sure I am a ghost."

"What else would you be?"

Shrug. "Maybe you're crazy. You did believe Kiki killed me for a while there."

"What else was I supposed to think? She was the logical choice."

"You've got a choice between a Romani girl and Greek girl and you figure the Greek girl is the killer? Greek blood is hot, but the Romani boil."

"I'm not crazy."

"What are you, then?"

Akili doesn't say. Trikeri is here. He docks the boat, jumps out, hits the concrete slab. That thing's so well built it doesn't even shiver. He's a man going places—like the *taverna*.

The beachside establishment is empty, unless he's counting the weathered face behind the bar. The bartender nods when he spots Akili.

"Stelios."

"Akili. Bring me anything?"

Akili sets the box on the bar. "Oil. Cheese."

Money changes hands, but he's not focused on that, is he? His gaze is scanning the *taverna*'s corners, skimming the beach, wandering along the path that leads to the small hotel.

The older man says, "They are not here."

"I can see that."

"Not here on the island," he explains.

"Where?"

Stelios carries the box into the kitchen. When he comes back, he shrugs. "Volos."

"Quiet here without them."

"Friend, you speak the truth. When a woman comes into your world, it is like a storm. *Clang, clang, boom, boom.* Then when she is gone, the silence eats you alive."

"They're gone permanently?"

"No, for the day. They will be back at seven."

Relief. For a moment he felt a pang of loss.

"I know what you mean," Stelios says.

❧ 37 ❧

Lucy

NEITHER OF THEM IS GREEK ENOUGH TO EAT MORE THAN A small *souvlaki* for lunch, so by dinnertime they're ravenous.

Lucy could eat a centaur—not in a porn-from-Denmark way, but with a knife and fork. "How about a pizza?"

Grandma laughs at her, so Lucy knows she's as transparent as a sparkling window. "Pizza, eh? Again? We just had pizza last night."

What can Lucy say? She likes pizza. And she likes Akili. So what if they've only met—what—three times?

It's not that he's sexy as hell and gorgeous (which he is, but the world is full of sexy, gorgeous men), it's his approachability. She's comfortable with him. He's old jeans and a favorite T-shirt. He's a favorite pillow. Sun-and-fresh-air-dried sheets.

And yeah, he's a scoop of hot coals when she's got the stones to look him in the eye. Which is something, considering Lucy isn't a woman who shies away from looking a sexy man in the eye.

"Any kind of pizza," she says. "Doesn't have to be *Akili's Pizza*."

Yeah, it does.

Grandma pats her arm. "I will tell you what. Tomorrow night we will make a date to eat pizza at Akili's. Today, I will take you to eat my favorite Greek food."

"What's your favorite Greek food?"

Five minutes later, they're standing in a bakery. Not a savory food in sight; these four walls are dedicated to the art of sugar.

Lucy's laughing, because this she didn't expect. "Desserts and cakes?"

"Desserts and cakes. At home I try not too eat too much cake, but we are on vacation, yes? And on vacation you eat cake, or it is not a real vacation." She leans towards Lucy as though they are sharing a conspiracy. "What shall we order?"

"One of everything," Lucy says, joking-not-joking.

❧ 38 ❧

Akili

AT THE EDGE OF VOLOS SITS A ROMANI ENCAMPMENT.
They've been here for decades—maybe longer—but nothing
they've built is permanent. They could pull up roots in day
and be gone, with nothing to mark their time here but a low-
moving swirl of dust and a few torn sheets of rolling newspaper. Tents everywhere. A few shacks, but it wouldn't take a
wolf to huff and puff them down.

Akili's been here before. Lots of times. But with Stavros
for company.

Today he's alone. Good thing he's got something to give,
because everyone's watching him the way lions watch prey.

They know his face. They know his face and they remember: He didn't bring trouble to the Romani, but he walked by
trouble's side. Now a Greek man is dead and one of their own
is sleeping on a hard, thin mattress in a women's prison.

She pulled the gun's trigger, yet it's Stavros they blame. And—by association—Akili.

But he'd do anything for the Boutos family, so here he is, offer in hand.

Drina lives in the first shack at the encampment's mouth. Outside, sitting on a tall stool, is a glaring barrel. Drina's father. He's twice the man Akili is—maybe more.

His eyes scan Akili; he's a primitive security system, but vicious when necessary. Words leak out of the edge of his mouth. "What do you want?"

"Is Drina here?"

"Why? What can you want with her except trouble?"

"That's between her and me."

The big man unhooks a foot from the stool's rung, stomps on the ground. A small dust cloud rears its head, then settles. "While she is on this piece of earth, Drina's business is my business."

"I want to give her a job."

"What job?"

"At my pizzeria."

"Doing what?"

"I haven't decided."

"So you just came to offer my daughter a job? A Romani girl? What, there are no Greek woman who want your job? Hard to believe, with the problems Greece has."

He figured it would go like this. "Hey, don't look at me. It was *Kyria* Boutos's idea. She asked if I had something for Drina."

The man softens, but not much. Granite to sandstone. "She has been good to my daughter. But only because she has no son."

Not true. He's known *Kyria* Boutos forever. Any initial hostility was the result of grief. True, she wouldn't have been happy about a Romani daughter-in-law at first, but

Stavros had a way of twisting life—and his parents—in his favor.

"As long as she's good to her, does it matter why?"

The Romani man's gaze fixates on a point somewhere over Akili's shoulder. Then he spits on the ground. Guy's got good manners—he spits to the side. Very considerate.

"People—especially the Romani people—should always question goodness. Goodness, kindness, they are excellent fronts for darker motives."

Jaded. That's how the Romani are. They see the worst in people, because that's what people show them. History, ancient and modern, tends to paint the nomadic people in a murderous, covetous light.

But it's a symbiotic relationship. Greeks and Romanies each get someone to look down on. Because some people need to know there's a body perched on a lower rung.

"Can I at least talk to her?"

Drina's father nods slowly, like it's one of his last. "Drina," he calls out.

The shack's door swings open. Out comes his best friend's widow, in her usual long, flowing skirt and T-shirt.

She's so young. Twenty-two. The universe can be a cold bitch, but it was a hot-blooded woman who turned her into a widow. Her own mother. The universe, God, they had no say.

Drina's mother swore Stavros was cheating. Akili knows he wasn't.

But knowing his friend, it was a matter of time.

Standing behind Drina is Stavros. He's staring at her ass. Death hasn't changed him much.

First time he's seen his friend anyplace but the sea.

"What's wrong?" the Romani man says. "You look sick."

Headshake. "I'm okay." No, he's not. "Drina, it's good to see you."

"Is it?"

Always they're like this. Stavros was the only one who didn't struggle with her, but even he had trouble in the beginning. Frustrating people. Akili didn't come for the riddles, for the interrogation, the word-twisting. So she's kind of got a point. It's not that good to see her. She's a reminder of the friendship he lost.

And she's the reason. Yeah, it's unfair and it makes him an asshole. But he can live with that.

"I've got a position open at the pizzeria if you're interested."

Arms folded, face shuttered. "Why?"

"Why what?"

"Why ask me?"

"Because *Kyria* Boutos mentioned you need work. And I need someone to work for me."

He doesn't, but he's seeing a time when Patra could be a problem he's got no other way to solve.

She nods, eyes on the wide blue ribbon in the sky. "Helena was wrong. I have work."

"Picking fruit?"

"It's honest work."

"Yeah, it is." Don't look at Stavros, don't look— "If you change your mind ..."

"I won't."

"Okay," he says, nodding. Stavros is circling Drina, inspecting her closely. His fingers dance through her hair. It doesn't move—it can't. His fingers aren't real.

"Tell her I'm sorry," he says. "Tell her I'm sorry about the baby."

Akili's throat dries up. "I can't tell her that."

Drina and her father look at him.

"Tell her."

"I can't," he says. "I'm sorry." The back of one hand wipes his mouth. "The job is yours if you want it."

❧ 39 ❧

Lucy

FIFTEEN MINUTES LATER, THEY'RE STAGGERING OUT OF THE *zaxaroplasteio* with several boxes bundled together with gold curly ribbon. Behind them, the sun is beginning its slow vanishing act.

"Now we will go to the ferry, okay? Maybe we will share this with Stelios, if he is lucky," Grandma says.

It's a short walk back to the dock where the *Flying Dolphin* is winding up for takeoff. Once aboard, they stow the boxes by their feet. Lucy dumps the bag of romance novels in her lap, hugs them tight. Can't have Stelios's gifts rolling around the ferry's floor.

Grandma eyes the books. "Maybe I should not have bought the vampire book. There is nothing romantic about sex with dead people. Who wants to have sex with a cocksicle?"

Good thing Lucy's not sucking down a drink, because she'd be wearing it now. Her splutter is—blissfully—dry. When she recovers she says, "Either he'll like it or he won't."

"I was talking about for me, not that old goat."

Sure you were, Grandma. Sure you were.

❧ 40 ❧

Fotini

THEY SAY SHE IS THE PSYCHOLOGIST, YET HERE IS LUCY looking through her as if she is glass. She cannot be anything but proud of her granddaughter's observation.

The concrete blocks on her shoulders are fading, her burden lifted by invisible hands as the distance between the ferry and mainland increases.

She cannot stand to be this close to her past.

Yet there's a morbid feeling awakening in her, a feeling of wanting to pick at the scab to see if the wound is as bad as she remembers it to be. Not an unexpected sensation; many of her patients have described the same thing—the wanting to uncover the past, poke at it with a stick to see if it still breathes fire.

Is she not doing the same thing every time she visits her Sarah, Lana, and Michael at the cemetery? It's the same nail dragging across a different scab, over a wound even deeper than her childhood.

Once you have lost a child and a grandchild, all other traumas pale.

Here comes the island. Trikeri. What a treasure it is. Greece, but not her Greece. It's a new Greece, one she never met before this visit. There, she is at a restless sort of peace.

And look, here is Stelios to greet them.

Only two people disembarking at the small dock: her and Lucy. The *Dolphin* is drifting away, readying its wings before she's had a chance to draw a deep breath of salty island air. There's a hint of sweet bitterness on the breeze, as though an orange leaf has been crushed between two hands.

"Were you waiting for us, old man?"

"No, I was checking on my boat. Making sure it is still here. And look, it is here. Happy day." He reaches for the boxes in her arms. "Let me take these for you. Cakes?"

"Cakes," she says.

"Are you planning to share?"

Of course, but this is the game they place, she and Stelios. Very high school, but it's invigorating. Here is youth; she can almost touch it again. "Share cake? Are you mad?"

Behind them, Lucy laughs.

Stelios swings around, grins at her granddaughter. "How was Volos?"

"Wonderful," Lucy says theatrically. "I jumped in front of a bus."

"Did it stop?"

"There was a bus stop, so yeah. Eventually."

"What is that on your arm?"

"What does it look like?" Fotini says, glancing back at Lucy and her loot. "Books."

He stops. "What books?"

"What books? Romance novels, of course."

He sets the boxes on the dock's concrete footing, shakes his hands at the sky. "Thank you, Zeus." Then he picks up the boxes and continues in to his *taverna*. "You want these in the refrigerator?"

"Some of them. But first let's take a look."

She likes the way he moves. Confident and steady. Strong. He's a man used to navigating his piece of the world with ease. Nice buns, too. He tries to make them shapeless with those loose pants, but she can tell. He's moving something inside her that hasn't been moved in decades—and not just her vagina.

With strong, careful hands, Stelios flips the lips open. "Have you eaten dinner?" he asks casually.

"What dinner? This is dinner."

He laughs. "Who eats dessert for dinner?"

She winks at Lucy, who's watching the exchange with a grin. "We do."

"It's true," Lucy says. "Grandma, I'm running back to our room to change."

"Go, go, and bring my slippers back with you."

"Can't handle all the walking?" Lucy asks.

She scoffs. "I like to walk, but walking likes me less than it used to."

❧ 41 ❧

Lucy

THE WINDING PATH THAT LEADS TO THEIR ROOM IS flanked by ankle-height solar lights staked into the ground. They're not glowing yet, but it won't be long. Night's already arriving a little sooner than it did their first day here. By minutes, but her body knows the difference between then and now.

When fall comes, it's not day by day, but in a rush. One day the sun-scorched air is gone and there's nothing left but the scent of oncoming decay, of leaves preparing to die. That day will be here soon.

Something in this world is always waiting for death. Either the summer or the winter, the night or the day.

At least they're reborn; unlike the seasons, people never come around again.

There she goes again, sliding into the hole, and not even with a white rabbit as an excuse.

Five minutes—that's all she'll let herself have.

Five minutes to indulge, wallow, feel sorry for herself. Then she's taking Grandma her slippers. Pulling her head out of her own ass.

Burying it in cake.

When she opens the door, something flutters to the ground. A small slip of paper. The sea breeze wants to whisk it away, but her foot's quicker. She tugs it out from under her shoe. Nothing on it but a smiley face and a picture of a foot, with an arrow pointed at the heel.

Akili was here.

She kicks off her shoes, shoves her feet into a pair of beach-worthy slides, then grabs Grandma's slippers.

Akili was here.

Fotini

"AKILI WAS HERE." ON THE BAR, STELIOS HAS LINED UP ALL the new books. One by one, he's inspecting the blurbs. He picks one up, looks at her. His eyebrows scoot higher. "Vampires?"

It's not easy, but she shoots for deadpan and wins. "Vampires."

"Why would I want to read about vampires?"

"Try something new for once in your life, eh?"

"Woman, I have tried many new things in my life. But back I come to the old things, because the old things are good, solid, honest."

"Like this island?"

"What is wrong with my island, eh?"

"Nothing. It is paradise," she tells him truthfully. "If I could stay here forever, I would."

He glances up at her. "Why can't you?"

Her laugh is blunt, its end snipped off by reality. "I have a business back home. A house. A life."

"A house, a business. You can have those anywhere. And life ... Life goes where you go. A life even follows you into Hades."

"What would I do here?"

Vampire romance waving in the air: "Open a bookstore. You can have it in the corner over there."

Very small corner. Big enough for one bookstand, one customer.

"What about healthcare?"

"There is a good hospital in Volos and a doctor in Alogoporos. I guarantee it is quicker to get to the doctor here than your doctor in America."

She settles onto the bar stool, slips her feet out of her shoes. Walking shoes they call them, designed by people who walk between the refrigerator and couch. "It is a nice dream."

"Think about it and I will read your vampire romance. But I will hate it—guaranteed. Vampires ..." He shudders.

"I expect nothing less. You said Akili was here?"

"This morning he came looking for you."

"You mean looking for Lucy."

"Of course I mean looking for Lucy. What would he want with an old woman like you?"

She tosses her shoe at his head. But he's quick and he's good. He catches it before it's barely had a chance to fly.

"Old women like you are for old men like me."

"All those romance novels and that is the best you can do?"

He shrugs. "I am still a man—what do you expect?"

She snatches a book off the bar, pretends her heart and head are not forming an attachment to this old barnacle. The embers they're poking must not be allowed to become flames. When their two weeks is up—hers and Lucy's—they must go home. There is no choice here, no possibility—just one certainty. Home is not here. It never was. Even before she escaped Greece it was not her home. If she casts a line into her deepest waters, all she'll catch are memories of a girl who considered Greece temporary, a place to be endured until she was old enough to run, and strong enough to keep going.

She has no memory of even one moment where she considered staying.

Not even for Iason. And in time she convinced him, too.

But leaving together was never meant to be. Fate had far worse plans for Lucy's grandfather.

"Ah, here is Lucy now!" Stelios crows.

It is Lucy, wearing different shoes and a smile.

"Akili was here looking for you," she tells her granddaughter.

The smile brightens. "I know. He left a note." Uncurling her fingers, she reveals the slip of paper. Very creative that Akili, she thinks. He's finding ways of communicating. Creative and romantic. It's the action of a man who knows what he likes. But what can they be, those two?

Bah! It is summer, it is vacation time, it is *Greece*. Let them have their fun. Lucy will take home some nice memories, and one day she will look back and smile.

"Is he coming back?" Lucy asks Stelios.

Stelios shrugs. "He did not say." Fotini gives him a look. "But I think he will be here tomorrow. Your grandmother bought a vampire book. I will give you some garlic later, eh? Just in case she has a secret."

Lucy laughs. It does her heart good to hear the sound. "I'll take any help I can get," her granddaughter says. "I'm going for a walk on the beach, okay?"

"Watch out for traffic," Stelios says. His mustache shakes.

They watch her until she's gone.

"Yes, he will be here tomorrow—guaranteed." He sets

aside the book, rests his elbow on the bar. "What do you think of that?"

"I think," she says slowly, "that we—Lucy and I—must be careful we do not become too attached to Greece."

Stelios snorts. "Life is change," he says. "Change is life."

❧ 43 ❧

Lucy

AKILI ARRIVES WITH THE SUN. SHE'S ON THE BEACH watching when his boat swims to shore.

Something's dancing in her chest. Feels like it's her heart.

She jumps up, picks her way across the pebbled ground. By the time she reaches the end of the dock, he's tying off the rope on what looks like a new boat.

Nice. Very sleek.

But she liked the old one better. Okay, it was uglier than sin, but it was more Greek. Too bad it went Titanic on them. Well, more like Poseidon, with the earthquake and the very short tidal wave.

"Nice boat," she says. His dark gaze smashes into hers, doesn't let go. Her eyes flick down, catch his smile. "God, I wish you could understand me. But maybe it's better this way. It's not like I can stay, and I'm not really the one-night-stand type. Not that I look down on people who have them—I've had a couple myself," she says quickly, though God knows why—it's not like he understands. "It's just not what I want, that's all. When I was younger it was different; now, with you, I'd be the kind who gets attached, you know? Why put myself through that? Anyway ... You want coffee?" She mimes drinking.

He nods towards the tiny *taverna*.

She leads, he follows.

She won't look back—she won't. But her skin feels hot, like his hands are already on her. If she stops, they'll collide. She wants the collision, wants to spin off her axis and into Akili.

It's not fair.

But when has life ever been fair to her?

Not lately—that's when.

The *taverna* is closed, but not locked, the way it always is in the mornings. Above their heads, the rooms are unoccupied. The Germans checked out late last night, and the others ... who knows? They were never in the room and now they're not on the island.

She performs the same routine as yesterday and the day before. Akili sits at the bar watching as she brews the American-style coffee and pours.

He takes the coffee from her, drinks, smiles. Then he starts to speak, and she is lost.

❧ 44 ❧

Akili

"I've been seeing ghosts. Okay, one ghost. My friend Stavros. I told you about him the other night. He's been dead for months, but I see him every day. It's like he's not gone, except I know he is. Must be crazy."

Lucy leans on the bar, in the exact same spot where Stelios always stands.

He gulps the coffee, winces when it burns. "Am I crazy? Sane people don't see ghosts. Makes me wonder if you see them, too. She told me about your sister, your grandmother did. I'm sorry for your loss. Stavros was like a brother to me. Now I'm lost. No compass to guide the way. Feels like I'm looking down at a map where the place names are all scrambled. Don't know which way to go."

Could be his imagination, but looks like she knows that map.

Footsteps. Then a bright, cheerful voice saying his name. Lucy slaps on a smile, aims it over his shoulder.

"Grandma," she says. Akili knows that's English for *Yiayia*.

He swings around on the barstool, tries not to let his disappointment show. Being alone with Lucy on Prasouda gave him a thirst for her exclusive company.

"*Kalimera*, *Kyria* Fotini."

She pats him on the shoulder. Feels comforting. "And good morning to you, Akili."

Lucy jumps up, pours coffee in another mug. This one's for her grandmother. It's relaxing (and arousing) watching her move. She's fluid, almost balletic in everything she does.

"I want to take Lucy to the coast, show her around. Can you ask if she wants to come?"

The older woman passes his message along. Lucy beams, nods. She reels off a long line of chatter, then bolts while he's waiting on a translation.

"She said yes. But first she's going to have a quick shower and change. Where are you taking her?"

"I was thinking up Pelion."

"Oh, you have a car?"

He shakes his head. "Gasoline prices are insane. Registration costs are for madmen. I'll rent a car for the day."

"That's sweet of you."

He shrugs. "Lucy is good company."

"Even though you don't speak the same language?"

What's he supposed to say? Lucy's grandmother has a way of unlocking the truth. He's not sure he could lie to her if he tried. "Language doesn't matter. With Lucy I don't feel like I'm alone."

She nods like she knows. "My Lucy is the best of people. She would fight to the death for someone she cares about—

and she almost has. You are both swimming in deep waters. Take care you do not drown."

Heavy. He tries lightening up the conversation. "I tried the drowning thing. Lucy saved me."

Lucy's grandmother laughs. "Yes, she did. Lucy would never let anyone drown. She has a good heart."

Stelios treks into the *taverna*, already laughing. "Listen to you, old woman. They are young, let them go without a lecture, eh?"

But it's cool. Akili gets it. From what he gathers Lucy and her grandmother have no one but each other. If he had a daughter—or a granddaughter—he'd want the best for her, too.

Akili knows he's not what's best for anyone, but ...

He likes Lucy. She's the best thing to walk into his life in a long time. What he's going to do when they pack up and fly home he doesn't know. Sell the boat. Open another pizzeria. Something—anything.

Whatever flips the pages of his life faster.

Lucy's coming. She's walking, but to his eyes it looks like dancing. She's in a red sundress that swirls mid-thigh. Her legs are pale, but there's a tan pushing through the dark pink on her shoulders and arms. Greek skin. Which means she'll be golden brown without too much encouragement from the sun before long. Her hair is up and away from her neck in a high ponytail.

He will never forget this moment, this day.

Which could be his undoing.

❦ 45 ❧

Fotini

STELIOS WALKS WITH THEM TO THE END OF THE DOCK. Together they wave until distance zaps the boat with its cosmic ray gun. Abracadabra, they're gone!

"What now?"

What now? A shower, that's what. A shower and a walk and maybe a picnic. "It's too bad there's not a handsome Greek man to take me on a picnic."

"I like picnics. But I only like them with ugly, old women. Preferably foreign and not too clever."

"Oh?"

"Clever women are a problem. First they make you think, then they make you worry."

"Worry about what?"

"That another man will also discover they are clever."

Always she wants to laugh with this man. "For you, Stelios, I will dumb myself down. I don't want you to worry.

Foreign ... I have an American passport. Is that foreign enough for you? I can't wave a wand and make myself ugly, but maybe you have a paper bag somewhere, eh?"

"It is a lucky man who has two paper bags, and I am that lucky man." She looks at him, waiting on the punchline. "One for your head and one for mine. In case yours slips off."

✻ 46 ✻

Lucy

AKILI RENTS A CONVERTIBLE IN VOLOS, WALKS HER TO THE passenger side. She offers him money but he won't touch it.

"I'm buying lunch then," she says, sliding onto the leather seat. "Don't argue."

How can he argue with that? He can't. Perks of speaking a different language.

She's had a dozen chances to pull out that travel guide, but flicking through the pages, looking for phrases that don't quite fit, slows things down. It's more fun doing things in complete ignorance.

He aims the car at Mount Pelion, sends it on a long hike up the twisty road. The city haze dissipates quickly, leaving them with all the fresh air they can swallow. Not that Volos is an unclean city, but it's a city. By nature they're more polluted than places beyond their cluttered borders. Pelion smells like one of those green juices super-healthy people chug. Grass, leaves, fruit. Occasionally, a hint of animal poop.

Did she say a hint?

She means a *hit*.

Because when it comes it's like a full-on frontal assault. Every few feet—it seems like—they stop for sheep, goats, for the shepherds that follow the livestock and their rash of droppings. And they do not smell like flowers.

(The animals. Probably the shepherds smell fine.)

Pelion is dotted with villages. Tiny capillaries bleed off the main artery and into villages slightly larger than postage stamps. Buses have no choice but to dump their passengers by the side of the road—or into small parking lots at the mouth of some villages. If there's no parking lot, it's the road for you.

Looks like there are worse things than walking, though. The village streets are cobbled and charming, even when they're covered in sheep shit.

Akili stops the car at the side of the road, not anywhere —as far as she can tell—near a village. He comes around, opens her door, then leads her to a water fountain doing its best to hide in the wild undergrowth of Pelion's forests. Someone has tapped into the rock and carved a lion's head around a small faucet, permanently set to ON. Water gushes out of its manmade mouth, traveling to lower ground.

Lana would get a kick out of the permanently puking lion.

Spring water. The travel guide mentioned Pelion holds reservoirs of water that farmers on lower lands funnel into their orchards and farms via stone aqueducts.

Her tour guide nods to the flowing faucet, mimes drinking.

"You first, buddy."

In case it's poison. You never know. Bad things happened

in Greek mythology when people drank running water that looked perfectly delicious.

Akili shrugs, bends, cups his hands under the flow. He drinks first, then offers her his hands.

"God, I hope you wash your hands when you use the bathroom."

Worrying about it doesn't slow her down. What she wins is a mouthful of sugar-sweet water, on the brink of freezing. That unrefrigerated water can be so cold in this heat is miraculous.

He's watching her drink. No, she can't see him (she's face down in his hands, remember), but there's a hot spot on back of her head that isn't from the sun. Her bones loose their normal cohesion and jellify. She pulls away before she melts in a puddle at his feet.

"Thanks," she says, wiping her hand across her lips.

He's watching that too, isn't he? Man misses nothing.

It's unintentional the way she bites her lip.

Honestly.

"Where now?" She flings the car door open, slides inside, just in case her body decides to pounce.

If he's disappointed it doesn't show. Akili leaps into the driver's side, making the jump look effortless. The car roars and they're off again, but a quarter mile or so up the road he takes a turn she almost misses. Rubber crunches the narrow cobbled street. They're driving around the edge of a charming (what else can she call it? This place was made for a calendar page—one of the summer months) village—more of a hamlet, really. Village is a serious exaggeration. Three-story Pelion-style houses, the requisite souvenir shop, and a village square where people just like her (foreigners) are drinking coffee and contemplating which souvenir will best remind them of this day.

Her driver kills the engine outside a hole in the mountain,

corked with a door and surrounded by a wrought iron fence and some flower pots. Red and pink geraniums say someone around here has a greenish thumb.

Not Lucy. She can't grow anything except mold.

"What is this place?"

Akili nods to the cross etched into the door.

"A church? In a mountain? Neat."

He opens the door. Cool air rushes at her, pulls her in, away from the heat and all its harshness.

Lights out.

Blink, blink. She closes her eyes. Opens them. Closes them. Opens them again, forcing her pupils to go into cat mode. The third time her eyes pop open she sees the flames. Small candles hovering in the dark, huddled together in this false night.

Mostly dead silence, except somewhere—deeper in the mountain perhaps—there's a distinct *drip-drip*. Spring water? Must be.

Good thing she doesn't need to pee.

Cat mode activated. Now she's seeing the church as it is. Past the narrow narthex, the church's nave is filled with wood pews. Simple. Unadorned. Even the altar is plainly decorated. Here it's easy to believe Christ started out as a carpenter. There's an icon stand with a portrait of the Virgin Mary and Jesus for those who belong to the Greek Orthodox faith to kiss, but she doesn't know how to do it, or if she even should.

Yeah, she was baptized Greek Orthodox, but baptism doesn't imbue a person with automatic faith. What if she kisses the glass-covered portrait and this whole mountain comes crashing down on her head?

It could happen. Look at the luck her family has. If there's a disaster, somehow they manage to find it.

Death's already tried to hook up with her twice this week.

Why invite it back for do-overs? So she holds back, lets Akili do his thing. Kiss, kiss, cross, cross.

Is he devout? He doesn't seem religious. When she thinks Greek Orthodox she thinks widows in their head-to-toe black, always crossing themselves because they're seeing signs on toast or in birds flying overhead. And when they're not crossing, they're spitting to ward away the evil eye. Grandma warned her about that years ago. Nine times out of ten, if a Greek is spitting on you it's a kindness, a courtesy.

But that tenth time ...

A door creaks. Light pours through a narrow slit at the top of—she sees now—steps cut into the rock. This church is like a puzzle box. It's made of hidden compartments. A man in a black cassock appears. He says something, but she doesn't understand.

"Sorry, I don't speak Greek," she says with what she hopes is appropriate reverence.

The man laughs. It booms through the tiny church. "If you need me, just knock. I am Father Kostas."

It's so dark she can't make out his face, not with the blinding halo behind his head.

"Thanks," she says. "I love your church."

"Thank you," he says in his lightly accented English. "The Holy Mother is the best church in all of Greece."

There's a voice behind him, the higher hum of a woman's voice. Then a baby squeals with delight. Father Kostas laughs again, but this time it's the child who has won his favor

"It's not very gold," Lucy adds. "I like that."

"It is very unusual in Greece for a church to be so unadorned, but that is one of the many things I love about my home. Would you like to see something else wonderful, American?"

"How did you know I'm American?"

Another laugh. "I have two ears. And my future sister-in-law is American." His hand reaches out, beckons "Come, come. Both of you."

She looks back at Akili, who shrugs. No way is she going to let him say no to even a small adventure. "Come on." Grabbing his hand, she pulls him along behind her. Up the steps, into the sun.

"Holy hell," she says. Then, looking at the priest, she winces. "Sorry."

Big grin. It lights up his face. He's attractive in an I-fought-the-world-and-I-won way. Hair the color of his cassock, eyes a warm shade of brown. Nose slightly off-kilter. "Don't be sorry. Hell is holy in its own way. Not that the Greek Orthodox church believes in hell as a separate physical location."

"It doesn't?"

"No. Belief in a physical hell is for people who want to scare their children into doing the right thing. In the Greek Orthodox church, hell is what you make it after you die. Although some people try to make life hell, too."

They're standing in a smallish apartment. Kitchen to the right, closed doors to the left. Directly ahead is her surprise, her adventure. The entire back of the apartment is windows and doors, and they're wide open. Outside, with support from one of the mountain's ledges, is a balcony large enough for a table, chairs, and a couple of potted plants—in those ubiquitous red pots. One is a cactus, the other is something she doesn't recognize.

"Laurel," Father Kostas says, following her line of sight.

Beyond the balcony is a view of heaven—Greece at its very best. The gulf is a sheet of blue-green glass. It's freckled here and there with boats, but they seem to be drifting without shattering the surface.

"Lucy?" a voice says. The woman she heard from inside

the church. It's her grandmother's friend's granddaughter (that's a mouthful!), Irini and her little girl.

"Irini!"

The priest's gaze jumps back and forth from woman to woman. There's a new smile blossoming on his face. "You know each other?"

"Our grandmothers are very old friends," Irini tells him.

Father Kostas laughs—seems like he does that a lot. "I should have known. Here everyone knows everyone. Irini and I are old friends, too. And now she works with my brother at the Volos Hospital."

Lucy asks, "Is this the brother who is engaged to an American?"

"The one and only," the priest says.

"Lucy Shake," she says, offering her hand. Then she jerks it back, inspects it for defects. "I'm sorry, but I don't know the protocol for meeting Greek Orthodox priests. Are we allowed to shake hands?"

Father Kostas and Irini both roar. The priest grabs her hands, shakes them both. "There," he says. "Now we are friends. I never expect a friend or a beautiful woman to kiss my ring. Irini would rather die before she would kiss it."

"I would not die," Irini says, winking at her. "But I would cut off his hand and shove it up his—"

"Irini," the priest says, still laughing, "this is a house of God."

"If you ask me, God could use the laugh. That," she says, pointing down the stairs, "is the house of God. This is just his sidekick's apartment."

"His sidekick!" Father Kostas says, faking horror.

Suddenly Lucy remembers Akili standing beside her. For a moment she got lost in the tornado these two people churn between them. "I'm sorry," she says. "This is Akili. And he doesn't speak English."

Father Kostas immediately switches back to Greek. As they get caught up in their conversation, Lucy drifts over to Irini and her daughter.

"Can I hold her?"

"Of course!" Irini picks up her daughter, sits her on Lucy's lap. Then she leans in close. "Where did you find *him*?"

Irini is immaculately dressed again. Blue skinny pants, crisp ruffled top, shoes that crisscross her feet and tie her ankles up with thin leather ribbons.

"He's the guy from the boat."

"The one that sank?"

Lucy nods. "That's the one."

"Wow. Lucky. Very nice souvenir. Will he fit in your luggage?"

They laugh.

"I wish. I know I have to leave him here, but ... I like him."

"Even though you do not speak the same language?"

Shrug. "I like what I like."

"So do I," Irini says. "So do I. Our heads love logic, but our hearts ... they cannot abide common sense."

Side by side, they sit staring at the sea. Behind them, the men chatter in a language she has no hope of understanding. Her grandmother's native tongue is a concrete wall, and it refuses to let her pass.

"How long are you here for?" Father Kostas asks as they're leaving.

"Ten more days."

"Leave me your number and I will arrange for Vivi—that's my brother's fiancée—to meet you. You will love her. Vivi is a remarkable woman. Also, she does not put up with my brother's shit ... or our mother's." There's a distinct twinkle in his eye.

Another exchange between the men, then the priest says, "Akili and Vivi know each other, too. His best friend was engaged to my cousin." He shakes his head. "That was a tragedy."

"What happened?"

"He was shot on his wedding day."

She doesn't look at Akili. It's too weird talking about him while he's standing right here. "Wow. Your poor cousin."

"Very tragic. But I know an alternate ending to the story, one where my cousin was lucky. Their marriage was arranged, and neither of them wanted to marry the other. So he married someone else—a Romani girl. It was her mother who shot him. And now my cousin is engaged to an old friend of mine."

Wow. What else can she say? It's so ... so ... soap opera-ish the way everybody here is connected by thin, almost invisible, strings. Pull one and they all jerk.

It's not like home, where everybody hustles to stay invisible.

Or to be seen.

❧ 47 ❧

Fotini

THE ISLAND UNFOLDS, ONE PETAL AT A TIME. A HIDDEN cove here, a patch of beach there. The land is dry but not dead. Life is sparse, yet it is everywhere. Here the olive trees have room to grow. They are not so desperate for sun; their twists are less arthritic, their canopies more rounded and full.

There are secret places, yes, but they want to be found.

They walk and see almost no one. Fotini and Stelios and the salty-sweet air.

When they do see a man, he's with a donkey. They're tethered together, man to beast, by several feet of fraying rope. Convention states that it's the donkey who hauls the burden, but in this case it's the man, a heavy brown sack thrown over his shoulder.

"Athanasio!" Stelios calls out.

The old man's face splits along its seam. "Stelios, you old

malakas. Where did you find this magnificent woman? How much did you pay her to keep you company?"

She laughs, but she cannot resist tugging on his leg a little. "Are you calling me a *putana*?"

"No! I am calling him a sorry excuse for a man. When he was a child his mother used to tie a piece of lamb around his neck so the vultures would play with him. Otherwise, he would have had no friends."

"*Gamo ti mana sou*," Stelios mutters, but he's grinning.

She looks at him, one eyebrow riding high. "Charming," she says, mostly joking. Greeks have a way of sexually violating everyone in their everyday speech. They think nothing of saying, 'I fuck the Virgin Mary,' or, 'I fuck your mother'.

The second one is what Stelios confessed to.

"I am a very charming man," the bartender tells her.

"But only in your own mind," she says.

The man with the donkey shakes his head. "You and every man on the sea has slept with my mother, friend.

"What's in the sack?" She nods at his shoulder.

"Flour. Very heavy."

"Why not get your donkey to carry it?"

He glances back at his beast, shrugs. "She is old. She likes the walks, but the load is too much. So I carry the flour and let her enjoy her life."

"You are soft," Stelios says. Fotini elbows him. "What?" he splutters.

"This is a good man," she says.

The bartender seizes the handbag off her shoulder, slides it over his. Pats the leather. "Look, now I am a good man, too."

He is a good man, but it is fun to play with him. Snatching back her bag, she smiles at the other man. "It's good to meet you, Athanasios. Enjoy your walk."

"If you have an opportunity to run away from him," Athanasios says, "I have a warm bed."

Stelios looks at her. "Do you want to run?"

"Who can run with these knees? Walk fast? Now that I can do."

Stelios laughs. He does her heart good.

THE MONASTERY IS OPEN THIS TIME, BUT IT'S ONLY THE two of them and the old woman who cares for the place. She's as old as these bricks, looks like, only the bricks are white, painted with a forgiving hand, while her clothes are the stale black of all Greek widows.

Shame reaches out, weaves its fingers through Fotini's hair, over the shell of her ear. *Where is your black?*

The woman scurries away, leaving the two of them to walk the monastery's grounds. Nature is doing its best to repel the flagstones laid upon its dirt. Between stones, weeds push up through the crumbling grout in search of sun and sky.

She and Stelios walk under the porch's cover, a series of arches adding strength and beauty to the structure. When they come to the star mosaic at the porch's entrance, she walks around it. Yes, it's made for feet, but better feet than hers.

Then inevitably, thanks to the design of this place, they arrive at the open mouth of the chapel.

"Wait." Stelios stops her with a hand. "I must tell you something. I cannot go in there with lies in my heart. God will know and—" He smacks his hands together. "*Kaput*! I would prefer not to go *kaput*, you know?"

"Speak up, man." The words are plain, bold, but behind them is an undercurrent of dread. Confession is only good for the soul spilling the truth. For everyone else, it can be uncomfortable at best, a soul-tearing disaster at worst.

Lives and futures hang on the curl of a confession.

"I lied," he tells her. "I was married. Once."

"So was I." She swallows the sudden fire in her throat. "So was I."

❧ 48 ❧

A (Minor) Interruption

THE STORY OF FOTINI AND IASON IS ONE OF GREECE'S shortest tragedies.

It's Romeo and Juliet, without the balcony, the Italians, and the suicides.

No, wait—there is a suicide, but it's in their story's epilogue.

But before that, there's a murder.

❦ 49 ❦

Fotini

THEY DON'T GO IN, WHICH IS FINE WITH HER. WHAT IS another church but a reminder that they are not good enough? People come to church to cleanse themselves so they have a shot at rubbing elbows with angels.

"What do you think of Trikeri's monastery so far?"

Stelios is waiting on her approval, as if her opinion matters.

Okay, he was married before. So what? Everybody has a past; only the shape and size vary.

Her past is the problem, not Stelios's. All these years in America, it was content to stay buried, but now?

Greece wants to dig it up. This country is fond of old things: rumors, stories, tragedies. Greece's past is stitched together with tears. The old gods were not happy, and before them, the titans cornered the market on misery.

She could diagnose them all with one disorder or another.

Virgin Mary, what is she to do?

Leave. As soon as possible. That is what.

But what of Lucy and her attachment to Akili? What of Stelios and his beachside *taverna*?

She is not a teenage girl again, running for her life and that of her unborn child. She cannot ... run *away*.

"I want to run away," she says, leaning against the monastery's warm outer wall.

Stelios thinks on it a moment. "Okay. Where will we go?"

An arched eyebrow. "We?"

"What, would you have me miss a good running away? What fun is that? So where do you want to go?"

Nowhere. Anywhere. Here the company is excellent but the location stinks.

"Who was she?"

"Who was who?"

"Your wife."

"Ah, is that why you want to run away?"

She shakes her head. The wall is hard behind her head, but its warmth and stability feel soothing. "No. I just want to hear someone else's sad story for a moment."

"Eh, it is not that sad. We were married, then she fell on a *poutso* that was not mine, then we divorced."

"She cheated on you?"

"Yes. Not just one man—all the men. She would go to Volos, shopping and making love to everybody."

Her mouth twitches. "Silly woman."

"What else could she do? She was not happy on the island. She was meant for bigger places."

"Did she find that bigger place?"

He nods. "Athens, for a time. Then she moved to back to Agria, remarried, had a family."

"Back to a small village?"

"Bigger than Trikeri, and her family was from there. She

was never a bad woman, just a woman who liked to wear her ankles like earrings. What about you?" Leaning against the wall, he nudges her with his elbow. A gentle move. Familiar, caring. "Do you want to tell your story?"

"It is a tragedy," she says. "You like happy, romantic endings."

His shoulders shake with laughter. "How can it be a tragedy? Who is it to say your story will not have a happy, romantic ending? Your story is still being written; you are here, yes?"

"Do you have to be so logical?"

"Of course," he says. "I am a man." His mustache twitches as he says it, which is just as well. Sexism, even the casual kind, belongs in another century.

Her hand closes the gap between them. It's a small space, but so what? When you want to be close to someone, even an eighth of an inch is two far between bodies.

"I can't tell you my story yet," she says.

"Cannot or will not?"

"The first one."

"But you will?"

"Yes, but not today."

"Okay. There is more than just today."

Is there? She remembers a time when there were yesterdays and todays, but no guarantees of tomorrows.

⚜ 50 ⚜

Akili

BACK TO AGRIA, WHERE THERE ARE SIGHTS TO BE SEEN.
They're all worn out to him, old, until he sees them anew
through Lucy's eyes and her enthusiastic smile.

She makes his world shiny and new.

Now they're inching along Agria's promenade, looking for
a place to park. Ice cream and a *frappe*, that's next on his list.

As soon as they get out of the car, Akili discovers he's got
a target on his chest. *Kyria* Dora's the one shooting his name
across the street.

"Akili! How are you, my boy?"

Her boy? Since when?

Since Effie Makri turned daily operations of the *Very Super
Market* over to her mother. *Kyria* Dora has been up and down
the promenade, making friends with all the proprietors. She's
known them all forever—still she's reacquainting herself with
everyone, as one of them.

He waves to the iron-haired woman squeezed into the black dress, but she's not letting him sneak away easily.

"Who is that with you?" She cups her hand over her eyes, squints. "I do not know her! Come over here, Akili." Lots of hand waving. "Introduce me to your friend."

It's the last thing he wants to do, drag Lucy into the serpent's pit, but it's too late now. His reputation will be dirt if he doesn't at least stop and say hello.

Agria doesn't forgive spurned greetings. Ever. It keeps an unofficial, verbal naughty list.

He crosses the street, steering Lucy by her elbow. There's traffic, but it's mostly slow moving, so they dart across the street in two bursts. Dora Makri has done as promised: She has set up a table and chairs under a wide, blue umbrella, and there's a sign in Greek and English, offering coffee cup readings for ten euros apiece.

He nods at her sign. "How is business?"

"Wonderful!" She beams at the two of them, though her eyes are laced with curiosity. "Everybody wants to know their future. I do not understand why. Even when I tell them, they never prepare. If I tell them bad things, they assume I am a charlatan. If I tell them something good, only then do they believe in the cup."

"Cassandra had the same problem."

Her laugh is big, bold boom. "Yes, but she was beautiful and crazy. I am old and ugly and not even a little bit *trela*."

POOR CASSANDRA HAD A TOUGH TIME. A PRIESTESS OF Apollo, a sworn virgin, and royalty (a princess of Troy, no less), she ended up in bad shape because she changed her yes to a last-minute no.

Apollo offered her the gift of prophesy if she'd pony up

her virginity, which sounded like a great idea right up until the ponying up part happened. Then the girl said no, and good guy Apollo, at his date-rapey finest, told her she could keep the gift except now it was kind of a curse. Yeah, she could see the future, but would anyone believe her?

Nope.

So she foresaw Helen and her hand in Troy's doom, the Greeks and their Trojan horse, and a bunch of other things nobody believed.

Poor woman was insulted, raped, and eventually killed after King Agamemnon took her for his concubine.

She foresaw that, too.

KYRIA DORA IS KNOWN AS A WOMAN WHOSE SCREWS AREN'T always tightened all the way down, but she's good people. She means well.

Mostly.

"This is Lucy," he says. "She's American."

When the older woman claps, her whole body shudders. "American! My niece is American. You should meet her."

Lucy looks up at him, eyebrows raised, smile ghosting her lips.

"Lucy doesn't speak Greek."

Lights up like an Easter candle, doesn't she? "Then I bet this is a *very* interesting story. I cannot wait to hear it." *Kyria* Dora unravels a string of English words. He watches Lucy relax and answer. Her voice is low, sweet. Too bad he doesn't know what she's saying. But it turns him on, anyway. He wants that voice in his ear, begging for more while he fucks her. English, Greek, doesn't matter, as long as she never quits talking.

Next thing he knows, Lucy's sliding into a chair at *Kyria*

Dora's fortune-telling table.

"Lucy—" he starts.

Kyria Dora taps him on the forehead. "It is just a little fun. Let the girl have fun. And sit. It makes me nervous when people stand around like that. You look like you want to chew off your foot and run away! You want me to read your cup, too?"

He jerks his head up, goes *tst*. Greek shorthand for 'no'.

She waves her hand and a waiter comes running over. He works for the *kafeneio* next to the *Very Super Market*. They must be getting some kind of kickback, he figures.

"Your Lucy looks a little Greek through the eyes and nose," she says, pointing sausage fingers at her own face. Then she repeats her words in English for Lucy's benefit.

"Her grandmother is Greek."

"Oh?"

Lucy's words fly.

"Oh! Her grandmother is from here! How wonderful. Who is her grandmother?"

"*Kyria* Fotini," he says. "I don't know her last name."

Chatter, chatter.

Kyria Dora taps a finger on her lip. "Fotini, she says. Interesting. We have had many Fotinis here. Some have come, some have gone, some are dead, some are still here. I would love to meet this grandmother. Who knows, maybe we are old friends. I love old friends—they always have new stories. And of course, all my stories are new to them if we have not seen each other in an age, no?"

She and Lucy chatter back and forth. Between them they try on different words, some of them not fitting perfectly the first time. But they find their way. And soon, the coffee shows up. Two cups and a *frappe*.

"The *frappe* is for me," *Kyria* Dora says, beaming. "The *kafe* is for the two of you."

"But—" Akili starts.

She waves away his objection. "I will give you a discount. Two for one. Very good deal, yes?"

Because it's always a good deal when someone gives you a price break on something you don't want.

But for Lucy's sake he'll play along. It's another memory of Greece, of time they're sharing. He digs in his pocket, slaps ten euros on the table. Lucy tries to shove it back at him, but he's more stubborn. She shouldn't have to pay for *Kyria* Dora's foolishness. Future in the cups! The future doesn't show itself until it's ready, and it's never ready until it's here.

That's a fact.

Still, let them have their little madness. What harm can come of it? She'll tell Lucy she'll find love, money, have great success in life. Maybe win a lottery, have many happy, healthy children. And she'll tell Akili a different version of the same lie. It's worth ten euro if Lucy walks away happy.

Her leg bumps against his under the table. She flashes him a smile, a small wink. He almost laughs, almost gets a hard-on. She knows this is bullshit same as he does. He should have realized they were on the same side, humoring the older woman.

Kyria Dora reels off a short list of instructions. English first for Lucy's benefit. Greek for his. Lucy makes a face with the first sip. She says something and *Kyria* Dora slaps the table, laughing.

"She says it is strong. Of course it is strong, it is Greek. Everything we make is strong, especially our cheese and our coffee and our women."

She chats with Lucy in staccato English for a few minutes until the muddy coffee is gone. Then—after they've both upturned the cups on their saucers and turned them three times, she picks up Lucy's cup.

51

Lucy

JUST BECAUSE IT'S BULLSHIT, DOESN'T MEAN LUCY DOESN'T want to believe. She's on the fence between Mulder and Scully when it comes to woo-woo stuff.

She's on the fence about a lot of things.

Kyria Dora, though, she's peering into the cup as though it's holding Lucy's truth. "I see water. Big water, like the ocean."

Must be the ocean—just a wild guess.

"The cup says you will go on a ... a holiday."

Very astute, given that she's already on vacation.

"Ah! Now here is something. I see a wedding. Maybe not your wedding, but a wedding. But now that I think about it, maybe it is a wedding that already happened because it is in the bottom of the cup. A secret wedding, I think. Who knows? The cup can be very mysterious."

Against her better judgement she leans forward. There's

pressure in her chest, the beginning of eagerness. "Whose wedding?"

"Maybe your parents, maybe your grandparents."

"Does it say anything about my wedding—one day?"

The Greek woman tilts the cup. "Wedding ... no. But I see an island. Or a blob of coffee grounds. Here is something else. I see crows—many crows. In the bottom of the cup and on the sides. Low. In the past. Some very far, some not so far."

"What does a crow mean?"

Kyria Dora shrugs. "Death. You have seen too much death, I think. Yes?"

Lucy nods. No more eagerness; what she feels are the remnants of dread.

"Good news! There are no crows in the future or present. So that is good, yes?"

Another nod. It's a cup; what can china know about the past, present, and future of anything beyond its thin wall?

It's all hocus pocus.

Isn't it?

She's seen death—too much of it; *Kyria* Dora was right about that. But she's given Lucy nothing tangible, nothing specific to guarantee even a modicum of authenticity.

"Great. Do you see anything else?"

"I see a ball."

"Is that bad?"

"It can be good, it can be bad, but mostly it is—how you say—" She thinks for a moment. "Neutral. A ball means completion. Of what, the cup does not say. Only you know." She looks at Lucy expectantly, clears her throat.

"Me?" Lucy sits back, stabs a finger at her own chest. "I don't know. That's why I'm asking you."

"Heh-heh." She says something to Akili in Greek. Then: "I told Akili you are a very funny woman."

She's not funny, but she's not quite serious either. This is how fortune-tellers are: short on meaningful answers. Maybe the older woman sees something in the cup, but its interpretation is all on Lucy.

Still, it was fun.

"Do Akili's cup now."

✣ 52 ✣

Akili

KYRIA DORA ABANDONS LUCY'S CUP FOR HIS. HE'S DYING
to know what she told her. Funny reaction for a guy who
doesn't believe.

"Interesting life, your girl here," she says. "Let us see what
lies ahead for you, eh?" She picks up his cup, tilts it towards
the sea.

"I see the truth," she says. "Nothing more."

Okay ... "What's the truth?"

The coffee cup reader's attention is wandering west,
further down the promenade. It's sharpening, pinpointing on
a woman standing outside the shoe shop, her arms folded.
She's staring out to sea.

The Bulgarian woman who works there.

"That woman," she mutters. "Why is she still here?"

Nobody knows—or if they do they're not saying. She
arrived some years ago and hasn't left.

Another one of Greece's many mysteries.

"That's it?"

"Yes," she muses. "That's all your cup is saying. It does not have a very big mouth."

Unusual for Agria.

❧ 53 ❧

Lucy

She reaches out, dances her fingers through the spray Akili's boat makes. The *Flying Dolphin* ferries are great, but everyone is kept encapsulated for their own safety.

Who wants to lose passengers at those speeds?

Part of her wishes Volos ran the old-style ferries, the ones that hum along using a lesser motor. It would be nice to stand up on deck, lean against the railing and watch one shore disappear while another materializes in the distance. There's a kind of magic in that sort of vanishing act.

"So what did she tell you?" she asks Akili. "Any warnings? Doom and gloom? Or did you get the version with lottery winnings and happily ever afters?"

He looks at her, totally clueless. Every bit as clueless as she is when he opens his mouth.

So she pulls a notepad out of her handbag, unclips the pen

from inside the wire coil that holds the pad together, and draws a picture of a cup.

It's not a good cup. Could be a bucket from this angle.

Or a funny hat.

She draws a handle. Then a saucer.

Now it looks like a weird UFO.

Lucy knows her talents don't include drawing. In kindergarten she failed finger-painting. In elementary school, *Pictionary*.

Some people just don't have that art gene; Lucy is one of them. She's at peace with that, but it sure would be handy right now.

She points to the cup, then to herself. Then she doodles faces with the eyes crossed out. Above each one, she writes the dates they died.

Those dates are carved in her heart. No way will she ever forget.

The ball is next. She tries a bowling ball first (c'mon, how hard can it be? Who messes up a bowling ball? It's a circle and three little circles), but when she works her magic she winds up with a lopsided coconut. She shoots for a beach ball next, with three monochromatic stripes. When Akili looks at it and blinks, she moves to charades.

She mimes someone much more athletic than her bouncing a ball.

"*Bala*!" Akili says, snapping his fingers.

Shaking both hands at the heavens: "Yes! *Bala*!"

Now to item number one, which she's left until last. Because how the hell is she going to dress or act out a wedding without Akili thinking she's cooking up a plan to drag him to the altar?

Draw first. Worry later.

First dress looks like a tent.

Second dress looks like a mathematical problem. Something to do with geometry, which was never her thing—obviously, otherwise she'd know what to call this dress ... shape ... thingy.

Third dress looks like something *Porn Star Barbie* would wear.

Finally she slumps against the side of the boat. "Forget it," she says.

Akili takes the pen and paper. He sketches for a few minutes then hands back the notepad.

It's a map. A street map.

"Is this where you live?"

He points to himself, to the square on the map several blocks from the main road.

Is he inviting her home for sex or to meet his parents?

Lucy's not big on meeting parents. Not when she'd give anything to see her own.

———

GRANDMA AND STELIOS ARE AT THE *TAVERNA*. THEY WAVE, but they keep their distance.

Nice of them.

Grandma will grill her later.

Not that she can talk, cozying up to Stelios that way. They're cooking up something, those two. Probably world domination.

Akili walks her to their room. Very romantic.

Is that what this is—a romance? How can it be when they've never exchanged a coherent word without a translator?

But it feels like a romance. Her skin is flashing hot and cold. Her heart is alternating between skipping beats and doubling up. And when Akili fixes that dark gaze on her she wants to rip off her clothes and sacrifice herself on his altar.

Or his bed.

Or hers.

Come to think of it, she'd be okay with those bushes or this wall.

Thinking comes to a halt when Akili backs her up to that very wall, curls one arm around his waist, cups her neck with the other, and reels her slowly in.

Doesn't feel like he's in any hurry to let her go. His body is making all kinds of demands, but his eyes are watching, waiting for her okay.

"If you don't kiss me, you're going to get kissed."

That's all he needs. His mouth comes crashing down on hers, he pushes her against that wall, all of him hot and hard. Two people sharing the same desperation.

Oh God. She needs this—needs him and all his fire. He's burning her down, starting with her mouth, her tongue.

Then he breaks away, braces his hands against the wall, either side of her head. August is hot, but her body cools. There's another kiss; this one is gentle, tender, a butterfly's kiss.

Why is he moving so slowly when there's already so little time left?

Too bad she can't ask. She really needs to know.

"WHERE DID YOU GO?"

"Pelion."

"What did you do?"

"Drive."

"Lucy, you are maddening." Grandma chases her words with a grimace. Lucy busts out laughing.

"Okay, okay." She gives Grandma, Stelios, and Father Yiannis (who has wandered in for his nightly bottles of stupefaction) the extended version, editing the kiss, throwing in some dramatic reenactments for her audience's pleasure.

They laugh, she laughs, they all laugh.

But her mind is on the mainland, in Akili's bed.

❧ 54 ❧

Akili

HE SHINES ALL THE WAY HOME, UNTIL HIS FATHER FLIPS HIS switch. Barely in the door after a too-short day with Lucy and a long night at the pizzeria before the old man starts hounding him. He follows Akili to the bathroom, just him and his wheels.

"They say you are seeing a girl," he says through the door.

Can't he piss in peace? "Who is?"

"People."

"People say a lot of things here. It's what they do."

"Sometimes they are right."

"Sometimes."

"Are they right this time?"

"Maybe."

"Maybe, maybe," he says in the mocking tone that makes Akili want to punch him into the street. "Why won't you tell me? Is she fat and ugly?"

ALEX A. KING

Akili zips up, flushes, shuts the door behind him. The old man is waiting on answers. Got entitlement issues.

"I don't discuss my personal life with friends. What makes you think I'd share it with you?"

"Maybe there is something good in it for you if you tell me."

"Like what?"

The old bastard cackles. "Maybe I will find somewhere else to go."

"Where? Who would tolerate your *skata*?"

"There are places for people like me. Places for fathers with ungrateful children."

Takes everything he's got to push, not shove, the wheelchair outside. He parks his father on the far side of the round table under the grapevine. Then he sits, too. The busy night melts away. The bits with Lucy stick with him though. Her company, her kiss. Thinking about it would be getting him hard, except he's got his father's drama to deal with.

"Who says I'm ungrateful? I loved watching you beat my mother, screaming at her, making her life hell. I'm glad you're here, reminding me exactly who I don't want to be. Life is good."

"*Ai sto dialo.*"

"Go to the devil? What for? He lives here in my house. I see him every day."

"If I hit your mother, it's because she deserved it. And you were a sniveling, fat, little bastard. I wanted a son and I got a little *skeela*. You were weak. And look, you are still weak."

Akili laughs. "Makes two of us."

The old man pulls that yellow packet of his pocket, rolls a perfect cigarette. He lights up, takes a long drag, blows out a personal-sized cloud of smoke. The night takes it, but before it does, the smoke drifts upward until it's a faint halo around his head.

204

"I won't miss that when you go."

"You will miss it," his father says.

"Not a chance."

"You hate me, I know. That is okay. I hated my father, too. But once he was dead, I found I missed the strangest things. That is how it will be for you, too. You complain about the smoke now, but when it is gone it will leave a hole in you, like an empty tooth socket." He sucks on the cigarette, blows another halo before he speaks again. "I want to meet her."

"Who?"

"This girl."

"No."

"Okay. Then I am staying right here."

"Right there?"

"Right here."

Akili pushes out of the chair. He's sick of the old man, tired of battling this blend of guilt and white-hot anger. Tired of the perpetual black cloud that bastard keeps tethered to this house.

So he stomps inside, shuts the door behind him.

Locks it tight.

Congratulations, old bastard, enjoy your *'right here'*.

But he can't do it. Doesn't have a cruel streak stitched to his nature. Won't leave a disabled old man to sit outside all night, no matter how much the bastard drags up their bruised and battered past.

He flicks the lock open.

Out in the yard, his father cackles. "Soft, boy. Weak." He coughs in his gray tobacco cloud. "Bring her here and I will go. You will never see me again, I promise."

CAN'T SLEEP, SO HE'S THINKING, AND LUCY'S THE ONE filling his head.

She's a beautiful distraction. This afternoon he almost couldn't stop. Took everything he had to break away before they went too far. He wants her, but he wants more than the week or so left before she flies back to her life. If he fucks her now he'll be following her onto that plane like a lost dog. Thing is, he belongs here and she belongs there. They both know it.

Sex isn't clarity, it's clouds.

Doesn't mean they can't keep things sweet and friendly. A good time is still a good time, even when there's no sex. Earlier he drew her a map, jotted down his address, hoping she'd write when she went home. Maybe they can write to each other, read letters they don't understand.

So where's the harm in bringing Lucy to meet the old man? She won't understand him, he won't understand her.

In return he'll win his freedom.

(Not that's he's convinced.)

Where's the old man going anyway? There's no family nearby—not anymore.

Virgin Mary, why does he care?

Gone is gone is gone.

𝕷 55 𝕽

Lucy

LUCY'S THINKING SHE COULD GET USED TO THIS, WAKING UP alongside the sun. At home she needs a crane and a howling, screeching fishwife of an alarm to leverage her out of the sack.

It's not a work avoidance thing; work doesn't start until the late afternoon. And she suffers (ha!) from the same malady on days off, doesn't she?

Normally Grandma's the one who beats the sun out of bed. Now she's hiding under the covers, employing her boogeyman shield as a day deterrent.

Not Stelios, though. He's at the *taverna*, brewing coffee, setting out what looks suspiciously like muffins.

"*Kyria* Maria's?"

"Who else?"

"Want to know what I think?"

Twinkle, twinkle, little stars in his eyes. "I think you are going to tell me anyway, so tell me."

"I think you made them."

"That is an interesting theory."

"Isn't it? But don't tell me—I love a good mystery."

He laughs. "Like your grandmother, you are one of a kind, Lucy."

A boat motor slices the air and sea into noisy chunks. She perks up. Very dog-like, she knows it.

"Akili," she says.

"How can you tell?"

Just one of those women's intuition things. When she says it out loud, Stelios laughs. But it's a warm sound, not the mocking caw of a non-believer.

"Go, go," he says. "I will make more coffee."

Lucy runs, dress flapping above her knees. It's not desperation, the act of a woman clinging to any man who shows her attention. She doesn't have that kind of reserve in her. She likes him, he likes her, they kissed—so why hold back?

It's definitely Akili. He's inching the new boat up to the dock.

She stops where the concrete kisses the pebbled shore, gets busy enjoying the view.

Best view in Greece.

Keep the mountain vistas, the sunsets, the snapshots of Greeks living the way only Greeks do. They're beautiful, but they're not Akili. There's poetry in the way he ties off the boat, the sun framing him in its early morning spotlight.

Her fantasies start battling for temporary Lucy-world domination. They all want Akili play-acting the scripts they've written. It's not easy keeping herself fully dressed, but her head fights that war and wins.

When he walks her way it's with a touch of swagger. On

him it looks good. Not arrogant, just confident. Big smile on his face softens up his hard surfaces.

"Coffee?"

He nods.

Now they're holding hands, and Lucy has no idea who reached for who first—only that it happened.

❦ 56 ❦

Fotini

FOTINI WAKES WITHOUT A SCHEMATIC FOR THE DAY IN HER head. Let today be whatever it wants to be.

What it wants to be is a trip to Agria in Akili's boat.

"Go," she told Lucy at first. "I will stay here."

Not the best idea, Akili reminds her now. Sightseeing is one thing, but Agria is still Agria, and if he takes Lucy home alone people will talk.

He doesn't want people talking about Lucy—not in a way that splashes scarlet paint all over her reputation.

Agria lives in a different century; sometimes she thinks it's located on a different planet, one where some social mores are concrete and others have the solidity of running water.

"Agria is ridiculous. It runs on the power of gossip," she says, after she's agreed to go.

"So do cities," Stelios says. "But they use newspapers and the television to spread gossip."

"There's a difference between news and gossip."

"The only difference between news and gossip is the size of the target."

"Stop being so logical."

"Only if you promise to stop being so illogical."

Infuriating, wonderful man.

AGRIA'S BACKSTREETS ARE THE SAME AS ITS FRONT STREETS, but with more potholes and bigger mouths. Everybody they pass stops Akili to ask about his companions. They measure the two of them with questioning gazes, stockpiling any information they collect. She—or he—with the most information wins here.

Fotini sucks in her stomach, hoping they will describe her as five pounds lighter—or two kilos.

It was difficult switching from metric to imperial—but now she's having trouble moving back into this century. America clings to its miles and pounds as if they are a security blanket. *Lest we forget how we used to measure.*

She looks for signs of recognition in the passing faces, but finds none. It goes both ways. If her name is familiar, they don't say.

But her last name wasn't acquired in Agria.

Walking these streets is a shot of *deja vu*. She's been here before, in a nightmare she once lived. She straggles behind Lucy and Akili, hoping the town won't notice her and reclaim her as one of its own. The roads transition from faded blacktop to dirt, then back to blacktop. Greece should have paved it all when it was pretending to have money.

The houses are similar—mostly white, all shuttered. Flat

roofs are still king. Television aerials reach for the sky with their metal fingers. Fences and gates are every shade between freshly painted and stripped naked to their steel bones.

It's not a difference between haves and have-nots; some of Agria's wealthiest residents live like paupers and never let a euro go without a fight.

"Here," Akili says.

His home is like the others, but with fewer potted plants. The pots need painting and the greenery needs a thorough wedding. There could be a triffid in here and no one would know until it lashed out its tongue and fed off their body.

The good host, Akili invites them to sit, offers coffee and cake.

"May I use your bathroom?" she asks.

"Of course." He gives her directions then disappears into the kitchen, pulling Lucy behind him. The house is small but not uncomfortable. The air is slightly stale, the rooms a fraction too warm.

The house is holding its breath.

"What are you doing in my house?"

She swings around, gasp lodged in her throat, sees the man with wheels. "I am sorry, we are here with—"

Inside its bone housing, her heart is getting ready to evacuate. Her lungs push and pull, fall and rise, but the oxygen refuses to budge. There's a thumping in her head, the roar of rushing blood in her ears. Dark spots block her vision, but it's too late: she's already recognized him.

Her brother.

"Yiorgos," she says, with a thick tongue. The name comes out malformed.

He cups one time-speckled hand over his eyes. "Who are you?"

"Do you not recognize me?"

That hands fall away, his throat moves, and one work croaks out: "Fotini?"

She nods, takes in the dark room with its green walls and marble floors that might pass for something more than morose, if only someone would throw the shutters wide and invite the sun inside. All this stale air, this darkness ...

The stars come out, but only behind her eyes. She staggers backwards, crashes into the wall. Funny, a moment ago there was no wall there.

"*Kyria* Fotini?" Hands steady her. Not a wall—Akili.

"Grandma, are you okay?"

Lucy.

Her head shakes, contradicting her words. "Yes, yes. I am fine. I need air, that is all. I have to go."

"But we just got here," Lucy says.

"And now I am leaving."

Akili's confused, poor boy. Look how his gaze shifts from face to face, trying to piece the clues together. But you cannot complete a puzzle with half the pieces missing. You can guess at the picture, but you don't know unless you are the one holding the box.

"I have to go," she repeats.

"Fotini!" the old man in the wheelchair barks.

She runs.

Lucy follows.

𝕤 57 𝕤

Akili

THE STORM INSIDE HIM WON'T REMAIN CONTAINED. "WHAT did you say to her?"

The old bastard shrugs. "Nothing. You were there."

"I was in the kitchen with Lucy."

"That woman, where did you find her?"

"Trikeri. You know her?"

A heavy nod. "I know her. She is my sister."

"But ..." Inside his gut, in his heart, his throat, a steel-capped boot is kicking holes. His *sister.* Since when did the old man have a sister? He heard about the one who died, but *Kyria* Fotini isn't dead. "She can't be your sister."

"Oh? Why not?" He's rolling a cigarette right here in the house, licking the paper, perfecting his already perfect craft. "If you say she cannot be, then you must be right."

Back against the wall, Akili bangs his head in a slow *thunk thunk* rhythm. "Tell me."

"Tell you what?"

"Everything."

"Everything? You are entitled to know everything, eh? I do not think so."

Akili's done with this old bastard. Wants to roll him to the village's concrete edge and shove him into the sea. Let Poseidon do what he will with him.

"I want you out of here. Go into a home. Go live with the Romani. I don't care. Just get out."

"Where will I go? I have nobody."

"Who's fault is that? You were a *kolotripas* to everyone, and now the world is an asshole right back to you. And that is a world you made with your two hands."

Akili storms out. He's at the gate—no clue where he's headed—when the old man calls out after him. "What do you know about your grandfather?"

He stops. Turns around, sees the old man struggling out the door, cigarette balanced on his damp lip. "Nothing. Not your father or Mama's."

"Come back and I will tell you."

Stay or go?

If he stays, the old man is going to reel out some bullshit story, repackaging stories he's already told. Go, and the chance might be lost. This could be the moment of moments, that one opportunity to discover the truth.

Just like *Kyria* Dora saw in his cup.

His father is old, and he's not growing younger. He could die before another opportunity comes around.

"Okay." Using his hand as a rag, he wipes the sweat from his forehead. "Tell me."

❧ 58 ❧

Fotini

OKAY, SO SHE CANNOT RUN FAR, BUT SHE CAN WALK. THESE walking shoes were not so good for Volos, but they have become accustomed to her feet now. They make quick work of the uneven pavements and the patchy stretches of road.

"Grandma?"

"What, Lucy? What?"

"What's going on?"

"You would not understand." She stops, looks at her granddaughter. The poor girl is pale and pinched. There's genuine terror on her face, the horrified expression of someone who is about to lose their one final lifeline. "That's not fair, is it? You would understand, I think. But, Lucy, my love ..." Her eyes are going Niagara Falls over the planes of her cheeks. Lucy—sweet Lucy—is there with a pocket-pack of tissues, wiping her face. "I am all right, I promise. I will be okay. I need to lie down for a while, that is all. Then we will talk."

Lucy handles everything. As soon as they hit the main road, she steers them towards the taxi stand, where a short line of taxis are waiting while their drivers smoke and gossip. She commands one to drive them to Alogoporos, and when they pull up at the village's dock, she darts to the payphone to call Stelios.

In no time, Stelios is steering his boat their way.

"Let us get her on board first, then I will ask what happened, okay?"

Old fool, he lifts her as though she is nothing more substantial than a small pile of his books. But does he stagger? No.

"Did you love her—your wife?" she asks.

He laughs. "Women. That is what is important to you right now?"

"Just curious."

He sets her down on the boat's narrow seat. Lucy slides in next to her, then they're leaving the coast behind. In the past, where it belongs.

Soon, though, she thinks it will chase them across the sea. Akili will follow. Maybe not today, but soon.

Will her brother tell the boy? Will he tell his son—her nephew—that he helped kill her husband?

Will he tell Akili that he and Lucy are cousins?

❧ 59 ❧

Lucy

IT'S GOING TO HAPPEN AGAIN, LUCY KNOWS IT. THE universe is going to arch its back and flick Grandma off the roller coaster, leaving her with nothing but a plane ticket back home and a big house she doesn't want to inherit anytime soon.

Okay, melodramatic maybe, because Grandma was walking just fine—no huffing, puffing, aches or pains. Just bloodless skin and all those tears.

But for Grandma, that's major. She's the ultimate non-complainer, even if she does get sick.

Which she doesn't—ever—except a cold here and there. But even those don't hang around long. They've got lesser mortals to infect and annoy with their constant *drip, drip, drip.*

The boat slices and dices the sea at the speed of paint drying. It's not really that slow, but after Akili's new boat, and the sea-skimming speed of the *Flying Dolphin*, everything else seems to crawl.

She can't take her eyes off Grandma. Another exaggeration—very Greek of her—because she does notice that Stelios keeps flicking worried glances at her grandmother. When he not doing that, he's a marble statue, watching the sea.

Grandma notices too. "Stop looking at me like that, you two. I'm not china—I will not break."

Stelios grunts his thoughts on the matter. Good; Grandma needs someone who can force her spine to flex a little.

Here comes the island.

Stelios docks the boat easily, then he leaps out and reaches for Grandma. Lucy gets her other side, helps her out of the boat.

"You two do know I am not an invalid?" Grandma asks.

"*Skasmos*," Stelios says. Then he glances over Grandma's shoulder at her. "That means 'shut up.' "

"I will give you '*skasmos*.' See if I will let you keep those romance novels now, you old goat."

He shrugs. "Maybe they have vampire romances on *eBay*. I will look next time. *Taverna* or your room?" he asks Lucy.

"Our room—please."

"Okay. I will take her there. Go to the *taverna* and bring some brandy."

They part ways at the Y that leads to the *taverna* one way, their small hotel the other. As usual, the doors are open. There's an empty beer bottle sitting on the bar, beneath it several euro. Enough to cover the beer and the tip, even though tipping isn't really a thing here like it is back home.

They're good people around here. Honest. She can't think of too many places where the bartender could leave and come back to an empty bottle and money. Most places they'd strip the bar clean.

At *Shenanigans* she'd be lucky to find a shattered glass, left behind after the looting was done.

No brandy snifters, so she grabs a regular glass. The closest thing to brandy she can find behind the bar is *Metaxa*, and that's not one hundred-percent brandy.

Too bad. It'll have to do.

Greek words flood into the *taverna*.

It's the monastery's lone priest, Father Yiannis, ready to deliver another sermon to his drink. No Stelios around, so she snatches a cold *restina* out of the fridge, dumps it in front of him.

"To your health," he says, lifting the bottle.

She grabs the *Metaxa* bottle, the glass, and bolts along the path, taking the other leg of the Y.

"Here she is," Stelios booms. He's got Grandma lying on the bed, propped up with enough pillows to open her own *Bed, Bath, and Beyond*. He takes the bottle from Lucy, pours a generous inch, shoves it into Grandma's hands. "Drink!"

"I hate brandy."

"It is a good thing then that *Metaxa* is not just brandy."

Grandma sniffs the glass. "It smells like brandy to me."

"This woman," he says to Lucy, shaking his hands at the ceiling. "She was put here on Earth to make me bananas."

Lucy stifles a grin.

"Did you learn that expression in one of your romances?" Grandma asks.

"Of course—where else?"

"Hmm." She eyes him over the rim of the glass, but she sips the liquor, doesn't she? Stelios must be some kind of Greek sorcerer if he can get her grandmother to do something she doesn't want to do.

Lucy needs to package some of that to take home with them.

"Okay, now tell me what happened. I came to get you, I give you my wonderful *Metaxa*—"

"Vile *Metaxa*," Grandma says, making a face.

He looks at Lucy. "Only your grandmother calls it vile. To everyone else it is the liquor of the gods."

"I don't know what happened," Lucy says. "One minute we were at Akili's house, about to meet his father, then she ran away."

"Who is telling this story?" Grandma asks.

"It is a good thing Lucy is telling me, because I did not hear you volunteering, even after I gave you my *Metaxa*."

Grandma bursts into tears.

"What did I do?" Stelios looks at Lucy, genuinely mystified.

Lucy shakes her head. No idea. Grandma's being decidedly not Grandma.

"Oh, Lucy, my dear girl." He voice comes out thick and clogged with tears. "I know Akili's father. I have known him my whole life."

The warm August night turns cold. "How do you know him?"

"Yiorgos is my brother."

Oh.

Ooooooooooooh.

That's impossible.

No it's not—is it?

There goes her happiness, swirling around the toilet bowl.

"Could it be a mistake?" She sounds breathless, broken. "You've been gone a long time."

Grandma shakes her head. "I know my own brother, even after all this time."

"But ..." The situation twists and turns in her head. Every

time she reaches for something solid, it liquifies. "Didn't you know when you saw Akili?"

"He must look like his mother. There's nothing of my brother in him that I can see. I could not believe it when I saw him—it was the last thing in the world I expected. I thought maybe I had died and gone to hell—Westboro Baptist hell, where there is no mistaking the fire and the brimstone and those crazy people who protest soldiers' funerals and hate everybody."

Lucy drops onto the cool marble floor cross-legged, tries to put the puzzle together. This makes Akili her cousin—her first cousin.

There's no loophole here. They're blood. As close as blood gets without being siblings. That kiss was Jerry Springer material.

"Oh, Lucy, I am so sorry."

She looks up at Grandma in disbelief. "What for? It's not like you knew."

"But I encouraged you to enjoy his company. I pushed you together. If only I had minded my own business."

If only, if only, if only.

So many "if onlys" they're orbiting her head like satellites. If only Mom and Dad hadn't been killed. If only Lana had sought a second opinion sooner. If only that stupid doctor had paid attention in medical school. If only she hadn't flipped out and gone banging on Kellerman's door, cradling a dead cat, rock in her back pocket. If only she had left Lana's diaries alone.

"I need to think," she mumbles. "I'll be back."

"Lucy—" Grandma starts.

She closes the door carefully behind her, setting out to God knows where. She takes the road less traveled, the one leading away from the *taverna* and the beach, toward the Monastery of the Virgin Mary.

Akili can't be her cousin. He can't.

Don't people have some hardwired defense against lusting after their own family members? Don't they know on some deep, instinctual level that they're paddling in the same gene pool?

Away from what passes as a village around here, the air changes from salt and sea to something light, faintly sweet. The path runs out. What's left is dirt regularly traversed by the handful of locals and the tourists who want to see Greece stripped to its bones. It's more like the suggestion of a path.

Who cares? It's going her way.

What are they doing now, Grandma and Stelios? Is he asking questions, trying to draw more of the festering story out of the wound? Or is she opening up and letting it pour, now that Lucy's gone?

She wants to hear the story; in a way, it's her story, too. Her history. And because it's part of her history, there's no way Akili can be involved in her future. At least not as anything more than a cousin.

Maybe not even that much.

Shit. She fantasized about him, for crying out loud. Maybe he fantasized about her, too. A few hours ago ... wowza! Her panties would have burst into flames at the thought, but now it feels like someone shoved a bucket of ice up her gyno zone.

Her heart is stumbling from one beat to the next.

She should be used to this—the losing.

But every new loss is as fresh as the first.

✢ 60 ✢

Fotini

"My father, he was the *baboulas*. But unlike the boogeyman, he did not have to hide under our beds. Why would he when he could sit in our kitchen any time he pleased?"

Warm in the room, yet she hitches the sheet to her chin.

Stelios says, "I do not like this man already. Still, you were a child, and children see things bigger and worse than they are."

"No. Children see things as they are. Children and animals, they see truth in a person. A monster cannot fool a small child or a dog the way he can fool a grown, experienced mind. And my father was a monster. Never a kind word out of his mouth."

"Did he beat you?"

"Sometimes. And sometimes he would burn us. There

were nights he tied my brother to a tree and made him stay until morning."

"Your mother?"

"Those were different times, Stelios—older, crueler times. A man could hit his wife and children and no one would interfere because a man's family was his property."

"I know," he says, his face like thunder. "I was here during that time, too. My father took the belt to me more than once, but ... I deserved it."

"No child deserves that."

"You never met me. I was a terrible child. Always naughty. My mother would send me to get groceries from the mainland, and I would not come home until night—without the groceries. That poor woman thought I would grow up to be a criminal. In those days we did not have time-outs and groundings. It was the belt or the wooden spoon. And if I cursed, Mama would pour pepper on my tongue."

"Our mother never did that. She never punished us at all. I don't think she could bring herself to do it, even when we were awful, because she knew, in time, my father would punish us for no reason at all."

"There is more to this story than a bad father and a beating—yes?"

"You are perceptive."

"Eh, I read a lot of books. I know when there is a secret." He leans in close, whispers, "Is there a secret baby?"

She laughs, but it's a shadow of its normal self. "You and your stories. Why do you keep trying to jump to the end? I am not done. Just listen to the story—I will not tell it twice."

"Not even to Lucy? She should be here for this."

"I meant to you. I will tell her, of course. This is her story, too. I made it her story by coming here. And it was I who encouraged her with young Akili." She buries her face in her hands. "What have I done?"

"What did you do? You got on an airplane with your granddaughter—that is all. Everything else ... Eh, it is fate, perhaps. Or a coincidence."

"Coincidence is a terrible plot device. It's bad in a book, but even worse in real life."

"You are the fun police," he says, but there's a twinkle in his eye that says he's tugging her leg.

"If you beat a dog, at first it will forgive you, but in time it will become vicious. That is what happened to my brother—Akili's father. I wonder now what kind of childhood that boy had, what kind of life his mother had. That cannot have been a happy home. Akili looks haunted—yes?"

"His best friend was killed not long ago, remember?"

"Poor boy. But I think the pain goes deeper. He has that weary resignation of someone who has been carrying a burden for many years. It has become a part of him. You cannot simply set something aside a piece of yourself. I know," she says. "I know too well."

"Tell me so I know, too. That way the problem is cut in half. When Lucy comes back, tell her and it will be cut in three."

"When I tell Lucy it will be doubled—for her. As I said, my father was the *baboulas*. I cannot recall one night where all of us went to bed without tears. My brother and I, we shared a bedroom wall with our parents. Her muffled crying was our lullaby. We could hear everything they said in that room. That man—our father—he would tell her we were all cursed, and he was cursed, too, because he was trapped with us.

"I was too young to understand it for a long time, but he refused to have sex with her any normal way because he did not want another chain preventing him from succeeding in life. When I was old enough to menstruate, he refused to give my mother money to buy sanitary napkins for me. He said I was destined to be a whore, so why not bleed like one?"

Stelios's face is turning red. It's a good thing her father is not still alive, or she thinks this man would snap his neck on her behalf.

"When I was sixteen I met Iason. He lived in Drakia and caught the bus down to the school in Agria. You remember how it was, so many of Pelion's villages did not have schools past grade school. If you wanted to go middle or high school, you had to bus to Agria or Volos. He was about to graduate high school and I had already dropped out of school to help support the family. My father like to pretend he was about to die any day—always this hurt, that hurt, he was dying, yet we all expected him to work, he said, when we should be taking care of him. Mama took in laundry to make money, my brother went to work on a fishing boat, and I went to work at *Kefalas Olives*—this was in the old days before they had machines to do everything. Despite always being at work, I met Iason. His father was one of the company's suppliers. Big olive groves up on Pelion. He came to deliver a check, pick up a check, I don't remember which. It doesn't matter. What is important is that we met, and we fell in love and then we ran away and were married."

"You eloped?"

"Of course. How else could we marry? His family did not approve of my family, and my father did not approve of Iason or his family. My family did not have money or a good reputation, thanks to my father. He was known in the area as having a temper, of being an unreasonable man. Because of that, he stained us all. But Iason did not care. We fled to Thessaloniki. And when we came back a week later we were married. His parents were not happy, but they accepted me. What choice did they have?

"Iason wanted me to come and live with his family until we could afford a place of our own, but I did not want to leave my mother. My father's daily storm tripled in force. He became a hurricane. She was always bruised after that, eyes constantly cast on the ground, and I was afraid he would kill her. I think maybe she was hoping he would. At least that would mean the end of his fists. He was furious with me for—as he put it—marrying above my station in life. People with money were suspect in his eyes. Always they were criminals, because my father's mind was limited and he could not conceive of an honest way to make money. My brother, at this point, was also becoming like our father. What other role model did he have? It was from our father that he learned to be a man. So I stayed at the house close to Mama while we made a plan to leave forever—Mama, Iason, and me, to America. We were to leave, but my father came home with my brother before we could go. Mama decided she could not go, so Iason and I turned to leave. But my brother ... he ... he and my father attacked my husband. They beat him to death and then they took him ... I don't know where. He was found a day or two later, and the story was that he had been attacked and killed by the Romani."

"My God."

"You speak of God, but he was not there that night," she spits. "I discovered I was carrying my daughter one week after they found Iason's body. I knew then I could not stay; my father and brother, they would kill me and my unborn child. I could not let that happen. So I left, without even saying goodbye to my mother. She would not have betrayed me intentionally, but *he* would have beaten it out of her. A silent exit was best for both of us. And that—" She looks up at Stelios, her face wet, eyes gritty. "—is a good story for a soap opera, but not so good for a romance novel. Although I suppose there was a secret baby."

"What happened to your mother?"

"My friend Irini in Platanidia wrote to me and said my mother died not too long after I left. She hanged herself from the wood stove's exhaust pipe. Maybe he put her up there, but I don't think so. A man like that needs somebody to subjugate; he would not have killed her except in a fit of rage. I believe it was suicide. Death was her America, her freedom."

"She could have gone with you."

"Some people do not have the fighting spirit. They let life happen. Then they let it leave."

Poor man, his eyes are wet. She's not even sure he realizes he's crying with her. She pulls a tissue from the box beside the bed, dabs his cheeks.

"You have a good heart," she tells him. "Your wife was a fool."

"We are all fools. But women are always more foolish than men."

Ah, there is the twinkle in his eye she has come to know and rely on. What will she do without him? He is becoming part of her, twisting his branches in hers. What a mess they will both be when it is time to take the final boat to Volos.

"That's because men make us foolish."

"Can you think of a better reason for silliness?"

"No," she admits. "I cannot."

❧ 61 ☙

Lucy

THERE WAS NO ORGASM, BUT WHAT SHE FEELS IS A LITTLE death.

Make that a lot of death.

Which is sort of messed up for a guy she's only known a few days.

But maybe it's not him. Maybe it's a culmination of all the loved ones she's lost. Akili is another link in her doom chain. The shiniest and freshest.

What now?

Lights in the tiny harbor wink and glimmer. She's standing on a rise, somewhere between the sea and sky, watching the water while the stars watch her watching.

(Very *Star Trek: The Next Generation*.)

(Very Juvenal—the old, dead, Roman poet.)

Are they up there, she wonders, Mom, Dad and Lana?

If not, where are they?

"Where are you, Lana? I need you here."

Suddenly she can't stand the idea that people die and that's it. Something can't become nothing—even physics says so.

And potential love, where does that goes when it dies?

If you're lucky you're left with a handful of mementos to remind you that something could have been, something that's no longer possible.

She kicks a rock, waits for the satisfying thud before deciding what to do.

Listen to Grandma's story first. Then she's packing up, going home. Going back to where there are fewer stars, but at least the sky is familiar in its darkness.

Grandma can stay out the vacation. Stelios is sweet on her, and she's just as sweet on him—Lucy can tell. But what's going to become of them when it's goodbye time?

She leaves the hill, its view of the harbor, and those snooping stars. Somewhere near sea level there's a story being told, and she needs to hear it.

———

STELIOS VANISHES, BUT NOT WITHOUT MAKING A thoughtful promise first.

"I will make some food, yes? Souvlaki, I think. It is a souvlaki kind of night. When you are finished talking, come to the *taverna* and eat. Or I can bring it here ...?

"We'll come to you," Grandma says. "Will you be joining us for dinner?"

"Of course," he says, "I have to eat. Just do not talk too much while we are eating, otherwise how can I read?"

"You read while you eat, too?" Lucy looks at her grand-mother, eyebrows raised. Peas in a pod, those two.

"All the smartest people read while they eat," Stelios says.

"What else is there to do? It is dinner and entertainment. Good for digestion."

✣ 62 ✣

Fotini

FOR THE SECOND TIME TONIGHT SHE TELLS THE STORY. HER granddaughter doesn't need to know her great-grandfather was a monster whose sole achievement in life was creating a second monster in his image. In a way, he was Frankenstein, his scalpel and stitches made of cruelty and beatings. But she tells Lucy anyway.

Let there be no more secrets between them.

❧ 63 ☙

Lucy

"How did you meet him, Grandma?"

She sighs. "It was very romantic, very Hollywood or Disney. I did not tell Stelios all this because I think he has an attachment to me."

"Wow, you think so?"

"Sarcasm, Lucy my love?"

"I learned from the best," she says, grinning.

"That I cannot deny. Stelios is a good man. In another life and place, I would let myself love him."

"Yeah, I don't think that's how love works."

Says the woman who has never really been in love. There have been guys—of course—relationships, but all the deaths in her family had a way of unpicking the fragile stitching of those relationships before they'd climbed the rung from *like* to *love*.

"Do you want to talk about Stelios or your grandfather?"

"Granddad first. Then Stelios."

❧ 64 ❧

Fotini

THE WAY LUCY'S SITTING ON THE END OF THE BED, LEGS folded, elbows poking into her knees, chin resting in her hands, she is a girl again. This is a kind of Christmas to her, where the gifts are words and stories, not toys.

She can't help being swept up in her granddaughter's enthusiasm. That is the nature of excitement—it's not content to be alone.

"Oh, Lucy, your grandfather was so handsome. A beautiful young man. When I saw him the first time, I was breathless. He had light hair—that is where you get it from—and eyes the color of dark honey. And he was tall. The top of my head only came to his shoulder. I dropped the box of empty olive containers I was carrying, and he hurried over to help me. I couldn't say anything. I scurried away like a little mouse—can you imagine?"

Of course she did. Iason was handsome and clean. Meanwhile she was a sort of Greek Cinderella, who reeked of olive brine and received her beatings from a father instead of a wicked stepmother and stepsisters. Her brother was wicked, but he never laid a hand on her. That tongue of his, though ... By that stage it had already spent years grinding its edge against their father's rough stone.

She unspools the whole beautiful story, and Lucy listens, entranced, until she reaches the part where the happy ending became an impossible dream.

Lucy looks like she wants to rip off someone's head. Maybe stuff it up his ass when she's done. Could be she would help her granddaughter with that one. Be her assistant and her alibi.

"My great-grandfather is dead?"

"I assume so."

"But your brother is still alive."

"Apparently."

"I want to wring his neck for hurting you, for killing Granddad."

"Lucy ..."

"I know. Wanting isn't doing—I'm not that rash." Moments tick by while Lucy massages her temples with her fingers. Then she looks up, a new light shining in her eyes. "What about Granddad's family, are they still around?"

"I think they must be. Where else would they go? They had significant property on Pelion—olives and other fruit."

"Would they want to meet me, do you think?"

Instant dizziness. Bees in her ears. This she didn't anticipate.

Foolish old woman, what was she thinking? Lucy, who has lost nearly everyone, is naturally going to want to meet a clutch of new relatives.

"I want to say yes, but I don't know. They believed I was responsible for Iason's death—and maybe now they are dead, too. It has been a long time, and I am not as young as I used to be. They would be much, much older if they were still alive."

"But there could be others. Cousins, aunts and uncles."

"Yes. There could be."

Lucy gives her a look that rattles her soul. The girl is going fishing, she can tell.

"Lucy, no."

"I get it, Grandma. I really do. But what about me? You're all I have. What if something happens to you? I don't want to be alone."

LUCY'S SCOFFING DOWN HER *SOUVLAKI* BEACHSIDE, nothing for company but pebbles and the night. Not her and Stelios; they're on the porch eating, while Father Yiannis hunches over the bar with a drink.

"What is she doing?"

"Planning," Fotini says.

"Planning what? A war? Because it looks like she is planning a war."

"Eat your *souvlaki*, you old goat."

"It is like we are already married."

For a long time, she believed that just because Iason was dead did not mean she was single, free. She still believes that—most of the time. Stelios is shaking those stubborn roots buried in her rock.

"Ha! Women do not marry old goats. Lucy is planning to find the rest of her family. Her grandfather's family."

He bites into the souvlaki, wipes his mustache with a napkin. Swallows. "Oh?"

"What do you think, old man?"

"It is her family."

"I know."

"Do you?"

It is a good question. But her answer is wrapped in painful memories and bitter string. It is anything but untainted.

❧ 65 ❧

Akili

COUSINS.

Drumming in his head, drilling in his heart: *Cousins*.

Akili's starting to get the feeling he's on God's shit list. He's on track to becoming a contemporary Iob—

IF YOU'VE EVER FLIPPED THROUGH A BIBLE YOU KNOW about Job. Good guy his whole life, then God whisked away His protection to prove His point.

See, God and Satan were having debate about good ol' Job. Presumably this meeting took place over coffee, somewhere between Heaven and Hell. Probably in a Starbucks. Satan's theory was that Job maintained his goodliness to keep God's protective arm around him. God said, "Hahahaha—no. Watch."

He snatched His arm away, leaving Satan to steal Job's wealth, kill his children, and ruin his health.

Job, God-loving man or idiot (depending on whether you're pro or anti religion), cast his vote for Team God, cursing the day he was born instead of the guy in the sky.

In return God restored His protection, Job's wealth, his health, flipped Satan the bird and said, "I told you so."

Job's kids?

Yeah about that ... God's not big on resurrecting other's people's kids—just his own. Perks of the job.

—EXCEPT HE'S AT PEACE WITH BLAMING HIMSELF FOR THIS mess. Should have put the old man in a home years ago. Should have warned Stavros to stay away from the Romani.

Should have admired Lucy from a safe distance.

"Can't unpick the past, my friend."

Stavros—again.

He's ahead of Akili, walking backwards on dry land again, shaking his head. Got a look on his face that says he's sorry about the premature death thing.

"That does not stop me wanting to try. So what if it makes me a fool."

"You are not a fool, friend. You are human."

He stops, shakes his head, hopes it'll chase away the ghost of friendships past. Stavros isn't taking the hint, though, is he?

"Drina's coming to see you today. She changed her mind."

"Good."

"You mean that or are you saying it because I'm dead?"

"Both."

"Don't blame her," Stavros says. "It's not her fault."

"Whose then?"

Stavros's shrug is swallowed by a car parked on the street.

"Are you talking to yourself, Akili?"

The question springs from a different source: *Kyria* Dora. She's rushing at him from across the street, like a bowling ball in a black dress. He's the pin in this scenario.

"A ghost, *Kyria* Dora."

He figures she'll mistake it for a joke, but her face turns serious.

"I understand. I talk to my dead husband all the time, but he lives in a can of olives and refuses to come out. It would be nice if we could take a walk together, but what can you do? He is more stubborn dead than he was alive, except now I cannot punish him by withholding the sex."

Akili blinks. He's in *Kyria* Dora territory?

Can't be a good sign.

"Come," she says. "Let us walk together." She thrusts a bag into his hands; it's filled with crochet and magazines. "I will even let you carry my bag for me. Tell me," she says, when they're moving again, towards the waterfront road, "how is your friend Lucy?"

Cousin, cousin ...

Cousin.

❦ 66 ❧

Fotini

O<small>H, LOOK: ANOTHER BEAUTIFUL DAY ON</small> T<small>RIKERI.</small> H<small>OW</small> common.

How magnificent.

Too bad she's fretting into this steaming cup of coffee, trying to see the future in a pool of joe. Unlike Greek coffee, American coffee's fortune-telling powers are limited, but much more accurate. For instance, she already knows she'll need to pee—a lot.

She and Lucy, they're on their room's small balcony, enjoying the view.

Okay, no they're not. They're on the balcony, yes. But the view? Forget about it. Both of them are more interested in the way the coffee refuses to remain stagnant in a cup. It shifts and shudders, vulnerable to the vagaries of the moon, just like the tides.

(Not really, but it is a good metaphor—no? Okay, no.)

And also because Lucy is jiggling her leg under the table.

"Lucy, I hate to tell a grown woman to sit still, but sit still or I will cut off your leg and throw it into the sea."

That leg of hers keeps on dancing in its seat.

"Lucy!"

"Huh?"

"Your leg."

The leg stops. "Oh."

"Where were you, my love?"

"You know. Around."

Yes, she can guess where her mind is. In Akili's pants and up that stupid mountain, hunting down the other branches on her family tree.

Maybe not in Akili's pants. Lucy turns pale green when anyone mentions his name now. It's for the best; a vacation baby or disease is a hundred time worse if it originates with a cousin.

Iason's family though, they are definitely in her granddaughter's thoughts.

"No," Fotini says. "It is a terrible idea."

"Grandma?"

"What?"

"Get out of my head."

"I'm not in your head. But your face, it is easier to read than a billboard." She looks into the cup for help. No help; just coffee. Which is fine if the help she needs is help waking up—not so fine when she could use some wisdom. "Lucy, your grandfather's family, they blamed me for his murder. I am sure they would love you—who wouldn't?—but ... This is why I did not want to come back to Greece. Too many ghosts. There is nothing here for me but pain."

"It's okay, Grandma. I won't go."

"Really?"

"I promise. Maybe I'll just send them a letter or something."

"A letter is good. Less of a shock."

You selfish old woman, let the girl go.

These days when her conscience speaks, it is with Stelios's voice.

❧ 67 ❧

Lucy

LUCY'S GOT WHEELS. RENTED WHEELS, BUT STILL WHEELS.
Wheels with a drop-top. Why not? A convertible was the way
to go when she was out with Akili.

"A convertible, Lucy? A convertible?"

Lucy shrugs at the shiny, yellow car. "Why not?"

"Bugs. Birds. Pollution."

They're cruising along Agria's rim, headed for Pelion.

Not to hunt down long lost family—Lucy promised, damn
it—but she really wants to see Makrinitsa. Grandma—and
the travel guide—say it's really something.

"Lucy!"

The big booming voice belongs to *Kyria* Dora, the woman
who—*wink wink*—read her cup. She's at her beachside table,
sipping *frappe* under the blue umbrella, free hand gripping a
crochet hook. She shoves aside the coffee and the hook to
wave at Lucy.

Grandma lowers her sunglasses "Who is that?"

"Some woman I met with Akili the other day. She reads coffee cups. Have you ever had your cup read?"

"Yes. I worked with a woman who liked to read our cups when I was working at *Kefalas Olives*. But it was nonsense."

"*Kyria* Dora is nonsense, too." Obviously. Didn't see two cousins sitting in front of her, did she? "But she's entertaining. I'll introduce you." She zips into an empty spot outside the *Very Super Market*. "Come on."

"Lucy ..."

Lucy flashes all her teeth in a combination grimace-grin. Very sharky. "That's my name, don't wear it out."

Grandma rolls her eyes for dramatic, humorous effect. "Okay, let's go."

She grabs Grandma's hand, propels them both across the street between bursts of traffic.

"Lucy, my love!" *Kyria* Dora crows like they're old friends. "Is this your grandmother? It must be—you have her nose." The big woman in black delivers a kiss on each of her cheeks, then Grandma's. "I am Dora Makri. And you are *Kyria* Fotini, yes?"

Grandma is the epitome of grace. "I am. It is good to meet you."

"It is very good to meet you, too. Lucy did not tell me too much about her family, but then it looked like Akili wanted to snatch her away and keep her for himself."

Akili. Does she have to say his name? Here she is trying to scrub him out of her brain. Last thing she needs is a reminder, even though Agria itself is one big, fat reminder. And Volos. And Pelion. And—oh hell, Greece is Akili, Akili is Greece.

Can she go home now? Please?

No. Apparently not. Because the conversation is moving

on without her and Grandma is helping herself to one of *Kyria* Dora's chairs.

"What are you doing?" she asks, heart bopping around her chest in mild panic.

"Dora is going to read my cup."

"But—"

Grandma said it was nonsense, didn't she? So what's she—

Itsy Bitsy Spider climbs up her neck. Not really, but that's how it feels. Long, black legs hiking up her bone rungs. So what does she do? Turn around to hunt for the source, that's what.

"Look!" the Greek woman says with an overabundance of enthusiasm. "There's is your Akili!"

Huh. So it is. Would you look at that? Very nonchalant, Lucy. Very smooth. So why is her heart tossing pots and pans in her chest now? He looks like a popsicle on a blistering hot day, good enough to lick in his cargo shorts and T-shirt.

The incest stick beats her over the head.

Cousin, Lucy. COUSIN.

Focus on something else. Say, the girl he's talking to. She's lovely. Petite. Long, dark hair—almost waist-length. Fine, beautifully carved features. She's not smiling, but then neither is he. Whatever they're talking about they're both consumed with it.

Jealousy punches her in the stomach. She and Akili never had that. Even if they weren't cousins—which they are—there was no way they'd ever be able to share an intimate conversation without doodling and charades. Even if she took Greek classes, it would be months—maybe years—before she could ask him for more than a glass of water.

Better for him to be with some girl—woman, whatever—he can have a real conversation with. Which is exactly what he's doing, so good for him.

It's so high school, but she can't help thinking he moved on quickly.

Okay, so she could be a friend, an employee, a relative (like, uh, her), but the immature numbskull living inside her head has already painted the girl as competition.

Which she's not.

Because they're cousins.

Good thing he hasn't spotted them yet, otherwise he might come over. What then?

Her brain does a little freakout dance.

"My Virgin Mary" *Kyria* Dora says. "Look who Akili is with." Then she laughs. "Of course, how could you know? I forget that everybody is not a part of Agria and its stories. That *tsigana* girl is Drina—"

"Gypsy or Romani," Grandma translates for Lucy's benefit.

"Yes." *Kyria* Dora nods so hard her body makes tsumani-grade waves under her dress. "A *tsigana*. Akili's best friend was murdered. Drina—that girl—was his secret wife. Very big scandal. His friend was engaged to a lovely Greek girl, but he did not come to the church when they were to be married because he was busy being dead. For a while, everybody thought it was his intended who killed him. But it was Drina's mother!"

"Why did she kill him?" Lucy asks.

Kyria Dora shrugs. "Because he had a certain reputation with women. Very good accountant, but with women he was a very generous dog. Stavros liked to share his salami with all the women."

Grandma's lips twitch.

"Very interesting," the round Greek woman continues. "I wonder what she is doing with Akili? I will find out." She raises her hand, shakes it in the air like she's summoning a storm.

Lucy lurches across the table to stop her. "No!"

Too late.

"Akili!"

He glances over, waves. *Kyria* Dora rattles off a chain of Greek words. He tosses out a few of his own.

Grandma's gone pale. "I'm so sorry, Lucy. He says he is coming over, as soon as he's done talking to that girl."

Lucy slides down in the chair, a move that doesn't go unnoticed by the Greek woman. Grandma warned her about people here, and their inability to turn a blind eye toward anything except their own actions.

"What is wrong, Lucy my love? Be happy! That girl is no competition for Akili's affections. Probably they are talking about Stavros. What else could it be?"

Lucy shoots her grandmother a pleading look, one that says she's about to chew her own foot off and run. Well, hobble. Hobbling is better than nothing when you're trying to escape.

Kyria Dora clutches her chest. "My Virgin Mary, did you and Akili have a fight? What is wrong?"

"It's nothing," Lucy says.

"Of course it is something, otherwise you would not be white like the ghost."

"He's Lucy's cousin," Grandma says.

Lucy really, really wishes she hadn't. She wanted to clutch the secret in her fist just a little longer. Delay reality.

The Greek woman almost leaps out of her chair. "You are that Fotini! Fotini Doukaki! I remember you!" Frantic crossing. Then she shakes her hands at Grandma and the sky. "My God! Everybody thought you were dead!

"Dead?" Grandma says. Her forehead crumples with confusion. "I was never dead. I ran away."

"*Po-po.* Everybody in town believed the *tsigani* killed you like your husband, and buried you who knows where! That is what your father told people."

Not for the first time that week, Grandma bursts into tears.

❧ 68 ❧

Fotini

DEAD?

What made them think—

The answers come pushing through the door. They've been waiting for years to have their say, and now they refuse to shut up.

She fled on the heels of one death—what were they supposed to think? They assumed that she, too, was dead. And so they believed it when her father threw his bullshit in their faces.

Dora shovels information into some of the blanks. "No one saw your mother after you disappeared. She took to the house and refused to step outside, even to get groceries. Then one day she was dead, too. The poor woman died of heartbreak, they say. But they say a lot of things."

Wouldn't Irini have told them she was safe in America?

No. Her family had already moved to Platanidia before

she ran away. In those days, another village was as distant in the minds of people as another country.

"I was not dead," she repeats. But there were times she wanted to be—before and after she left.

And then Sarah was born and the sun began to shine.

Now here she sits on that same old shore, and what's left of her past is just a few blocks away, while Lucy looks to her for answers.

"I think it is time to go home," she says.

Lucy leaps up. "To Trikeri? Come on, I'll drive us back to Alogoporos."

"No. Home."

🏵 69 🏵

Lucy

GRANDMA SITS ON THE BEACH, JUST ANOTHER UNFINISHED pebble. If she stays there long enough, eventually all her edges will erode.

Lucy doesn't want her edges to erode. Pebbles are dull, smooth things. A rock? Now a rock has character. It can be any shape it pleases.

"I'm worried about her."

Stelios raises his head from his book. He won't admit it, but she can tell he's digging the vampires.

"Of course you are. But your grandmother is tough, like Greece. Greece has a way of making its women strong."

"Not my great-grandmother. She killed herself—did Grandma tell you?"

He nods. "Your great-mother killed herself, yes. But that was the final moment of her life. Up until then, she ..." He goes in search of the right word. "... endured. Your grandmother tells me her life was very difficult, but she held fast, the way a rock holds fast."

"I think she was too weak to leave."

"Or too strong."

That's not how it works. "You can't have it both ways. Either Grandma was too strong to stay or her mother was too strong to leave. It's a contradiction."

"In the same person—yes. In two different people—no."

She grips the edge of the bar, bangs her head on its high sheen. "You're maddening."

"That is what your grandmother says." Beneath the mustache he's smiling.

"Did she tell you I want to meet my family—my grandfather's side?"

He nods. "She did."

"What do you think?"

"Does it matter?"

"No. But I want to know."

Bookmark wedged in place, he pushes the book aside. He speaks to her, but his focus is on the woman on the shore. "You should know where you came from, but I like your grandmother, and I see that being in Greece is difficult for her. When you care for somebody it is not easy to watch them suffer."

She doesn't want Grandma to suffer. Still, this might be the only chance she gets to know where she came from.

"I could go without her," she says slowly.

Two palms up: "You could."

"Do you think she'd feel betrayed?"

"Who can say? You know her better than me."

She nods at the sea and Grandma's stalwart back. "I'm going tomorrow morning. Early. Can you take me to the mainland—please?"

"Of course I will take you."

"Ten bucks says I can get them to adore me. And if they adore me, maybe Grandma will want to see them, too."

There's a lot of humor and a healthy slug of doubt in the shake of his head. "Lucy, you are a very ambitious girl."

"Not really. If I was I'd be doing something amazing with my life." Lucy says it matter-of-factly—which she is. Who knows her weaknesses better? Nobody, that's who. The ambition boat sailed by, and she stood on the shore and waved while everyone else waded out to sea. Then she swapped spit with her cousin.

Trump that, high school reunion!

"Maybe you already are."

Optimistic, isn't he? It's part of the reason she likes him so much.

"Nope. I'd know if it I was. That's how you know you're doing something amazing: you're amazed."

Stelios laughs—but in a I'm-a-cool-dude way. "If you say it is so, then I believe you. But do not be surprised if you wake up one morning and discover you are amazed."

"I haven't been yet."

GRANDMA MOVES. IT'S ONLY HER MOUTH, BUT IT'S A START. "Did you change our flights?"

"Nope."

"Lucy ..."

"I'm going to, I promise. I just want a few more days."

"What for, my love? There is nothing for us here."

"Uh ..." *Think fast, Lucy. Come on.* "There's Stelios."

"Stelios." Grandma snorts.

"This island. You could stay here for the rest of the trip. No mainland. Just quiet beaches." She flicks a wink. "And

Stelios. Lana would be pissed if one of us didn't get a vacation romance."

"Are you trying to be a matchmaker?"

"Ha. No. Anyone with two eyes can see you guys don't need one."

"And what about you, Lucy?"

"I don't need one either."

❦ 70 ❦

Lucy

THE DOOR BARELY COMPLAINS AS SHE CLICKS IT BACK INTO its frame.

Outside, the light is thin, but it has potential. She stays barefoot until she's at the *taverna*, then she slips into her sandals.

"Are you sure?"

"Nope. Which definitely means I should do it."

Stelios laughs. "You are a very funny girl."

"I know. It's such a burden."

He gives her a look. Sarcasm doesn't always cross the language barrier.

"Never mind. To the mainland, my good man!"

LUCY DRIVES. ALONE. NO ONE IN THE PASSENGER SEAT TO

tell her she's headed the wrong way. Which is good and bad. What if she gets lost?

Hey, it could happen.

Then she'd be stuck in Greece forever, searching for someone who speaks English and knows geography.

But either there's some kind of DNA memory at work, or she unconsciously memorized the way, because it's not long before she's at the foot of Mount Pelion, wondering if she's got the moxie to scale its leg.

What the hell are you looking for, Lucy?

Good question.

Short answer: missing pieces.

Long answer: the missing pieces of a puzzle, with Lucy's picture on the box. On some level, she's always been three-quarters of a person, and lately she's had one foot on dry land and the other in Lana's grave.

The road up to Drakia through Agria is smooth, less twisty than the road she and Akili traveled. The way is barren at first, but before long trees creep closer to the narrowing capillary. They're a tangle of olive, and oak, and other botanical specimens she doesn't recognize.

It's times like these Greece could be another planet. It's similar to home in some ways, but never the same.

Would Lana see it through the same otherworldly lens?

Focus, Lucy. The road.

Right, the road. It's smooth, but slow going. Lots of live-stock crossing the road to get to the other side. Not a chicken in sight, though; maybe they already crossed, found whatever it was they were looking for.

When civilization reveals itself, it's in one sudden chunk. First nothing, then the cosmic magician whips away his cloak of trees to expose a village nesting on the rock. The sidewalks are cobbled, the street a stretch of faded blacktop that feels out of place, as though someone has slapped modern touches on an old masterpiece. The shops and houses are a combination of brick and stacked stones. Atop almost every building is a roof of rough tiles, reminiscent of a shell collage. In the air is a hint of lanolin from a shepherd's flock.

Now that she's here, she feels faintly ridiculous. Who marches into town—a total stranger—asking for directions to a place she doesn't know, to meet people who have no idea she exists?

The Lucys of the world, that's who.

May as well work with what she's got.

She parks next to a ...

Actually, no idea what it is. A small stone building without windows or doors—that she can see. A tall wall? Whatever. She's parking here. There's no sign that says she can't.

Therefore, she can. Logical, right?

She marches over to the nearest shop, hands pushed deep in the pockets of her cargo shorts. The sign is Greek but the sparkling window is written in the language of bread—as in loaves stacked in warm, haphazard piles.

Deep breath, Lucy.

In she goes.

The bakery isn't much bigger than a phone booth. (Not the TARDIS—a real phone booth.) Okay, so that's an exaggeration, but not much. Sitting atop a wide table is a short stack of paper, the unbleached kind favored by delis. There's a fiery mouth cut into the brick wall. The baker is prodding around inside with a long stick. When he pulls it out, there's a metal hook on its hot end.

Besides that and the bread in the window, the store is empty. It has one purpose: cook bread, sell bread.

She waits, hands clasped in front of her, until the baker notices she's alive. When he does, he just stares at her, unblinking.

"*Yia sou.*" She dishes the greeting with a lame wave, just in case her Greek is incomprehensible. "I'm looking for ..." She looks at the paper in her hand, reads her great-grandparents' names. "... the Manatos family. My great-grandparents were—or are—Orestis and Katerina Manatos."

Does he say anything?

Negative. Not a word, a grunt, or a twitch.

What he does do is stomp past her to the door and thrust his head out into the street. He hollers something she's got no hope of understanding, then he returns to his station on the cool side of the oven.

She's starting to think all is lost when she hears footsteps on the street.

"Hello?"

English. Thank the patron saint of tourists who suck at speaking Greek.

It's funny, she thinks. At home, a person's own language is ubiquitous. It's part of the scenery and goes unnoticed most of the time. But when they're in a foreign country, even a single word in their own language stands out from the background like a bright thread. This is her bright thread, and she wants to grab and pull until a whole conversation unravels.

"Hi!" She bounds over to the door just in time to collide with a woman around her own age. She's more rounded than Lucy, with a warm beaming face, despite the black she's wearing from top to toe. They're fashionable clothes, on the conservative edge of trendy. There's a vague familiarity about her, as though they've passed each other on a quiet street or sat side by side on a crowded bus.

"You are looking for the Manatos family?"

"I am!" She sounds like an overexcited puppy, doesn't she? "I'm Lucy. I'm American."

The other woman's gaze is wary but not unfriendly. "It is good to meet you, Lucy. I am Katerina. How do you know the family?"

ALEX A. KING

Oh God, she probably thinks Lucy's a bill collector or something.

"My grandmother used to know them." Katerina starts to smile. "She was, uh, married to Iason Manatos, before he ... before he ..."

Katerina's smile dies.

Stupid, Lucy. Stupid. "I'm sorry," Lucy says. "I shouldn't even be here. My grandmother will hate me when she finds out I've come. But, I had to try to see them."

The baker is watching them, arms folded, legs akimbo. Very bouncer-like. She really doesn't want to get bounced out of town.

If that's even a thing.

Do they do tar and feathers here? Or something more Greek, like honey and stinging nettles?

"It's really nice to meet you, Katerina, but I should go. In fact ..." She squeezes past the woman in black. "...I'm going right now. Have a great day! Like you could have anything else —it's so beautiful up here." There goes her mouth, doing its own thing. She swings back around again, looks at Katerina's black ensemble. "I'm, uh, sorry for your loss. I don't know who you lost, but I'm sorry."

"It was a year ago, but it was my grandfather," Katerina says, her words slow and careful. "And I think maybe your great-grandfather."

262

❧ 71 ❧

Lucy

LUCY KNOWS MOURNING; THEY'RE OLD ACQUAINTANCES, the kind who bump into each other randomly at the parties of mutual friends. She's mourned her father, mother, sister, and now she's in a distant sort of mourning for the great-grandfather she never knew.

Someone with no clue she existed.

Isn't that pointless, mourning someone who never knew she was alive? It's like watering the lawn during a downpour.

"I'm sorry. I didn't even know him, and you did."

She's in Katerina's kitchen, watching her cousin make coffee. Her place is small but cozy. Reminds her of a Hobbit hole with its warm wood and muted throw rugs.

Her cousin. How strange. She arrived in Greece with none, and now she's has two—maybe more.

"It is a pity you did not know him, too. He was a good

man. I would have liked another cousin—a girl. Everyone in the family has boys."

"You would have had two if—" Here comes that old, familiar lump in her throat. "—I had a sister. Lana died six months ago."

"I'm sorry."

"Thanks. Me too. All the time. Losing a sister is like losing a limb."

"Can I ask you something?"

"Anything!" There she goes again, reacting like an overly friendly puppy.

"Why come to Greece now? Why did you want to meet us?"

"It wasn't my idea—at first. After my sister died ..." Tears bubble just below the surface. She chokes them back, lets them know they'll get their chance later when it's just her and her pillow. "I wasn't myself after she died, for a long time. My grandmother suggested I get away to clear my head. Greece was at the top of my sister's bucket list."

"Bucket list?"

After a brief explanation, she fills in some of the blanks, the parts without Akili and his dreadful father, or the kisses they would have shared.

Katerina sits at the table. She passes one cup to Lucy, keeps the other for herself. "Everybody in the family talks about uncle Iason—your grandfather. If they mention your grandmother, it's a whisper. I don't know the whole story. They say she was a good girl, but her family was bad—mostly her father. We are strange when it comes to blood, here in Greece."

"It's like having a serial killer in the family, now that I think about it."

Katerina's face goes blank, so Lucy explains. Then her cousin laughs. "You are funny." She gestures to the cup she set in front of Lucy. "Drink your coffee, then I will take you to meet some people."

"Who?"

"Our family."

Now she can place it, the familiarity in Katerina's face. She's seen it in her mirror and in pictures. Not just her own— but Lana's.

She knows family when she sees it.

Too bad she didn't recognize the sameness in Akili.

❧ 72 ❧

Fotini

IN HER DREAM SHE'S TRAPPED IN GREECE; AMERICA WON'T let her come home. When she wakes, she's still trapped in Greece, and America has no idea how desperately she wants to leave.

It's not easy dragging herself out of bed, but she does it. And with that accomplishment achieved, the next thing on her to-do list is coffee. Forget the cup—she wants to slurp it out of a swimming pool.

Stelios better have a pool in that *taverna* of his. Even a paddling pool will suffice. But when she gets there, there's no pool filled with coffee and no Lucy. Good thing she enjoys Stelios and his handsome face.

"Where is Lucy?"

"She went for a walk. You want coffee?"

"Make it a bucketful. American style."

He laughs, nodding. "A bucket it is."

When he comes back, it's not a bucket. But close.

"Liar."

"I bring you coffee and you call me a liar? Give me that." He reaches for the cup and she slaps him away.

"You are a liar. Lucy might be walking, yes, but not on your island."

"Who is lying?" He throws a glance over each shoulder. "I do not see any liars here."

"We have a saying in America: 'Liar, liar, pants on fire.' Your pants, they are on fire."

His chuckle is good-humored, warm. "If I burn, who will bring you coffee, eh?"

"I have two hands, I will get it myself." And she would, but she'd miss his coffee. It comes with a serving of good company. "Would you ever come to America?"

"What for?"

"For a vacation."

For me.

She almost laughs at herself. What an old fool she is. Love affairs do not happen at her age. They're for the young and other immortals.

"What for do I need a vacation? I am already in paradise. What does America have besides people and noise?"

"Books. We have bookstores filled with books."

"There are bookstores here."

My, what big ears he's got. Perfect for flicking. She's about to give the closest one a good flick, when he laughs. "Relax, Fotini. I am joking. For you, I might consider leaving Greece for a small vacation."

Her frown settles back into a smile. "I would like that."

"As would I." He reaches across the table, takes her hand in his.

"Where do you think she is?"

"Lucy?"

She nods.

"Looking for answers."

Just as she feared.

❧ 73 ❧

Akili

SHE'S A HARD WORKER, DRINA. MAYBE SHE'S TRYING TO impress him on the first day of work, but he doesn't think so. Drina isn't a woman out to impress anyone—least of all him. She balances trays effortlessly, ferrying them to their tables. She's charming to his customers, and polite to the rest of the staff.

"She's hot," Thanasi says.

Akili glares at him "No. Hands off."

"Why?" Patra asks, looking too interested in his answer. "You want her for yourself?"

Ha. Not likely. For a million reasons.

Yeah, a million reasons that begin with Lucy and end with his dead best friend. He wants to talk to Lucy—needs to. But that's impossible without a middleman. Or woman.

"No."

"Why not? She's pretty."

"Pretty?" Thanasi scoffs. "She's gorgeous."

Akili opens his mouth. Closes it.

Patra's staring at him, brows raised, waiting on him to screw up and say the wrong thing. Then she'll snap.

"Not interested. And not interested in discussing it."

He goes back to the dough, punches fist-sized dents in its pliable surface.

Better than a punching bag.

HE CAN'T STAND TO LOOK AT THE OLD MAN, SO HE DOESN'T.

"I want to see her."

"Who?"

"My sister. Fotini."

"I doubt she wants to see you."

"Bring her here."

"Forget it."

He shouldn't have brought the women here to begin with. Not going to do it again; why make good women suffer?

"I promised I would leave for good, and I will. But first I want to see her one last time."

"You promise?"

The old man nods, head stirring his smokey halo.

❧ 74 ❧

Lucy

Her great-grandparents' property is intimidating. Big house, too much land, more trees than she can count.

"It will be okay," Katerina says, opening the house's screen door. She ushers Lucy into a wide, dark hallway. In the foyer's corner is one of those Greek icon stands (no home is without one, according to her travel guide and Grandma), and the pale pink walls are heavy with paintings of old people. She follows Katerina down the hall to sunlit room at the back of the house. Looks like what they used to call a drawing room.

Now she's standing in front of a woman who is allegedly her great-grandmother. She's almost the stuff of Greek legends, with her weather-and-time-beaten face. Round and wrinkled. Reminds Lucy of one of those canteens cowboys carry around in westerns. Her clothes are black, her hair halfway to gray, and one claw is clutching a walking stick.

"So. You are my great-granddaughter." It's a rich, full voice, as though it's squeezing out of a much younger mouth.

"I ..." Wait—was that English? Because it sounded suspiciously like English. "You speak English?"

"Am I speaking to you in English?"

Trick question. "Uh, yes?"

"There you go. We are speaking in English."

"How do you speak English? You're ..." Old. Decrepit. Ancient. Pick one.

"The same way you speak it: with my mouth. Is a good trick, yes?" She doesn't wait for an answer—probably doesn't have enough time left to wait on anything. "The language of the business world is English. My parents insisted I learn English, French, and German. A person who speaks many languages, they told me, will always succeed in life."

Maybe that's one reason Lucy's going nowhere in such a hurry.

The old woman doesn't give her time to dwell on it. "What are you wearing? It reminds me of my dead husband's underwear."

"Cargo shorts."

"Cargo shorts? What cargo is it carrying? Your bottom is skinny, like a greyhound."

Lucy looks down at her shorts. Nothing wrong with them. They're fashionable enough. "They're comfortable."

"So is a dress."

"No pockets in most dresses."

"Buy a handbag."

"I have a handbag."

"Yet here you are in shorts made for a man."

"Jesus," Lucy says to Katerina. "Is she always like this?"

Katerina's lips twitch. "Today she is on her best behavior. Be thankful."

The old woman is watching her. "What do you know of your family?"

"Almost nothing. Grandma never said much until we came here."

"She kept us a secret? A family as good as ours? *Po-po* ..."

"I don't think it was you she was keeping secret. More like her own family."

The old woman scoffs. "That I believe. I would keep that father of hers a secret, too. And her brother. Sit." She pats the vacant chair beside her. It's one of the wood and lacquered straw chairs that seem to be a Greek favorite.

Katerina nods, so Lucy slides into the offered seat.

"For years, I hated Fotini," her great-grandmother says. "Not at first—at first my husband and I disapproved, but we did not hate her. She was just a girl. But after my son was murdered, I hated her. Every night before bed I cursed her name. In church, I asked the Virgin Mary to send goats to rape her and shit on her head."

Katerina buries her face in her hands. "*Yiayia!*"

"Oh, Katerina, I am an old, old woman." She taps her walking stick on the hard marble floor. "If I cannot tell the truth now, when can I tell it? After I am dead? Who will listen? You will all be too busy spending my money to listen."

"Dead people aren't known for their conversation skills," Lucy says. "I know, I've tried."

Her great-grandmother cackles. "I like you. You remind me of me."

"Really?"

"Why would that be so strange? We are blood. Where was I? Ah. Goats shitting on her head. Yes, I asked the Virgin Mary to visit all kinds of terrible fates upon your grandmother. A grieving mother, you understand, must blame someone. In my head—" She points at her loose bun with its silver threads. "—Fotini had lured my son to her marriage bed with a magical *mouni*."

Katerina cringes.

Lucy glances from woman to woman. "*Mouni*? What does that mean?"

"*Mouni, mouni, mouni*. I can say it because I am old. A *mouni* is what is between your legs if you are a woman."

Must be the Greek translation of the C word. Or the T word. It has a less clinical ring than *vagina*. Whatever. If it's good enough for her great-grandmother to say, then she can say it, too. "*Mouni*."

The oldest woman in the room slaps her lap, laughing. "*Mouni!*"

When the laughing is over (and the cringing, if you're Katerina), Lucy says, "I don't think Grandma's is magical. I'm pretty sure it's just regular."

"I believe that now, but at the time ... Witchcraft. Sorcery. My Orestis and I guessed her father had killed my boy, but what could they do? There was no proof. Just his abandoned body in a ditch. Today the police have ways of finding murderers, but not in those days it was not so easy. His son and wife were his alibis. They said he was home, eating his dinner while my son was dying. Not your grandmother, though. Fotini would not speak to the police. She would not lie to them or speak against her father. *Po-po* ... It was so long ago.

"Everybody thought she was dead, you know—your grandmother. One day she was here, then—*poof!*—gone. We believed her father had murdered her, too and buried her body where no one would ever find it. And still I hated her."

"What changed?"

"Your grandmother's father died. Did she tell you that?"

"No. I'm not sure she knows for sure."

The old woman grunts. "He died. I went to see him when

he was sick. He told me he killed my son—and he smiled as he said it. So I kicked him in the *poutsa* and told everyone he makes love to sheep. And when I heard he died not long after, your great-grandfather drove me down to Agria so I could piss on his grave. First, I had three *frappes*. After that, I forgave your grandmother and stopped asking the Virgin Mary to have her violated. But your great-grandfather? I asked for him be sexed in the mouth by Turkish demons for all eternity. I hope he is enjoying his afterlife."

Lucy dissolves in a puddle of giggles. She can't help it. Her great-grandmother has an unusual way with words. This should be a solemn occasion, seeing as they're talking about death and murder, but she can't seem to quit laughing.

"Forgive her," Katerina says, her face looking like she wants the earth to open up and say, 'Ahhhh.' "She is old, she does not know what she is saying."

Lucy's great-grandmother points a finger at her. "The older I get, the better I get. I am sharper than a needle. And wise—more wise than anyone in this family."

"Of course, *Yiayia*."

"What's *Yiayia*?"

"Grandmother," Katerina says. "But to you she is *Pro-Yiayia*—great-grandmother."

Outside, the gate squeals.

"Who has come? Katerina, go and see who it is."

Katerina vanishes from the room. There's a moment of low, excited chatter, then she returns. "Romani women," she says.

"What do they want?" the old woman asks.

"Money, of course."

"Invite them in!"

"*Yiayia*! We cannot invite them in."

She leans over to Lucy. "She thinks we cannot invite them in because they will steal."

"That's not true!" Katerina says.

"Of course it is. I will go and invite them myself."

Lucy leans over to Katerina. "Really, she's always like this?"

"The older she gets, the worse it is."

Worse? Great-Grandma seems pretty great to her. "I like her. She's funny. I know you and I know her—what about the rest of the family?"

"This weekend we are making a party. You have to come. Then you can meet everyone."

"Cool. What's the occasion?"

"No occasion. For fun. That is what we do."

"How big is the family?"

Katerina grins. "Very big."

❧ 75 ❧

Akili

HE WANTS TO SEE LUCY.

He doesn't want to see Lucy.

Which is why he's pointing the boat toward Trikeri.

"She's not on the island," Stavros says. "And by the way, thank you for hiring Drina."

"You're not real," he mouths.

Stavros pats his shoulder. "One of us is not real. But sometimes I think it is you."

Akili clears his throat, shakes his head.

Stavros is gone.

HE TRUDGES INTO THE *TAVERNA* WITH ONLY ONE QUESTION. "Is Lucy here?"

Stelios grunts. "Does it look like she is here?"

"I mean on the island."

"No, she is on the mainland."

"Doing what?"

"I do not know, but this is the second day she has gone there alone."

Easy, man. Don't get crazy. She's not yours—she never was.

"And *Kyria* Fotini?"

"She is there." He nods to the beach where—sure enough —Lucy's grandmother is hiding under a floppy sunhat, her nose in a book. "That woman reads as much as I do. We read the same books, you know."

"A perfect match."

He nods. "A perfect match. Except we are two people who belong in different worlds."

"Are you?"

"Look at her. She is America, I am Greece."

"You are too ugly for her anyway."

"Ugly! I am still as handsome as Alain Delon. I could be on the cover of a romance novel. Fabiopoulos. All I need is to grow my hair."

"I'll bring a wig next time."

"Fotini will not be able to resist me."

"Are you two ...?"

"She is a good woman. Very good company. What more is there?"

"Passion."

"Passion. Ha! When you get to my age, passion is finding a woman who enjoys the same books."

❧ 76 ❧

Fotini

THE SOUND OF HER NAME STARTLES HER. GOOD THING SHE doesn't need to pee.

"Akili! Lucy is not here."

"That's okay. I came to see you."

Birds flutter inside her chest. What can he want with her?

Her brother. Of course. He is the reason for these birds flapping and pooping inside her.

"Do you mind if I sit?"

"Of course not. Sit. Ask Stelios to find you a chair."

He nods to the ground. "This is fine. My father told me what happened."

"The whole story?"

Shrug. "Who knows? He's not known for being a reliable source."

What is he like, my brother?"

The weight settles on Akili's shoulders. That father of his

is the source of so much stress, she can tell. "He's not a good man," he says, scooping pebbles into piles. "Or even a decent man. He was ... My parents' marriage was difficult."

"He is a product of the marriage he saw every day when we were children."

"Maybe. But you're a good person. You are kind. Lucy loves you so much—I can see it when she looks at you."

"I had advantages my brother did not. I left."

"No, he'd still be rotten. Some people are born rotten and life does not change that."

"As a therapist, I would tell you to see the good in people, to believe they can change if they wish for it hard enough and work toward that goal. As woman who grew up in the same house as your father, I know you are right. Some people are doomed from the womb. Their building blocks are cobbled together with wet sand. Your father is such a person—and I could not be more sorry."

There is a question twisting his handsome face. She knows it before he speaks it.

"He wants you to come and see him. Will you?"

"No." There is no way she will jump into that fire. There is only pain inside.

"I don't blame you. He's shit. He turns everything he touches to shit. But he asked me to pass along the message, so here I am."

"I understand. You're a good man, Akili. And I wish very much that things could be different, but ..."

"They're not."

"They are not. Lucy likes you very much. Do you know how much I loved seeing her happy? It has been too long since that girl made one real smile. But here? She has changed, and it began with you. And I am grateful. But the price? It has been too expensive. For Lucy, for me, and for you, I think. The best thing we can do now is go home and forget about Greece."

Forget about Greece? Ha-ha. You cannot forget Greece—she has tried. But this is tough love she's showing Akili. Poor boy, as if he has ever known any other kind, with his father in the house.

"I need to talk to Lucy."

"About what, Akili? You are cousins, you can never be anything more."

"Fotini!"

That's Stelios, barking across the beach at her, as if he is a dog.

"What do you want, old man."

"Let the boy speak to her."

"I am not stopping him from speaking with her. I am trying to stop them from hurting each other more —saving them."

"Leave them alone."

"Mind your own business. This is my family, my blood." She casts aside the book, the bartender, the boy, and beach, trudging uphill in search of a view that doesn't face her past.

❧ 77 ❧

Akili

THE OLD MAN POUNCES—AS MUCH AS AN OLD MAN IN A wheelchair can pounce.

"Where is Fotini? Is she coming?"

"No. I asked but my aunt said no. Can't say I blame her."

"I sent you to do one thing and you fucked it up. What is wrong with you."

"What can I say, my aunt's knows what you are. She's smart to stay away."

The old bastard laughs. "Why do you call her your aunt? She is not your aunt."

"But she's your sister."

"Yes, she is that. But how can she be your aunt?" He leans closer, the whites of his eyes tarnished. His breath is sour, metallic. "Why do you think I hated you? Why do you think I let your mother give you her father's name? You were never my son."

"What?"

There's a squealing in his ears. A kind of ringing. The old man's mouth is moving but Akili can't make out his words. He stumbles, but the chair is there to catch him.

"Not your son?"

Slowly, his hearing returns.

"I married your whore mother when she was already pregnant. She did not think I knew, but I knew. But I wanted a house more—one I did not have to work for. I saw what Greece was becoming, that property would become expensive and taxes high. And so I got this palace and a screaming brat."

A whirlwind of thoughts, one big, bold word spiraling in his head: "Good."

"Good?" the bastard echoes.

"Better than good. Now I won't feel bad throwing your *kolos* out in the street."

"You are not man enough to make me go."

He gets up in his—

Not his father. So what is he? Stepfather?

—stepfather's face. Finger pointed, underlining his meaning: "Get out. Go."

"Where will I go?"

"Let the devil care where you go, because I don't."

Rolling out of the room, the old bastard shoots more barbed words into the distance between them. "You will be sorry when I am dead. I am not your father, but I am the only father who would take you. What of your real father, eh? He did not want you. He threw you and your mother both out like trash. Smart man. I would like to shake his hand and congratulate him on his escape."

"Who was my father?"

He stops, shrugs. "Who knows? Maybe there were so many men your mother never knew."

Akili's fist yearns to fly. It wants nothing more than to sail across the room, crash-landing in the old bastard's teeth. But he's a man, not a kid. A man controls his fists; they don't control him.

"Get out before I push you down the hill myself."

"After everything I have done for you," the man who is not his father mutters.

What's he done for Akili?

Nothing. Except condemn his mother to a lifetime of misery.

And, with a handful of words, set Akili free.

Lucy isn't his cousin.

There's almost no time left to make her his, but he needs to try.

❧ 78 ❧

Lucy

HERE COMES THAT MOMENT WHEN THE SEASON CHANGES
without the calendar's rigid approval. When the change
comes, there's a hint of death in the air, as if summer knows
its passing is imminent.

She's not sure if it's the same everywhere, but it's true in
America and it's true in Greece, too.

She's walking the grove with Katerina, on her third trip to
Drakia, soaking up the knowledge her cousin is sprinkling in
the air. Olives. Their cultivation. Her—their—family history.

There's peace out here. An all-encompassing calm. She
hasn't want to punch anyone in days. Not even Kellerman.

"Katerina! Lucy! Look at this!"

From her peripheral vision she sees Katerina mirroring
the upward tilt of her chin, all the way up the tree's spine to a
long, wide branch. *Pro-Yiayia* is up there, straddling the
gnarled limb, cackling.

"My Virgin Mary," Katerina says, shaking her head. "What are you doing up there?"

"Ask Lucy!"

Katerina swings around, question in her eyes.

"Living?" Lucy guesses.

"Living," her great-grandmother crows. "Life looks beautiful from this tree."

"How did you get up there?" Katerina asks.

"How does anyone get up in a tree? I climbed."

Katerina closes her eyes. "She climbed."

Lucy slips her arm through her cousin's. "If we're lucky we'll be climbing trees at her age."

"Ha!" the old woman says. "You cannot climb a tree even now!"

Lucy shields her eyes with one hand. "Is that a challenge?"

"Why would I challenge the weak?"

Well played, Great-Grandma. Well played. "Move over, old lady. I'm coming up."

It's been years since she climbed a tree, but she's sure her body remembers the moves. It's like riding a bicycle, but with a greater risk of limb breakage. Hers—not the tree's.

Katerina obviously has her doubts. "You are going to climb up?"

"Sure, come on!"

"I will stay down here. Somebody has to call the ambulance when you fall."

"Nobody's falling."

"You, maybe not. But *Yiayia* is old. What if she breaks a hip?"

Lucy looks up at her great-grandmother. "She's right, you know. As old as you are, those hips could smash to dust."

Her great-grandmother chuckles. "There are worse ways to go."

Goodbye, shoes. Hello, rough bark. It's exercise, pleasure,

and exfoliation all in one. Branch by branch, she works her way up to where her great-grandmother is perched, looking like she's ready to start collecting nuts.

Starting with Lucy, probably.

But when she settles onto to the thick limb, she sees it: the view. Thousands of trees plunging into a shallow valley (reminds her of a push-up bra), forming a loosely knit blanket of silver-green.

"I could stay up here forever," she says in wonder.

"You could," the old woman says slyly.

"I wish."

"Why not?"

"Because I'm all Grandma's got. I can't—I won't leave her alone with no family."

"You are a kind-hearted girl, Lucy. Family is important to you—that is how I know you are Greek."

"It's important to Americans, too."

"Not the way it is here."

"No," Lucy says, with absolute certainty. "Grandma is important to me the way family is everywhere. Greece doesn't have a monopoly on family values."

❧ 79 ❧

Fotini

She does not like it.

Lucy doesn't say where she goes every day, but Fotini knows. *She knows*. And she does not like it.

"The old woman will brainwash her."

"They did not brainwash you."

"No. But I was accustomed to bullying."

"Lucy is accustomed to you."

"What are you saying?"

"You are a force of nature, Fotini."

"I have never manipulated my granddaughter."

"Maybe not directly, but Lucy listens to you. She absorbs everything you say, everything you show her. Children do not stop being sponges after they reach twenty-one."

"I do not understand what you are saying, Stelios."

"And that is how I know you are upset with me. Usually I am the old goat."

"None of this is your business."

"So you keep saying. Yet you keep talking about it."

"We have to go home."

"Not for a few more days."

She could change the tickets, leave today, but she hasn't, has she? Not today, not yesterday, not the day before that.

"Come on, Fotini, let us go for a walk. I will pack a picnic and some books and we can go. If you prefer, we take the boat instead of walking.

———

THEY MAKE SECRET LOVE ON A SECRET BEACH. NO ONE watching but the sky and the sea, and they are known for their discretion. The water keeps its knowledge, and so to do the heavens. Ask any astronomer, anyone who makes a science of space and all its artifacts.

If love is for the young and other immortals, what is she doing on this beach?

Some hypotheses, she supposes, are made to be flawed.

❧ 80 ☙

Lucy

SATURDAY. PARTY DAY.

She arrives unfashionably on time, to find the party has already started without her.

On the wide front porch they've set up long tables, accompanied by wood and lacquered-straw chairs (of course). Vehicles of every flavor scattered on the pebble and grass-sprinkled lawn. People everywhere; some familiar, but mostly not. The immediate family she knows, the rest are strangers. To them, she figures, she's the stranger.

Isn't that how a lot of good stories start out, when a stranger comes to town?

"Lucy!" the women cheer.

"*Yia sou, yia sou.*" Does she sound ridiculous? Greek words don't roll off her tongue easily. How did Grandma do it, learn a new language well enough to get an excellent education and have an amazing career? And not just her, but her great-grandmother, too.

She works her way around the table, delivering a pair of kisses on every two cheeks. Except for Katerina and *Pro-Yiayia*, all the women present married into the family.

"When are you leaving, Lucy?"

The woman asking is a cousin's wife. She's heavily pregnant with offspring number four.

"Wednesday."

"That is too bad. Why can't you stay?"

She laughs. "I have a job. I have to make money somehow."

"You cannot go, Lucy," her great-grandmother says from her seat at the head of the table. "The family has plans for you."

"Plans? What plans?"

"This is a family short on daughters. In your generation there is only you and Katerina. Even though she is a grand-daughter and you are a great-granddaughter, you are of a similar age. Katerina is already engaged to a good man. There is a boy I want you to meet—very important family, very rich."

The penny drops. "You want me to marry him?"

"Eh, if you could. Yes."

"No."

The old woman glances around, appealing to the other faces, before snapping her gaze back to Lucy. "How can you say no? You have not met him."

"Still, no."

"*Po-po*. Children today. In the old days we married who we were told to marry. But now? Everyone marries who they please—and what happens? The divorce. Divorce here, divorce there."

"Nobody tells me who to marry."

"Meet him, at least. Then decide." Sly old fox. That expression she's wearing is pure fabricated innocence. "Look, here he is."

How 'bout that. She could drop dead from the un-shock.

Least she can do is look at him—right?

Yeah, about that ...

Hair by *Crisco*. Skin with more craters than the moon. Sunken chest. Built like a boneless ferret. Clothes torn out of *Saturday Night Fever's* wardrobe department.

Make that a double helping of 'hell no'.

"I have to pee," Lucy says.

"No, you do not," *Pro-Yiayia* says.

"It's my bladder, I should know. What kind of impression will I make if I pee on his shoes?"

The old lady considers her words. "Good point. Go."

Lucy scurries off to the bathroom, flattening herself on the safe side of the latched door. This room never makes sense. It's opulent with its marble floors, pale walls, and hand-embroidered towels. The fixtures are the genuine sort of old and well-made, the claw-footed bath real porcelain. But the toilet ...

It's a fancy hole in the ground, with wavy, ridged panels on either side, that looks like shoe soles. Which is exactly what they're for.

Squatting over that thing makes her feel like a dog. So now she won't pee here unless her plumbing is about to spring a serious leak.

All their money and her family couldn't afford a real toilet?

Where do they *read*?

(Maybe they don't; she hasn't seen any bookcases.)

Well, she can't stay in here forever, can she?

Maybe she can shimmy out the window and race to her

car before anyone notices. Too bad the window is over the—ha!—toilet.

She eases the door open. Standing directly outside is Ferret Guy.

His face lights up like July Fourth. "You are Lucy?"

"Unfortunately."

Blank stare. Not too bright, this one. At least when Akili stared at her there was motion in his brain and a spark in his eyes.

He points to his puny chest. "I, Lambros."

Very Tarzan.

She points at her own chest. "I, Jane."

His face scrunches up like an old lunch bag. "No Lucy?"

Oh God, he's about to do the disappointed puppy dog thing, that woebegone, hangdog move she's pretty sure guys learn when they're in diapers.

There goes his chin, his brow ... Argh!

"Yes, Lucy," she says. "I was just being apparently not very funny." He doesn't look like he has funny bone anyway, despite the exaggerated protrusion of his elbows.

Now what? He's standing there every bit as blank as a paper sheet.

If she's expected to carry this conversation ... "Come on, let's go check out the food." She grabs his arm, pulls him out to the porch where food is arriving after its short trip from the kitchen. Not far from the house, under the dappled shade of the olive trees, the family's men are turning some kind of dead animal on a spit. Below, a nest of coals glows.

"You like sheep?" Lambros asks, with all the enthusiasm of a caffeinated, sugar-dosed preschooler.

"That's a sheep?"

"Yes, sheep. *Baa-baa.*"

"Huh."

"You like?"

"I like it better when it's headless." She draws a grisly line across her neck, lets her tongue loll out of the side of her mouth. Lambros's expression collapses into mild horror.

Good. Maybe he'll protest any stupid ideas he's got about marrying her.

But no. It's not that easy, is it? He herds her round to the back of the house where there are more trees and bushes than eyes. Hopefully someone will hear her if she screams. With luck, they won't mistake the sound for happiness.

"Tell me about America," is the next thing out of his mouth.

What is there to tell? "It's exactly like in the movies."

"What movies?"

Lucy waves her arm in a broad arc. "All of them."

"I no see that one. Is good?"

She's going to be here awhile, isn't she? "Best movie ever. You'll love it."

"Is on DVD?"

No Netflix here, huh? "Uh, sure."

"Maybe we see together."

Suddenly she feels like hell. He's just some poor sap they've thrust on her. But they've thrust her at him, too.

"Maybe, Lambros. Maybe. Tell me how you know my family."

ANY ESCAPE THAT DOESN'T INVOLVE CHEWING OFF A BODY part is a good one.

Somehow she manages to detach herself from Lambros's side and hide amidst the fruit tress, away from the women and all their matchmaking.

She doesn't leave unnoticed, though. One of her cousins snaps off the group of men to wander her way. He's in his early thirties, built like a dumpling, with legs ripped off a corgi.

"And here is cousin Lucy!" He sidles up to her. "Come to secure your share of the inheritance before the old woman dies, eh?"

Say what? Is he high? "Inheritance?"

Gripping the beer bottle, he casts his hand wide, encompassing the house and its grounds. "The house and all its land. Not to mention the business. Big money."

"I'm not here for your money."

"Of course you are not." He winks at her. "It will be our secret, eh?"

"I don't care about the money!"

"I believe you."

Yeah, right. He's the proverbial wolf, wrapped up in the fluffy hide that the twirling sheep back there no longer needs.

Hands on hips, she says, "Act like that and I might just start caring."

He looks at her, stunned. Then the spell comes crashing down. "Try, Lucy. We will see if you are really my uncle's granddaughter."

"What?"

"Your grandmother ... Who knows who your grandfather was? Her father was a bad man. Maybe your grandfather is also your great-grandfather."

Eww. There's a limit, Lucy figures, to how much shit she can tolerate.

"Do you have children?"

"Two sons." He says it like having two sons is the pinnacle of manhood.

"Good, then you won't miss these."

Up comes the knee, landing square in the family jewels.

"If your wife gets knocked up now, *you'll* be wondering who the father is."

"Owww," he wails. "What is 'knocked up'?"

Hey, he was asking for it. All she and Grandma have is each other. When Grandma's not here to defend herself, Lucy's got her back.

Yeah, yeah, there's all this new family, which is awesome. But they're still an unknown quantity. Their horns haven't come out yet, except on old whathisface here.

"Which one are you again?"

"Orestis," he cries.

"Sorry not-sorry about your balls. But that's what you get for insulting my grandmother. Insult me ... fine. But not her. Never her. *Capishe?*

"I don't understand!"

Of course he doesn't.

She helps him up off the ground and he staggers away, newly hunchbacked. Then she returns to the porch where the women are watching Orestis limp back to the men under the trees.

She flops into a chair, lets out a big sigh.

"Why is he crying like a girl?" her great-grandmother wants to know.

Lucy tells her, carefully editing out the incriminating details.

"Huh," *Pro-Yiayia* says, scratching her chin. "I did not know he had any. This is why I am not ready to die. Every day there is something new to be learned."

"You've got that right," Lucy says. She nods to Orestis's wife, a lovely woman who deserves a guy several shades less scummy. "I'm sorry about his balls."

Her cousin by marriage shrugs. "For years I have been wanting to do the same thing. Right now, you are my hero."

A motor is rumbling in the direction of the house. A moment later, a small convertible rounds the corner, crunching to a stop near the other parked cars.

"Ah," Katerina says. "Here is someone you will want to meet. She is American like you."

Not one new arrival—two. A petite dark-haired woman and a pretty blonde girl, maybe sixteen or so.

"That is Vivi and her daughter Melissa. Vivi has a business that is growing very quickly in Agria. The family supplies her with olives. Vivi!"

The dark-haired woman waves. She's wearing a big smile. "*Yia sou!*" The conversation turns Greek fast, until she and her daughter are on the porch and Katerina introduces her to them.

"American!" Vivi says, basically pouncing on her. "Whereabouts?"

"California."

"We're practically neighbors." She points to herself. "Born and raised in Oregon." She turns around, tugs her daughter over. "This is Lucy. She's American."

"I know, Mom. I heard." Her tone is genuine bored American teenager, but her smile is real. "Hi, Lucy. Did you come to Greece on purpose, or did someone drag you here?"

Vivi rolls her eyes. "When I'm on my deathbed my daughter will remind me that I forced her to come to Greece, thus proving that she is completely Greek. Greeks never let anything go—ever."

"Actually," Lucy says, "I dragged my grandmother here. I bet she was even more reluctant than you were."

"No way," Melissa says, winking behind her mother's back. Vivi reaches back, gives her daughter a playful slap.

"Way," Lucy confirms. "Totally way."

"You missed all the fun," the family's matriarch says. "Lucy just kicked Orestis in the *arxides*."

Vivi laughs. "What did he do this time?"

Lucy gives herself a mental head-slap. "I just realized who

you are," she tells Vivi. "You're that woman's niece—the one who reads coffee cups."

"Dora Makri?"

"That's her. I met her with a ..." Wow, uncomfortable. What's she supposed to call Akili? "Another cousin of mine introduced me to her. Akili."

"*Akili's Pizza* Akili?"

"That's the guy."

"Oh God." She rubs her hand over her face. "Do you know what Greece's unofficial national sport is?" Lucy shakes her head. "Gossip. Nobody gossips harder, longer, or louder than Greeks."

The rest of the women in the family have returned to their own conversations. Clearly this one isn't that interesting to them.

Good.

"My aunt," Vivi continues, "has been all excited—"

"Picture a dog peeing all over itself," Melissa tosses in.

Vivi nods. "That's an apt description. She's been all worked up because she thought you were Akili's girlfriend, but now it turns out you're cousins. Your grandmother is from Agria?"

"Originally. She ran away from home years ago."

"Her and a lot of other kids. Greek parents—especially in small villages like Agria—were borderline psychotic with their need to control their children's lives. My fiancé was actually this close—" She holds up her finger and thumb. "—a pubic hair away from marrying a woman his mother chose. Meanwhile, at the time, his brother was in family exile because he ran off to be a priest instead of going to law school."

The story has a familiar peal. "Is his name Kostas Andreou?"

"Yes! You know him?"

"Akili took me to his church."

"You're her! He gave me your number but he must have written it down wrong."

Lucy facepalms. "No, I just realized I gave him *my* number—my cell number, not the number at the hotel."

Vivi laughs. "Oops."

"Uncle Kostas is the best," Melissa confirms. "Not that he's my real uncle, but still."

"Where were we?" Vivi asks. "Oh yeah, your grand-mother. Apparently everyone thought she was dead, but now it turns out she's not. So people are talking." She winces. "Sorry."

She likes this woman. She's cool, easygoing, funny. A woman who's really got it together.

"We'll be gone in a couple of days, so they'll have to get over it. What made you move to Greece?"

"My husband left me for another man, so I ran away with my daughter. If you stick around long enough someone will tell you anyway, so I'm beating them to it."

So she didn't always have it all together. Good to know. It gives her hope.

"Ian. Ugh." Melissa pokes her finger down her throat, fakes a gag.

Vivi rolls her eyes skyward. "As you can see, our daughter doesn't think much of the situation."

"It's not that he's gay," Melissa explains, "it's that Ian is basically Satan's butthole—with herpes."

"Melissa!" But that reprimand comes with a smile.

Lucy's great-grandmother leans across the table. "What are you talking about?"

"Gay men," Vivi says brightly.

"What is that?"

"Gay men. Men who like men."

"Oh, them. They are everywhere now. You know because

they are very well dressed and they take good care of their teeth. *Poustis* have the best parades."

Lucy blinks. *Pro-Yiayia* didn't show up for the picnic with all her sandwiches neatly packed in the basket, which definitely makes life interesting.

"Anyway," Vivi continues, "you're definitely one of the newest topics of gossip. There's not much you can do about it. Like you said, you'll be leaving. And sooner or later, someone else will do something scandal-worthy and eclipse you."

"They don't even know me."

"That doesn't slow the gossip machine down. They had a field day when we moved here." She gives Lucy the condensed version, right down to the part where she spent a night in jail with her mother for a murder they didn't commit.

"It sounds like there are a lot of murders in Agria."

"There are murders everywhere," her great-grandmother says, leaping into the conversation again. "Greeks are good at murder. We invented it."

"Pretty sure we didn't," Vivi murmurs.

"I heard that." The old woman points at her. "Then who invented murder, if not the Greeks?"

"Cain and Abel?" Vivi tries.

"Greek."

"They weren't Greek, they were—" The end of Lucy's sentence breaks off. "Actually, I don't know what they were. They could have been Greek—before Greece was Greece, though."

"See." Her great-grandmother stabs the air with a pointy finger. "Greek."

"I think it was in Persia," Melissa says. "Which is Iran now. That's one theory."

The old woman sucks her breath in through her gums. "Persia! They did not invent anything except carpets. And now that I think about it, they stole that from the Greeks, too."

"I'm sure you're right, *Kyria* Manatou," Vivi says. There's a shadow of a smile on her lips and a twinkle in her eyes.

"Agria is very uncivilized," *Pro-Yiayia* says. "And murderers do not like civilization, so they go to Agria. In Drakia, we are civilized. Only a hundred years ago, Agria belonged to Drakia. We used it as a port, because it was not fit for anything else."

Not that she's biased or anything—right?

LAMBROS IS AMBLING THEIR WAY. NOW HE'S SPORTING A pair of blowfly sunglasses.

"Oh God," Lucy mutters.

Vivi looks up. "What is it?"

Lucy fills her in.

"Greek families—*oy*. Stick to your guns. Don't let them bully you into anything, because they *will* bully you."

"Good thing we're leaving in a few days."

"You don't sound like that's a good thing."

It doesn't, does it?

"Besides Grandma, I've had nobody since my sister died a few months ago. So being around family is kind of neat." She waggles her eyebrows. "Even if they are functionally insane."

"Functionally insane. That describes this country perfectly at times."

Lucy cracks up. "I know!"

"Hello Lucy, *Kyria* Tyler." Here comes Lambros, strutting over like a bantam rooster.

"Vivi. Just Vivi. Otherwise I feel ancient."

"What ancient?"

"Old," Lucy tells him.

Vivi clues him in with her Greek skills.

"Oh, you not old. I show respect." His shrouded gaze swings around. "Lucy, walk?"

"I'd love to, but my leg hurts. I think it's got a bone in it."

Masterful the way Vivi swallows her laughter and manages to translate. She's betting she left out the bone bit. Too bad; she thinks he would have swallowed it anyway.

"Okay. Tomorrow."

"Tomorrow."

Then he slinks away, looking like she whacked him over the nose with a newspaper.

"Poor guy," she says.

Vivi threads her arm through Lucy's. "No—no 'poor guy'. 'Poor guy' will lead you to the church in a big, white dress."

"Seriously?"

"Lucy, they will do anything to stuff you into that marriage if it's for the good of the family—in their estimation. They'll play hardball. Make sure you do, too. Old families with money are that way."

BEFORE THE TYLERS LEAVE, VIVI GIVES LUCY HER NUMBER. "Need anything, call me. I can help you jilt the groom if need be."

"Thanks," Lucy says. "I appreciate it."

"Greece can be a lonely place. I should know, I live here."

❦ 81 ❦

Fotini

"WHAT ARE YOU AFRAID OF?"

No beach this time. They're in Stelios's bed, in the house she hasn't seen until now. She can see why he keeps it a minor secret. It's straddling the line between large house and mansion. Big windows. Wonderful views. Furnishings by someone with a good eye and deep pockets.

This is not what she expected. He is not what she expected.

"Your house is huge."

"Yes."

"Your *taverna* is tiny."

"Yes."

"And you dress like a fisherman."

"How does a fisherman dress?"

She laughs. "Like you."

He rolls over, pulls her to him so they're nose to nose. "You did not answer my question. What are you afraid of?"

"Sharks. Heights. Especially those Plexiglass platforms. They built one over the Grand Canyon. You look down and there is nothing but fresh air."

He shakes with silent laughter. "That is not what I meant and you know it."

Clever man. Too clever. Here is someone, at last, that she cannot sidestep. When she tries, he's there to catch her.

"I know what you meant." A sigh works its way out of her soul. "What if they blame me for Iason's murder? In a way, it was my fault. If we had not married, he would have lived."

"And you would have had no daughter, no granddaughters, and you might still be stuck in Greece in a life you feared and hated."

"No," she says. "One way or another, I was leaving."

"You are a warrior, Fotini. Fight. Go with Lucy, see them, make your peace. You have tried to find peace the other way, stuffing the past into an old box, but that did not work, did it?"

"Sometimes it did. But not always."

His hand is warm on her back, her hip. It's starting to roam again, heating her one handful at a time. "If they blame you, they blame you. Give them the *moutsa* and leave."

If she was a woman who giggled, she'd giggle at that. The idea of showing them her open palm, rubbing faux poop in their faces, is childish but funny.

She doesn't giggle—she laughs.

"There is my Fotini, my light. Light is the shadow of God, you know."

"A romance novel?"

"Plato."

❧ 82 ❧

Lucy

GRANDMA'S GOT A SURPRISE FOR LUCY. "TODAY I THINK I will come with you."

The way she freezes, you'd think Lucy had been zapped with a ray gun.

"Oh?"

"Yes. Why not? I could use a trip to the mainland."

"But every time we go over there you get weird."

"Only the one time."

"No, all the times. You go spacey."

"This time I won't, I promise."

What's she going to do? She can't tell Grandma no, can she?

"Okay."

Stelios takes them to the coast. He tucks Grandma's hand into his and keeps it in his pocket the whole way there. Then he helps her off the boat, swinging her into the air as if they're both teenagers.

"So, where are we going?" Grandma asks when she's settled in the passenger's seat.

"Up Pelion."

"Up Pelion where?"

"Just up."

Her hands are *Play Doh* on the wheel. They feel malleable and squishy. The rental car climbs Drakia Road slowly. Probably it knows the way by now. Lucy could almost walk there, blindfolded.

She eases the car through the blip on the map that is Drakia, then onto the narrow dirt road that leads to her great-grandmother's home.

"I know this place."

"Oh really?" Lucy glances over. Grandma's all pale, like a Japanese geisha.

"I changed my mind. let's go back."

"Too late. You wanted to come, and we're already here."

She cuts the engine directly in front of her great-grandmother's house. No one else is visiting today, looks like, so the whole driveway is theirs. No sound but the faint rattle of leaves as a Zephyr passes through. It's hot, dry, and the grass is dying, but it dies quietly and without ceremony or melodrama.

Grandma says, "I hate you."

"I know. But I can live with that."

"You say that now, but wait until I disinherit you."

"I'm your only heir."

"Have you seen that commercial with the poor, shivering dogs? I will leave them everything. Then they won't shiver so much."

"That's a big heart you've got there, Grandma."

"I know."

❧ 83 ❧

Fotini

SHE COULD JUMP OUT OF THE CAR, EXCEPT HER PASSPORT says she's at the age when jumping out of a moving vehicle could snap a bone. Probably her hip.

Or hips.

Imagine what a flight back to America that would be.

"Don't make me go in, Lucy."

The front door opens. An old woman hobbles out, her mouth pinched, her back almost as bent as the handle on the walking stick she's using for support.

Iason's mother. Katerina Manatou.

"Too late." Lucy jumps out of the convertible, comes around to open the passenger door. "All you have to do is say hello. It'll be okay, I promise. Things have changed."

"People do not change."

"Of course they do. They change all the time. Just not

always for the better. But she has. She doesn't even hate you anymore. She used to—but not now."

Well there is a blessing. The thought is slathered in sarcasm, with a snarky spit shine.

Out of the car. Suck in the gut. Pull those shoulders high, Fotini. Want to swim with sharks? Do not bleed.

Were they really sharks, though? Or did they seem that way because of her biased lens? It's hard to see the good in people when you're on the brink of womanhood and your name is bitter on their tongues.

Today—here—she's a fully fledged woman. A woman who has loved and lost and learned more than the girl she was ever dreamed. Stand up to one old woman? Definitely.

The place has changed some. Evolved. New layers on the house. A sprawling porch. The line of trees has inched closer to the house.

Lucy curls her arm around her waist, hugs her. "Together," she says.

"Together."

There are moments when her heart overflows with love for Lucy. This would be one of them, if only her grand-daughter had turned the car around.

Hand shielding her eyes from the sun (never mind that she's in the porch's benevolent shade), Iason's mother watches them trudge up to the house.

"Lucy, who is this?"

As though she doesn't know. Wily old buzzard.

Lucy, bless her, looks slightly puzzled. "It's my Grandma."

"Oh, your grandmother." An offhand tone. "How is she?"

Can a woman on the far side of menopause roll her eyes? Why yes—yes she can. She's doing it right now. "I am well, *Kyria* Manatou. And you?"

That hand lowers as they step onto the porch.

"We meet again, Fotini."

"It's been a long time."

"You got old."

"So did you."

Iason's mother cackles. "Time is deaf. It does not hear us when we tell it to stop or turn around." Her gaze is as discerning as ever. It's like standing in front of the airport's x-ray machines, except this old woman is looking for cracks and other weaknesses instead of bombs in her underwear. "Lucy, I have a gift for you. It is on the table inside."

Lucy vanishes into the house. When she returns, she's holding a shoe box. "Shoes?"

"Yes, shoes. Very beautiful, and a good price."

That old cheapskate. Something is wrong with those shoes, count on it.

When Lucy opens the box, her granddaughter gasps. White high heels, with lace uppers. They're dotted with tiny crystals that catch the light and fling it in their eyes.

Beautiful. What is the catch?

And there is a catch—guaranteed.

"Those are for your wedding."

See—the catch.

"My wedding?"

"To Lambros."

Lucy laughs. "I'm not marrying Lambros."

"Of course you are. You just do not know it yet."

That box could be on fire, the way Lucy drops it. "Come on, Grandma. We're going."

"Go where?" Iason's mother says. "You just got here."

"And now we're leaving."

The old bat looks to her for support. Ha! Put that on the list of things that will never happen.

Up she gets. "How about we take a trip to Makrinitsa?"

"Sounds great," Lucy says.

"Sit, you two. Sit. What is wrong with Lambros that you do not want to marry him?"

Lucy shoots lasers at her with her eyes. "Everything. Starting with the part where you want me to marry him. I choose the men in my life—no one else."

"That is not how it is in this family."

Shrug. "Then I'm not in your family. I did fine without you before. I'll do fine without you now. *We'll* do fine."

What a woman she is. In many ways she is her grandmother's daughter—a fighter. Throw that boulder of grief off her shoulders, she will be unstoppable in life.

Lucy leads the short parade back to the car.

The car sparks to life, leaving Iason's mother behind a cloud of Greece's dirt and dust. This Fotini understands: putting the past behind her, where it belongs.

"Who does she want you to marry?"

"A creep. Well, not exactly a creep. More like a dweeb. A dweeb with a lobotomy and zero fashion sense."

"What's his name?"

Lucy tells her.

She nods. "I remember the family. The grandfather was friends with Iason. Good family, very wealthy. But soft in the head."

"I'm not going to marry him."

"I know."

"They can't make me, can they?"

"No," Grandma says, "they can't make you. Not even here." And if she knows Lucy, the old woman had better not try. Otherwise she's liable to wake up one morning and find her olive trees have had a fateful encounter with a chainsaw.

THEY SEE MAKRINITSA, ENJOY THE VIEW OF ETERNITY from its town square, perched on the mountain's lip. They buy souvenirs. A peasant top for Lucy's coworker Betsy, hand-crafted ornaments to remind them of this day.

As if she can ever forget.

✿ 84 ✿

Lucy

BEAUTIFUL SHOES. VERY CINDERELLA MEETS PRETTY Woman.

Too bad she can't—oh, you know—*wear* them.

They're different sizes. One's a perfect fit. The other's someone else's perfect fit.

When she delivers the verdict to Grandma, her grand-mother busts out laughing.

"That is your great-grandmother. She can squeeze a rock until it bleeds. Those shoes were on sale for being mismatched or she wouldn't have bought them."

That explains the toilet.

"So what do I do with them?"

"Smile and tell her they are your favorite pair."

"I think I'll tell her they don't match."

"Lucy, you can't do that."

"Sure I can."

SHE DRIVES BACK UP THE MOUNTAIN, EVEN THOUGH SHE said she wouldn't. That's the nice thing about having your own mind: you can change it at any time—sometimes even consequence-free.

Her great-grandmother has a too-satisfied look on her face. Thinks Lucy's there for a remorseful reunion. Thinks she's given her a taste of the moneyed life, of how things could be if only Lucy would bend.

Not happening.

She sets herself in stone, arms folded, legs apart in the screw-you-and-not-in-a-good-way position.

"About those shoes ..."

"Oh? Do you like them? They were a very good price."

"Yeah, because they don't match. They're different sizes."

"How?"

"One is my size, the other one is too big."

"Lucy, my doll, that is why God invented newspaper."

Huh?

Good thing her great-grandmother's got all the answers. "Stuff the newspaper in the toe of the shoe that is too big and you will have a perfect fit."

"Newspaper?"

"Or a rag."

"Or a rag?"

"Are you going to repeat everything I say? It will be a very long conversation if you do, and I am old. Every conversation could be my last. But I do not mind, I will see my Iason and Orestis again. Although I will be very angry if I die in the middle of an interesting conversation. What if I miss the gossip?"

"Yeah, but imagine all the eavesdropping you could do as a ghost. You could listen in on everything."

"You are a smart girl, Lucy. I like that idea. But still I am in no hurry to go." She nods to Lucy's feet. "Now put on the shoes and let me watch you walk."

❧ 85 ❧

Akili

AKILI'S PLAN STINKS.

Yeah, he knows it. But he's working with what he's got.

What is it he's got?

His dead best friend's fiancée, Kiki. She's an English teacher and her husband-to-be is American. Well, Greek-American.

Which means he'll always be American to this crowd, unless he cures cancer or achieves something equally prestigious. Then he'll be Greekest Greek who ever lived.

Akili remembers Leonidas from school. Okay guy. Good at basketball.

There's no love lost between Akili and Kiki, though. Which is what happens when you accuse an innocent woman of murder. So it's his own fault.

Now he needs her, so he's preparing to go to her on his knees.

Akili doesn't go to anyone on his knees. So this is new.

And uncomfortable.

The grief starts before he pushes the Andreou family's gate open. Three generations live in this three-story house. Kiki's parents and *yiayia* have the bottom floor. Kiki lives on the middle floor. And her older sister, Soula, lives on top.

The two Andreou daughters are nowhere in sight, but their mother and grandmother are in the front yard. Margarita Andreou, Kiki's mother, is stabbing blue thread into a piece of white fabric stretched flat in an embroidery hoop, while her mother flips through a magazine.

"Look, Margarita," the older of the two women says. "The toilet must be broken, because here is some *skata* floating past."

He kind of deserves that.

"Mama! Do not be so rude. Leave that to me. You have no business here," she tells him. "Go away."

"Is Kiki home?"

"Not for you."

"May I speak with her?"

"Poor thing, are you deaf?"

"Wait—I will do sign language." Kiki's grandmother shows him her sign language.

He's pretty sure that's an insult in any culture.

"Mama! Enough! Go home, Akili. Or I will go inside and let my mother have you."

There's movement on the balcony above their heads. Kiki. She's watching the comedy duo, big grin on her face.

"Giving you trouble, are they?" she calls out.

"Can I talk to you?"

The grin fades. She's considering his request, so that's something.

Then she tilts her head towards the concrete stairs. "Come."

The gate lets out a thin whine.

"If you are rude to my daughter I will kill you with this needle, very slowly," Margarita Andreou says. "And my husband will bury your body."

"But I will piss on you before he does," her mother says.

"I promise I'll be good."

Do they look convinced? No. Which is why he keeps some distance between them on his trek from the gate to the stairs.

Kiki flings her door open the moment his feet strike the landing. "What do you want, Akili?"

"How are you, Kiki?"

"Never better. You?"

"I need your help."

She's lovely, Kiki is. Not his type, but he can still appreciate a pretty woman. Her sister Soula gives men whiplash, but Kiki's softer and more sweet-tempered.

He really messed up accusing her of Stavros's murder.

"What help?"

"I need a letter. In English."

"What for?"

"There's an American woman ..."

She's flinty, cold. "Are you talking about your cousin?"

He slouches against the concrete wall of the landing. Greek houses have skeletons of concrete and steel. Earthquake proof—mostly.

"She's not my cousin."

"I heard—"

"She's *not* my cousin," he repeats slowly.

He sees her doing the arithmetic, deriving an interesting answer. A smart woman, Kiki. "Oh. *Oooooh*." Her hard edges soften. "Are you okay? When did you find out?"

That's Kiki—she's kind. She always was.

Fact is, she'd have made Stavros an excellent wife—better

than Drina, who walks through life in frigid armor. But he knows—even Stavros knew it—that his best friend would have made any woman a lousy husband eventually—at least until he grew up. Guys like that don't change unless life forces change upon them.

"A couple of days ago. Had a fight with the old man and he let the truth fly." He laughs; sounds more like croup than mirth. "Too bad he didn't tell me years ago. Too bad *she* didn't. Would have been good to know we weren't blood."

Kiki gives him an opening of the physical kind: she steps aside, ushers him in with the sweep of her arm. "Come inside."

Her threshold is a metaphorical bridge. If he walks carefully, maybe they will be able to smile when they pass each other in the street. Maybe he will be able to call her without reservation if one of his English-speaking diners loses a wallet.

Been a long time since he was in her place. Before it was always too neat, too clean. It's still clean, but there are signs of life here now. Leo has unbuttoned her—let Kiki be Kiki.

"Where is Leonidas?"

"At the clinic, talking to Papadopoulos."

Papadopoulos is—was—the village's only vet. He's also a physician. Akili tries not to wonder too hard about which one he's legitimately licensed for.

"They going into business together?"

Kiki shrugs. "Leo wants someone to do pets. Euthanizing cats and dogs bothers him. Do you want coffee?"

Normally in Greece you say yes when someone offers coffee or food, but it's different with Kiki. She belongs to his generation, and they're less rigid, not so easily offended. So he makes the little *tst* sound that means no, couples it with an upwards jerk of his head.

Kiki groans. "I hate that. My kids do it all year along in class. Last time I was in America with Leo, I did it in a restaurant when the waiter asked if I needed ketchup."

Akili laughs. "What did he do?"

"Looked at me like I was from Mars." She waves a hand at her small balcony. The doors are open, the ceiling-to-floor sheers flutter. Greece is showing mercy today. "Let's sit outside." She leads him out to a small round table with two chairs. "So tell me about this woman. If she's not your cousin, who is she?"

The funny thing about Greeks is that they ask blunt questions.

How much did that cost?

How much do you make?

Are you getting fatter? You look fatter.

When are you having children?

When are you having more children?

Nothing is too personal.

But answers? Those Greeks don't yield easily. They're masters at sidestepping the truth. Why tell the truth when you can take a more interesting detour? Greeks prefer their conversations to be circular, rather than drawn in straight lines. Which is why they love debating politics.

But this is the first civil conversation he's had with Kiki in a long time. If they are to be more than enemies he must be honest.

So he tells her about the sinking boat, about the way talking to Lucy makes life sweet, even when they don't understand each other. About the way her hair is gold in the sun.

Very poetic. He didn't know he had poetry in him.

But then look at Stelios. Who would ever guess that old crust reads romance?

Kiki's eyes fill with a light mist when he recants the

conversations with Lucy's grandmother and tops it with his father's—no, his stepfather's snide revelation. He can trust her, he knows. His best friend's former fiancée might tell her current beau, but the story won't travel beyond these walls.

"My Virgin Mary," she swears. "What a mess."

"A big mess. Now I must clean it up, but my English ..."

"Non-existent?"

"Close." He snorts. "I should have paid attention in school."

"Come to my class when school starts. I can show my students what happens when they don't study." She says it with a tentative smile.

"Be glad to. So can you help?"

She vanishes into the house, returns with a pen and paper. "Write your letter in Greek, then I'll translate it for you."

"I NEED YOU TO COVER ME FOR AN HOUR. THINK YOU CAN do it?"

Thanasi shrugs. "Yeah, I can do it. It's pizza—not rocket science."

He's about to pounce when the kid says, "I'm joking. Go. Your pizza will be better than ever—you'll see."

Yeah, if Thanasi can peel his eyes off Drina's ass.

Still, the kid is a hard worker. Observant. Makes one hell of a pizza. And it's only for an hour.

He slaps Thanasi on the shoulder. "Thanks. Back in an hour."

Patra is arriving as he's leaving. She slams on her brakes, creates a traffic jam in the narrow doorway.

"Where are you going?"

Convenient, the way he ignores her question. "I'll be back."

"Fine, don't tell me."

He wasn't going to.

Yeah, it's cold. But women like Patra have a way of mistaking kindness for interest. Leading her on would be cruel. He's not the kind of asshole who needs the ego boost.

86

Lucy

THREE DAYS—INCLUDING TODAY—THEN THEY'LL BE GONE.

Lucy waits on the dock for something to change. The season is shifting—what about her?

What do you think of Greece, Lana? Is it what you hoped it would be?

No matter how hard she squeezes her memory, she can't recall which place was next on her sister's list. Greece was at the top; Lucy was blind to everything else.

There's a hollow in her heart, in her gut. A feeling as if something is boring bigger holes so it can nest. At the same time, her bones are jittery, restless.

She's not ready to go home. Something is unfinished.

Maybe it's her.

❦ 87 ❧

Akili

Stripes of foam etch the gulf's glass in random patterns. There's no rhythm to the temporary schisms, just the haphazard carelessness of people like him, piloting their boats to the shore of their choosing.

Trikeri comes. Her lights are pinpricks at first. Then they explode into full bloom, painting bright, shimmering pools on the water.

As the sun creeps away, the stars step into the sky to take its place. Each is the other's stand-in. The dock emerges from the shadow, and on it the slight figure of a soul as lost as his.

Lucy.

He throttles the engine, inches the boat towards the dock and woman.

She stands. Pulls her shoulders back. Draws herself into the firing position.

The boat sidles up to the concrete protrusion, until he's

standing directly across from her. Only a short distance between them, but it's a sea. He is Odysseus to her Penelope.

If he doesn't succeed now, years might pass before he sees her again—if he ever does.

Can he reach her?

He can't tell. Her face is working through its repertoire of emotions, trying to decide which one is suitable for ... for whatever box she has shoved him into. *Cousin? Friend? Stranger.*

No words—from either of them.

He holds out the letter in the envelope Kiki gave him. Lucy's face changes again, to bewilderment this time. She plucks it out of his hand.

Then she turns away, gathering speed as she runs.

❧ 88 ❧

Lucy

UNTITLED

Lucy carries the letter back to their room, assumes the lotus position on her bed, unpicks the envelope's tacky seam using her fingernails.

English. That's what strikes her first. A feminine hand. There's no way Akili's handwriting has this many swirls and loops. Whoever's penmanship it is, she makes an art out of writing.

Grandma's is smooth and angular; every letter reaches out and touches its neighbor. Lucy's own hand is rounded and childish. Her letters are loners. They stand on the page, hoping to be part of a bigger word. Alphabet with ambition.

The letter is addressed to her.

Naturally. Otherwise she wouldn't be reading it, would she?

Not Dear Lucy—just plain Lucy.

She reads from the top down to Akili's signature. Then, breathing ragged, heart running hurdles, she starts over.

❧ 89 ❧

Fotini

LUCY DROPS A LETTER ON THE *TAVERNA*'S BLUE TABLECLOTH. "It's from Akili."

Ah, he has found a way. Clever boy. "What does he say?"

Back and forth, the girl paces. "Read it. Wait. Let me tell you." She drops into the chair opposite, leans forward on her elbows. "His mother ... She was pregnant with him before she married your brother. Can you believe it?" Then she jumps up again, resumes pacing.

Very distracting.

But not so distracting that Fotini can't form a fascinating conclusion.

"Akili isn't his son?"

"Apparently not. He says his father told him during an argument."

"Who is his birth father?"

"He doesn't know."

"My God," Stelios says reverently. "We are in a romance novel. This was the big misunderstanding."

"Hush, old man. Let Lucy talk."

"Talk, talk. I will be here listening. Who can read when we are in a novel?"

He busies himself with rearranging the glasses hanging over the bar, but his ears are open.

"It changes everything." Lucy drops the envelope and its contents on the crisp blue and white tablecloth. "And it changes nothing. We're leaving the day after tomorrow."

Are we? she wonders. She thinks maybe only one of them will be boarding that plane.

She watches Stelios shifting stems. If she was smart, neither of them would go.

But Greece ... She and Greece are mortal enemies.

She cannot make peace with her homeland. They have hated each other for far too long.

Theirs is an abusive relationship.

"STAY WITH ME, FOTINI. WE COULD BE HAPPY HERE. YOU have met your old ghosts, conquered them. Now it is the season for happiness."

Stelios says it as she's on her way to bed—alone.

"I could love you," she says. "But Greece? We've had our time, and it was terrible."

❧ 90 ❧

Lucy

SUDDENLY, MORNING ARRIVES. ALL OF IT IN THE SAME crusty, seeping moment.

That's how Lucy knows she fell asleep after all.

Clothes. Shoes. Into the bathroom where she succeeds at making order out of chaos. She cleans up nicely. No way would an outsider know she feels just this side of crazy.

When she comes out of the bathroom, she realizes her stealth was for nothing. Grandma's gone.

Rock in her chest, grinding sparks and beats, she trots to the *taverna* for morning coffee. Stelios is there, reading.

"Where's Grandma?"

"Good morning, Stelios. How are you? Are you well? Good morning, Lucy. I am wonderful. How are you?"

She hoists herself onto the barstool. "Point taken. Good morning, Stelios. Did you sleep well?"

"Wonderful, thank you. Your grandmother went to the

331

mainland—early. I took her to Agria so she would not have to catch the bus. I will go again later to get her."

"What did she go for?"

He slaps his head. "My Virgin Mary, I forgot to interrogate a grown woman."

"You know what you need?"

"More books?"

"Besides more books."

"What?"

"A stick with a string and a hook to hold up your books. That way you can read and live at the same time."

"Reading is life."

"Yeah, but someone else's life—not yours."

"You could be a Greek philosopher. All of ours are dead."

"Is that sarcasm?"

"Yes. Do you like it?"

"Are you going to let my grandmother escape?"

"Escape? Is this the zoo?"

"You know what I mean—leave Greece."

He puts the book to rest on the bar. "Lucy, your grandmother is her own woman. If she wants to stay, she will stay. If she wants to go ... I cannot stop her."

"Sure you can."

"That is called kidnapping. I like the romance, not the thrillers."

"For the record," she says, "you suck."

His laugh fills the small *taverna*. "What about you, Lucy? Will you stay or go?"

"I don't know. It depends on Grandma."

"Ah, you are hoping she makes the decision for you. If she goes, you will go. If she stays, you will stay. I understand. You are afraid of being alone."

Plucking all the correct strings, that's what he's doing. "Who's the Greek philosopher now?"

"Bah! I am just a bartender who likes other people's stories. But let me tell you this. You make your own destiny. If you let others make it for you, you will be unhappy. But if you make your own, even if you fail you will be happy. Most of the time."

❧ 91 ❧

Akili

AKILI MAKES PLANS. PLANS KEEP A MAN FROM GOING crazy.

His plan is to work and work and work.

If Lucy wants to speak with him, she knows where he is. He made his move, now it is up to her. Doesn't stop him from calling Stelios.

"What is wrong with you?" the mustachioed man asks. "You give her a letter and then you stay away? How is that romantic?"

"Not meant to be romantic, old man. Don't want to scare her off."

"Scare her off." He mutters a string of curses. All of them sexual and religious. "Women want to be wooed. You want her? Come here and court her. So what if you don't speak the same language? You can learn."

"No. The next move is hers."

"*Po-po*. Where is your *poutso?*"

In his pants. Where it's staying, for now. Patra rubbed her ass against his groin earlier, said she was sorry but she had to squeeze past him. Yeah right. He knows a come-on. He's had more than his share over the years.

Thing is, these days his cock's not interested. It wants what it wants. He's not Stavros. One hole isn't the same as another. Women aren't interchangeable.

Lucy isn't forgettable.

❧ 92 ❧

Fotini

ONCE SHE HAS BEEN THERE, BUT SHE REMEMBERS THE WAY.

Okay, so she brought along the map Akili drew for Lucy. It is not cheating, it is smart.

Early. The sun is barely up, and Agria is still rubbing the sleep out of its eyes. One old woman nearing her twilight years is beneath its notice, she hopes. She hurries along the streets, walking shoes scuffing away the half mile or so between the shore and the Dukakis home.

Who is Akili if he is not Yiorgos's son?

Does it matter?

Not to her. Akili—from what she knows of him—is a kind man. Even if Akili was truly her nephew she'd welcome him into her family, provided Yiorgos didn't follow. But now, that is not a problem. She can welcome him as a friend—and maybe as something more if he and Lucy pick up where they left off.

If.

A pivotal word and concept.

As for her, what is she doing? Besides breaking her promise to herself, that is.

Not picking at the scab. Sealing a door—that's the plan. Solder the gap between Greece then and Greece now. Stelios's simple plea touched something inside her. It pushed her to a place she's never been able to reach in all her years as a woman or a therapist.

A place of peace.

And now here she is, ready to seal her past with fire.

She doesn't announce herself Greek-style. Used to be visitors would stand on the street and call your name—maybe they still do. This place does not like change, even if it is polite. She pushes through the gate, walks to the front door, knocks three times.

"Who is it?"

That tobacco-worn voice. Yiorgos sounds like their father.

"It is me. Fotini."

Swearing sifts through the door—not at her, but at everything that is suddenly in his path. That table, those chairs, that rug his wife had to have. Until finally he jerks the door open.

"I thought you were not coming."

She shrugs. "I changed my mind."

"Oh, you changed your mind? Lucky me."

"Congratulations, you are an asshole like our father. Not that I doubted you would be. Where is Akili?"

"Not here."

"I can see that."

"Why do you care?"

A fly finds its way into the Dukakis house. Her brother

337

snatches up a flyswatter, slaps it on the wall. For a moment, the dead fly clings to the paint.

Then it falls.

"He's a better man than you. I'm glad he is not your blood."

"So you know, eh?"

"I know."

"Are you going to let him fuck your granddaughter now?"

She shakes her head. What a mess he is. "You cannot make me angry now, Yiorgos. Not with words. Look at yourself. You are pathetic. A loser in life, in everything. Like our father. How does it feel to know that since our mother died, nobody has loved you, and nobody will ever love you again?"

"What is love? Our mother was too scared to love us. If she had loved us she would have protected us from him. She thought you were dead, you know. We all did. After ... After Iason died—"

"Do not speak his name. He didn't die. You and our father killed him. That is not death, it is murder."

"I don't remember—"

"How convenient your memory is. Our father was a monster, and you were his accomplice. I watched you both kill my husband."

"He made me do it!" Spit flies out of his mouth. Yiorgos slams his fist on the kitchen table. It scoots an inch left. "I am not the son of a monster! If I am, what does that make me, eh? What does that make me?"

"What does that make *us*?"

"You are a woman, it is different."

Clearly her brother has never seen *Mommy Dearest*. "I have struggled with this my whole life, too. Knowing what our father was—who he was inside. Maybe it goes all the way back through our family's history. A chain of monsters hiding inside our men. Or maybe our father was the first glitch, a mistake in our family's making. In another time they would have taken him to war and made sure he never came home. And they would have taken you, too, and you would have never come home except in a box, a man not fit to return upon your shield."

"Life has made you hard, Fotini."

"Greece made me hard. But America made me happy and soft in the good places." She looks down at her hands. How did they get so old? "I came to tell you goodbye. When you see our father again, tell him I spit on him."

Lucy

When Grandma shows up, it's with cake and books.

Romance novels—of course.

Lucy pounces on the cake. Stelios has already claimed the books.

Grandma laughs. "I wish you were both so happy to see me!"

"We are happy," Lucy says, mouth bursting with some kind of chocolate pastry cream. It's heaven in a horn-shaped flaky shell, that's all she knows. "You should have woken me up."

"I did not have the heart, my love. You were sleeping like a baby."

"That bad, huh?"

"Wrestling with the sheets all night."

Miles beneath Trikeri's beach, the ground begins to shake.

❧ 94 ❧

Akili

AN EARTHQUAKE DOES NOT COME IN PEACE. IT IS THE VERY symbol of antagonism. Tectonic plates colliding in a battle of wills.

This one arrives early, shaking Greeks from their beds. Their houses are (mostly) earthquake proof, still they huddle under doorways, under tables.

Then, just as they've become accustomed to the shake, the plates make temporary peace and settle into their new configuration—until next time. In that they are like Greece and its rival, Turkey.

SOME OLD HOUSES CRUMBLE—THEY'VE BEEN SHAKEN before, but this is their last resort. The new houses lose only a few important things. A glass here, a photograph there.

Agria has only one casualty this morning.

His fate is final.

HOUSE? FINE, SO *KYRIA* DORA SAID. ONE OF HIS neighbors told her, and so she had to tell her friend Akili the good news. He was grateful and he told her so. She waited expectantly for something extra, something more socially valuable than his thanks.

Yeah, he knew what she wanted: gossip. And there was Akili, fresh out.

That was ten minutes ago. Now he's taking stock of the pizzeria. A couple of chairs tumbled into the sea, but those will dry out. No harm done."You all okay?" he asks when his employees straggle in.

Yes, yes, yes. So it's business as usual. Great. Good. Now he can get going, back to Trikeri where he was headed before the quake interrupted.

First customer of the day is Detective Lemonis. The cop's face is set to grim.

Akili knows that expression. He's seen the man wear it before, at a wedding that never happened.

"Who is it?"

Lemonis scratches his chin, tilts his head toward the open door. "Walk with me."

Trikeri is going to have to wait. He tosses aside his keys, then he's out the door and they're walking to nowhere.

"It's your father."

"Is he okay?"

Headshake. "No. He was already gone when they found him."

"Who is 'they'?"

"Your neighbors. They found him dead in your home."

"What were they doing in my house? Nobody visits. Nobody talks to him."

"Where were you this morning?"

"I came straight here after the quake."

"Before that?"

"My boat. About to leave for Trikeri. Before that I was sleeping in the pizzeria."

"What's on Trikeri?"

"A woman." He looks at the sea. How can it be so flat when there's a storm brewing in his gut? "Heart attack?"

Lemonis shakes his head. "No. Can anyone verify your whereabouts this morning?"

So it's like that. The old bastard would be thrilled. "Just say it. You think I killed him."

"He was in your house."

"Good evidence. Well done, Sherlock."

"Akili, I am trying to help you."

He stops walking, looks at Detective Lemonis. Hand on hips. Legs in a wide, aggressive stance. Says, "You're a fuck-up. You keep pinning murder on the wrong people. And you're doing it again."

"I go where the evidence takes me. The neighbors said you fought the other day."

"We fought every day. Right up until I threw him out."

"Why did you throw him out?"

"Because he's been a bitter asshole my whole life. And that day I discovered he wasn't my real father, so I was no longer obligated to shelter the devil. He hadn't moved yet, so I've been staying at the pizzeria."

"He wasn't your father?"

"No. Thank the gods."

"So you hated him?"

Jesus ... "Did you know him?"

"A little. Mostly I knew of him."

"The little you knew, was it good?"

"No."

Akili tells the truth; it's not a secret anyway. "Yes, I hated him. Everybody did. Because the man was shit. But I wanted him out, not dead."

"So you say."

"It's the truth."

"You know who, in my experience, admits guilt?"

"Innocent people?"

The detective shakes his head. "Crazy people. Everyone else is innocent—especially the guilty."

Great. Perfect. The old bastard is dead and that should be the end of it. Except he's found a way to fuck up Akili's life even in death.

"What do you want from me?"

"Nothing. Yet." Detective Lemonis rubs his head. "They say you put him in that chair."

"Who?"

"People. You know how they are here."

"You're the police. You see black, you see white. Never gray. Some people are shit. And when bad things happen to them, it's because they deserve it. Sometimes the universe is just."

"Vigilante justice—"

"What happened to the men who killed your father?"

Detective Lemonis's gaze turns Arctic. His jaw hardens.

Everyone knows what happened. They don't know the how or the who, that's all.

LONG STORY SHORT, TWO BULGARIANS SHOT DETECTIVE Lemonis the elder when Detective Lemonis the younger was a high school kid. Pharmacy robbery gone wrong. The men were looking for good-time pills, until the detective interrupted them.

They never made it to trial. Guards carried breakfast in one morning, found their cell empty. No sign of a struggle. No sign of anything—unless you count a disappearing act.

Bodies showed up about a week later, bloated with seawater. Beach-goers fled the shore screaming, mistaking the men for Jaws.

Their murders are an open file nobody looks at too carefully.

"NOBODY KNOWS," LEMONIS SAYS IN HIS OWN FLIMSY defense.

"Somebody knows. And somebody knows who killed my stepfather. But not me. And not you, or you wouldn't be wasting your time."

Lemonis points at him. "Do not leave town. I would say I am sorry for your loss, but it sounds like you haven't lost anything."

"Wait—how did he ... how did he go?"

"It is a funny thing. The same way as his mother. He hanged himself, but how? A man in a wheelchair, a man paralyzed below the waist, there is no way he could have hanged himself this particular way without help."

❧ 95 ❧

Lucy

NOTHING BROKEN BUT SOME GLASSES. LUCY GRABS A BROOM and its dustpan, gets busy cleaning up after Earthquake Minor Asshole.

People should name quakes the way they do hurricanes.

Funny, the shaking didn't bother her like it used to. Things have changed. She has changed. Mostly she stopped being nine.

"I'm going to Drakia to say goodbye. Want to come?"

Grandma gives her a look. "Do snakes have legs?"

"Sure," Lucy says. "They're called lawyers."

Stelios laughs. "Lawyers, politicians, and bankers. Together they are destroying Greece."

"They're destroying everything," Grandma says. "But to answer your question: No. Your great-grandmother and I have no business together. We loved the same man—that is all."

346

It's too bad. She could use Grandma's backup. Not that she can't stand up for herself. Life's just easier with a kickstand, that's all.

"At least come for the boat ride with Stelios?"

"That I can do. It will be a pleasure."

Lucy claps. "Hooray."

❧ 96 ❧

Fotini

PERFECT DAY. THE BEST SO FAR. THE SKY IS BLUE, THE water is green, and sandwiched between the two is life. Already locals are diving for sponges, and a mixture of tourists and locals are flooding to the pebbled beaches.

This is what people here do best: live.

Stelios nudges her with his elbow. "What will we do today, Fotini?"

"Make plans."

"For what?"

"For the future, you old goat. What else?"

She should be packing. Instead, she's sitting in a boat, considering the impossible.

"You tell me, Fotini. What do you see in the future?"

"Trikeri. Maybe an old romantic fool who lives there."

"Are you talking about staying here?"

"What else?"

"But what about your home, your work? What about Lucy?"

"Lucy wants to stay. Can't you see it in her? I can. That letter from Akili changed everything, whether she realizes it yet or not."

He's giving her a strange look.

"What's wrong?" she asks.

"Nothing. I want you to stay, but I wanted to be the one to convince you. This way it is not very romantic."

"You were running out of time."

"In a romance novel, there are no big gestures until the end."

She laughs. "Stelios, we are not in a book. This is real life. And like love, real life is messy, ugly, and inconvenient at times. This is one of those times. Tomorrow I have to go back to America. I have a business, a house, a life to pack up. But I'll be back very soon—to stay."

"What will you do here?"

"Live, Stelios. I want to live."

❧ 97 ❦

Lucy

HARD TO BELIEVE IT'S THE LAST TIME SHE'LL THREAD A CAR through these mountain roads. Cornflower blue sky. Thirsty land with wide patches of cracked and peeling earth. Two weeks in Greece, she hasn't seen a hint of rain.

At least not in the sky.

Everything is wilting but the olive trees. Their roots must have mined deep down to the schisms in the rock where the water leaks from Pelion's springs.

The car inches to a stop. Her foot has its own mind; apparently it thinks the middle of the sky-bound lane is a suitable place to sit and idle.

Nuts, Lucy. You're going nuts.

Well, nuts-er.

Her foot, it seems, is waiting on a sign. And look, there's a sign.

A literal sign. It's pointing a wooden finger toward a chapel. *The Honorable Cross.*

Oh look, here's another sign. This one is a bus huffing and puffing up her ass. And honking. Also, she's not sure what the driver's hand gesture means, but it's a lot like a wave. So she shows him her open palm, four fingers and thumb spread.

YEAH, NOT A WAVE. THAT'S THE INFAMOUS GREEK *MOUTSA*, and it's got nothing to do with benevolent greetings or gentle hints about talking to the hand.

What it does have are two meanings.

In the first, you're a chronic masturbator who has gone soft in the head. All that monkey-spanking slowed down the rate at which neurons fire in you brain. The Greek equivalent of hairy palms or going blind.

In the second, the person showing you their wide open hand is rubbing metaphorical crap in your face.

SHE GETS THIS SHOW OFF THE ROAD AND ONTO A ... CAN she really call it a road? It's more like a sidewalk that used to be a dirt path, up to the moment somebody tripped and spilled their bucket of wet cement.

Greece must be hell on tires. Thank God this is just a rental.

The little car bumps and jumps along the road, until the road pools into a big patch of gray concrete sky. Standing off to the side, on a patch of wispy grass and weeds, the chapel waits to be noticed. It's the main attraction—the only attraction—yet it's acting like a wallflower.

Rough stone body. Aged beams hold up the roof on a slate

porch. Inside, standing room for a half dozen Americans or twelve Japanese tourists and their cameras. Under the porch's narrow protective arm, an ancient fresco waits for time and pollution to chip away its paint.

There's another sign pointing to the chapel from a sidewalk twisting between the olive trees.

Two paths, zero people. Well, other than Lucy.

This is what she likes about Greece: all its quiet pockets. They're all stitched to the greater garment, yet those stitches are so tiny, so neat, that the pocket lies flat. And there they wait to be discovered by the attentive and the desperate—the people who need them.

No prizes for guessing which one she is.

She kills the engine. Jumps out. Normally she'd take the civilized exit, via the door, but there's a kind of fragile magic here she doesn't want to break.

What is this place?

Yeah, yeah, she knows what the sign says ("*The Honorable Cross*"), but that's just a name. And like lots of names, it's nothing but an empty title. Doesn't say a thing about who built the chapel and why. She wants the story, the reason for its existence. Its purpose.

Grandma might know more—she grew up here, after all. But she and all her answers are on Trikeri.

As Lucy approaches the porch, she spies a small, rectangular plaque. Words, words, words. All them them Greek. How fitting. They're as mysterious as this concrete thicket and the tiny chapel.

In some far away distance, bells rattle. No chiming; they're not melodic in the churchy way. More like bells strung around a neck. Goats—maybe cows? No, not cows. Greece isn't cow-friendly. Not a lot of pastures. Too much rocky land and sparse greenery. Good for more nimble beasts. Goats and sheep.

There's the faint leathery hiss of wind stirring leaves. The air smells fresh and green. Lucy sits on the porch. Porches are for sitting, otherwise why build them?

"I don't know what to do," she tells the trees.

Their whispers continue, but they're like bitchy high school girls. They'll talk about you, but not to your face.

First Akili's a gorgeous Greek stranger, then he evolves into something more. Then they're cousins. And now they're not.

That's a crazy-making kind of change.

He wants to see her before she goes, Akili does. What's he hoping for? That they'll pick up the stitches they were forced to drop?

Can't happen. Not when tomorrow is plane-day.

Maybe they can be pen-pals, shooting emails or letters across the globe that the other can't read unless they run it through Google's wonky Translate page.

How long would it be before a day between emails became a week, a month, a lifetime?

"What would you do, Lana?"

The old woman isn't there, then she is. Wherever she's from, she arrived as silently as falling snow. She's dressed in the constant black uniform of all elderly Greek women who have lost their husbands, her hair pulled into the low bun her peers favor. Black and buns are their version of the *Uggs* and tights uniform of Lucy's generation.

Her hand is wrapped around the curved handle of a walking stick, but from the way she doesn't lean, it's more like a dramatic effect than a necessity.

"You will not find answers here."

Very English. Very cryptic.

"Know where I can find them?" Lucy asks.

The new arrival presses her hand to her forehead before turning away.

Lucy blinks, and the old woman and her stick are gone.

Maybe she vanished down that path. Or hobbled into the trees. Or …

Ghost.

Argh!

Her head freaks the hell out, but her body knows what to do:

Run.

"ARE THERE GHOSTS IN AGRIA?"

Watching *Pro-Yiayia* laugh is like watching JellO shake.

"I'll take that as a yes."

"Greece has more ghosts than people. Last week I was in the bathroom and I felt a pinch on my *kolos*. But I was alone in the bathroom."

Mental note: Need to pee? Hold it. As if the hole in the floor wasn't convincing enough.

Her great-grandmother squints at her. "Did you see a ghost?"

"No."

"So why do you ask?"

"Curiosity."

"It is good to be curious. But do not ask too many questions."

Is it just her or is that nearly a contradiction? "Why not?"

"Because most people are stupid and they have only stupid answers to give."

Having met some of the people her great-grandmother knows, Lucy thinks maybe her advice leans toward biased. Not without good reason.

"We're leaving tomorrow," she offers casually.

"Oh?"

"I might come back, someday. But not for a while, I think."

"Bah! I will be dead by then."

"Your loss."

The old woman's laugh fills her porch. "Lucy, Lucy. Finding you is like falling in love when you are old. You think life has no more surprises, then ... BAM." She smacks her hands together. "I do not want you to go. You are family. You belong here with your family."

"I have Grandma."

"And when she is gone, what then? Who else do you have?"

"Friends."

Does she?

Friends—her friends—were as substantial as mist. They stuck around for funeral *numero uno*, but by number three it was just her and Grandma standing graveside.

People know bad luck when they see it, she figures.

Pity. She misses friends. The secrets shared, the dissecting of life over coffee. When she gets home (which sounds foreign now), she needs to put herself out there, show the world some honey instead of her old vinegar. Make some new friends.

And try not to let anyone else die.

"Friends," *Pro-Yiayia* echoes. "What are friends? They come and go with the rising and falling of fortune. Stay here, Lucy." She waves her walking stick at the land she owns. "You are part of this."

"I can't," Lucy says. "Not for love or money."

IT'S A TEARFUL GOODBYE SHE SHARES WITH KATERINA. HER

cousin is made of a smoother, sweeter fabric than Lucy, but her core is a familiar steel.

"Write to me, okay?"

"Of course." Katerina nods frantically. "Do you have to go?"

"My life is there." Is it? "I have to go. But I'll be back to visit. You can even visit me."

Lucy leaves her a list. All the usual suspects on it: phone number; address; email; social media. She's not a *Facebook* fan, but everyone's on there. People who matter—people who matter to someone, but not her.

Cold? Yeah, but anyone on *Facebook* should be used to the chill and the false, warm front it shows.

She leaves Katerina with one last hug.

Katerina leaves her with a friend as well as a cousin.

❧ 98 ❧

Akili

AKILI'S SCRATCHING AT THE EARTH, HUNTING FOR ALIBIS.

People saw him. But did they *see* him? Hard to tell. He's part of this place; who notices the individual stitches in the embroidery?

They saw him, yes, but on that morning?

Eh, maybe.

Maybe not.

Most mornings are alike. And this morning was the same as the others, until the earthquake. But even in that it was not too different. Earthquakes come, earthquakes go, and life goes on. The planet will have to punch Greece's face much harder if it wants Greeks to sit up and take notice.

Detective Lemonis has been asking his questions, people tell him. They are happy to tell Akili what the detective wanted to know. Nikos Lemonis's reputation as a policeman is not exemplary. He is a good man and a good policeman from a good family, yes, but when he first points his finger at a murder suspect, people are starting to learn he has the wrong woman or man. So they know Akili did not kill his father—guaranteed.

Akili doesn't deliver the good news, that his father wasn't his father. They'll hear about it eventually. Like an octopus, information is nimble. Hide it in a sealed box and still it will escape.

His mind turns back to Lucy. Not that it's ever far away.

Oh, God. Kyria Fotini. Does she know about her brother?

He picks up the phone, dials Lemonis. Asks, "When you said don't leave town, is Trikeri on the no-go list?"

"Is this about the woman?"

"Her grandmother is my stepfather's sister."

He hears the shuffling of paper on the detective's desk. Then: "The one who went missing?"

"Not missing. She ran away. To America."

"And now she is on Trikeri?"

Lemonis sounds interested. Too interested. Warning bells clang in his head.

"Forget it, Lemonis. She's an old woman."

"Does she know her brother is dead?"

"Not that I know of."

"Then it's my responsibility to see that she knows. Stay there, Akili. In Agria."

NOT HAPPENING.

AKILI SPRINTS ACROSS THE STREET. UNLIKE HIS NAMESAKE, his heels are fine.

Hasn't been home yet, has he? Can't stand to, not when the old man killed himself there. No way is he going back in without calling a priest in to evacuate the unwanted. It would be just like the old man to hang around, flinging plates, knocking his mother's pictures off the walls.

So tonight he's sleeping on a couple of flour pallets again. This way if Lemonis throws him in jail, he'll be prepared for the mattresses.

"Akili, Akili!"

Virgin Mary, it's *Kyria* Dora. She's hurrying this way, her landmass heaving under her black dress. He waves, hoping that's enough to slam the brakes on her approach.

But like a nuclear warhead, she keeps on coming.

"I hear your father is dead!"

"Apparently."

"I am very sorry. They say you killed him. Is it true?"

He almost coughs out a laugh. The woman was born without an *edit* button. It's a common affliction around here.

"Sorry to disappoint you, but no."

"I am not disappointed, I am overjoyed!" She squeezes him in her arms. Now he knows what it's like to be on the business end of an anaconda. "If I see Detective Lemonis I will tell him you did not do it. *I* never thought you could, but you know how people are here. They like a good story about someone else's misery."

Kyria Dora is exactly how people are here. "Thank you," he says. "Excuse me, I've got to—"

"Oh, are you going to see Lucy?"

"*Kyria* Fotini."

"Fotini! Does she know?"

"Not yet."

"My Virgin Mary!" She crosses herself frantically, forehead to chest, shoulder to shoulder. "The poor woman. She comes all this way and now her brother is dead. How is your cousin?"

Her eyes shine with curiosity. Stories are like cake to this woman.

"Funny thing, she is not my cousin."

"Not your—" A light comes on. "Oh, that is right. Your mother was pregnant when they married. I had forgotten that old story. They used to say he married her so she could give her child—you—a name."

"You knew?"

"Everybody over a certain age knows. But it is an old scandal, one we keep in old, dusty boxes. We never forget the old stories, but the new stories can be a distraction."

An almost thirty-year distraction.

Great. Fantastic. Everybody knew except the one person who needed to know.

"I have to go."

"Go, Akili, go!" Her hands do that shooing thing. "What are you waiting for?"

The boat comes alive with the twist of his key. It chomps and churns the water, eager to stretch its sea legs. With almost no coaxing, it starts screaming its way across the gulf.

Is Lemonis on his way, too?

Maybe they'll pass each other.

All he knows is that *Kyria* Fotini deserves to hear the news from a friendly mouth, not some police detective with an agenda. He would have called, but you don't deliver that kind of news over the phone unless you're some kind of sadist.

Death is personal, even when the dead man is an asshole.

❧ 99 ❧

Fotini

FOTINI EXPLAINS HER PLAN TO STELIOS.

Go back to America. Pack up her belongings. Arrange for them to be shipped over. Ensure her patients are happily settled in other compassionate hands. Then fly back to Greece.

"What about your house?"

"That depends on Lucy." It's hers if she stays, otherwise it's For Sale.

Look at this view. They're outside the walls of the Virgin Mary's monastery again. Orange trees, olive trees, and the limitless sea. Boats bob on the water. From up here they're bath toys. Further out, bigger boats are starting their slow crawl away from Greece, towards wherever it is cement goes. There's a motorboat etching the gulf, on the direct path from Agria.

Coming here?

Her heart rolls over. "I think that is Akili."

"How can you tell?"

"Women's intuition."

"Ha! Women and their intuition. He must be looking for Lucy."

"Who else?" she muses. "Let us go and see."

"Be patient, Fotini. First we must ask for our miracle, eh?"

"Poor Akili," she says, following.

This time they don't linger in the courtyard. They go into the monastery, in search of the icon that stories say is miraculous.

Well, story. And it's all out of the priest's mouth—a mouth that enjoys its liquor.

The icon of the Virgin Mary is a grubby thing, resting in its frame against a clean pillar, blackened by age and handling and who knows what. A remnant of the original church, left to ruins by the island's original inhabitants in their haste to get away from pirates.

"What miracles has it performed?" she asks. Not the first time she's asked this question.

"Nobody has ever said. We should ask the priest."

Father Yiannis is in the courtyard, conferring with the decrepit caretaker. He's sober—more or less—and he looks up in surprise as they approach. "Visitors! Or should I say visitor. You're not exactly a visitor," he says to Stelios.

Stelios says, "Trikeri will soon be gaining a citizen. Fotini is moving here."

"Wonderful! I will see you every Sunday, otherwise your soul will be damned."

Don't look at Stelios, don't look at Stelios. Too late—she looked at him. His mustache jumps as he swallows his smile.

"We were wondering about the icon ..."

"Yes, it is very special." He beams at them. "Every year

people come to Trikeri for the Virgin Mary's festival. They hope for their own miracles."

"What miracles were performed?" she asks.

"Eh, miracles. Miraculous miracles, you know."

"Like what?"

The priest looks at his wrist, at the watch that isn't there. "Look at that. It is time for me to go. I have a ... a thing. Very important."

Then he scurries away.

They look at the old woman. She hurries away, too, muttering something about weeds.

"Heh." Stelios scratches his head. "I think maybe there were no miracles."

"Oh, do you think so?"

"Come, Fotini. Let us at least try for one, eh?"

WHAT MIRACLE DOES SHE WISH FOR?

Maybe they're like birthday wishes: If you speak of them they never come true.

"HERE COMES ANOTHER BOAT," SHE MUSES.

The monastery is behind them. It's a temporary farewell.

"All these people, we will be overrun." He speaks with conviction, but there is a telltale sparkle in his eyes.

"How does Trikeri cope during the festival?"

"Eh, we are peasants. Somehow we cope."

The laugh busts out of her chest.

Holding hands, they close the gap between the monastery and the *taverna*. She was correct—Akili is there pacing, and with him, wearing the face of a furious god, is a second man.

He's in his early thirties maybe. Tall. A good-looking man in a clean, chiseled way.

A policeman.

He's in plainclothes, but everything about his body language says this is a lawman. She would put good money on it.

Akili lunges toward her—stops. His hands fall slackly at his side as though he has suddenly found them boneless.

"*Kyria* Fotini—" he starts.

"*Kyria* Fotini—" the policeman says in the same moment.

She cuts into this macho dance, pre-empting them both. "Is my brother dead?"

The lawman says, "How did you know?"

Stelios is tense at her side. What an excellent guard dog he is, the dear man.

"Why else would Akili be here with a policeman? My brother is dead and you believe it was a murder."

"It could be Lucy," Stelios says.

No, it couldn't be. She would know. She remembers that feeling of loss, of an elevator floor falling away in the moment before the calls came, first with Sarah and Michael, then with Lana. When Lana passed in the hospital, she had gone to the bathroom for just a moment, leaving Lucy to witness death alone.

"No," she tells him. "It's Yiorgos."

"Detective Lemonis," the second man says.

Her memories shift around like snakes. They sound leathery, ancient. "Lemonis? Was your father a policeman, too?"

The detective nods once. "And my grandfather."

"I think I must have known your grandfather. He came when my husband was murdered."

"He was murdered?"

"Oh, yes. By my father and brother. So if my brother is dead, forgive me if I do not show grief. For him I have none."

"That is very cold, *Kyria* Fotini."

"He was an asshole."

Akili's gaze meets hers. "He was an asshole," he confirms.

"I did not know the man, but even I know he was an asshole," Stelios adds.

Detective Lemonis rubs his forehead. "*Kyria* Fotini, I have questions."

"Ask them."

"Somewhere private."

Stelios nods in the direction of his business. "Go in the *taverna*. Akili and I will stay here."

The detective points at Akili. "Do not go anywhere."

———————

THEY GO ONTO THE *TAVERNA'S* OPEN PORCH, NOT TO HER favorite table but another; why attach bad memories to good?

"Where were you yesterday morning?"

Both palms flat on the table: "I will not speak to you without my lawyer present."

"But you just agreed to answer my questions," Detective Lemons says, sounding slightly mystified.

"No. I said you could ask them. So ask them."

"But you won't answer them?"

"Do you see a lawyer?" She peers past him, shrugs. "I do not see a lawyer."

"Where is your lawyer?"

"America."

Exasperation pools on his face. "Would you consider a Greek lawyer?"

"If it is a good one."

A familiar buzz outside. The sound of the Sporades-bound ferry. It's slowing. Someone wants on or off Trikeri.

Lucy, she hopes.

A flash of spring flowers printed on white cotton. It's moving this way. Definitely Lucy, her steps springy and quick.

Lucy looks from Akili to Stelios, questions gathering on her face.

"Daughter?" Detective Lemonis asks.

"Granddaughter."

He likes what he sees, she can tell. Not just as a man, but as a cop.

"No," she says. "You leave my Lucy alone."

"*Kyria* Fotini, a man is dead. Asshole or not, it is my job to investigate."

Lucy's attention cuts to the *taverna*. She's got that take-on-the-world look about her. Her jaw is stone, her eyes cold fire.

"Lucy," she says, as her granddaughter storms into the *taverna*. "Don't say anything. Not one word without a lawyer."

Very obedient, Lucy is. Unusual for her. Which is how she knows she's about to—

Opa, there it goes. Middle fingers on both hands raised.

My Virgin Mary, this girl ...

Then Lucy grabs her hand, pulls her out of the *taverna*'s wood seat.

"I'm not—" the detective starts.

Lucy whirls around again. Performs a hand gesture she picked up ... God knows where. It's very Greek. Two hands chopping at her groin. She's telling the detective to suck it— the penis she doesn't have.

Outside, Akili and Stelios are breathless with laughter.

Detective Lemonis isn't nearly as amused. "You, you, and you." He points to everyone except Stelios. "On the boat."

Grandma translates.

Lucy shakes her head. "I want my phone call."

"Tell her she doesn't get a phone call."

"In America we get a phone call," Lucy says, hands on hips.

"Tell her she is not in America."

"Huh," Lucy says. "Is that why everybody here talks funny?"

"Fine," he says, exasperated. "Tell her she can have one call."

❧ 100 ❧

Lucy

LUCY CALLS VIVI, ASKS IF SHE KNOWS A LAWYER.

Yeah, Vivi knows a lawyer. Not a good one, she tells Lucy. But Lucy tells her at this stage a mediocre lawyer is better than no lawyer.

"It's not that he's mediocre, it's that he's an incompetent baboon who is also a crook. What's wrong? Wait—you don't have to tell me. I've been here too long. I'm getting incurably nosy."

Lucy grins into the phone. "Oh, you know. Murder, mostly.

"Oh God. Did you strangle your great-grandmother for trying to marry you off?"

Lucy tells her the short version of the bad news.

"Lemonis. That nitwit. Okay, he's not a bad detective, but he's getting a reputation. He put me in jail—and my mother.

368

Actually, he stuffed us into the same cell. As my daughter would say: Harsh."

"Is your mother that bad?"

"You met my aunt. She's like that, but with a sharper tongue."

"Jesus."

"Jesus," Vivi agrees. "Anyway, go with Lemonis. I'll have my cousin Pavlos meet you there. Sorry in advance."

❦ 101 ❦

Fotini

PAVLOS MAKRIS, THE LAWYER, REACHES INTO HER HANDBAG for loose change, using nothing but his eyes. Priest dipped him into the baptismal oil and water when he was an infant, and somehow he never dried out. Even his suit has that same slimy sheen.

"You must be Fotini and Lucy and ... I know you." His mind wanders off, in search of answers. "You own the pizza place. *Akili's Pizza*. What is your name?"

"Akili."

He snaps his fingers. "That is right! Very good pizza. Maybe you give me a free one, yes? Okay—" He looks at Detective Lemonis. "—what did they do?"

"His father—" He nods at Akili. "—is dead."

"Okay. And? Because people die all the time. Even now, someone, somewhere, is dying. None of us escapes life alive." Looks proud of himself, doesn't he?

"The manner of death is questionable."

"Oh? How did he die?"

"Hanging by the neck."

Pavlos scratches his nose with his pinky nail, inspects it when he's done. "Okay. I remember the last time somebody in Agria was found hanging from a tree. It was suicide, but you called it murder and arrested my aunt and cousin."

"I had reason to believe they were involved."

"And you have reason to believe these three are involved now?"

"They would not be here if I didn't."

"Okay." He looks at the three of them, picks up his brief-case. "Who is going first?"

Fotini raises her hand. Age before beauty, she thinks. Give Akili and Lucy a little time alone.

Very nice room. They spared no expense. What does it cost, she wonders, to decorate a room using the despair palette?

She sits in the cold chair at the equally cold table. Every-thing in the room is metal, except for the people. And she's not convinced Detective Lemonis isn't a robot.

Pavlos is greasy, yes, but he doesn't slide off the chair when he sits. "Do not speak to this man," he reminds her. He nods at the detective. "Ask your questions. Maybe she will answer them. Maybe not."

"They're only questions."

Pavlos gives him the stink eye.

"Where were you this morning?"

She looks at the lawyer. He shrugs. Very helpful.

"I went to the mainland."

"To Agria?"

"Objection!"

Detective Lemonis sighs like Pavlos is busting his balls. "This is not a courtroom."

"Have you ever been in a courtroom?" she asks her lawyer.

"Many times," Pavlos says. "I go all the time to watch."

"To watch?"

"Yes, to watch."

"Have you ever tried a case?"

"Uh ..." Shifty eyes. So confidence-inspiring. "One time I was very close. Then my client killed himself with a shoelace. But," he says quickly, "I have watched many cases—in the courtroom and on TV. I have seen every episode of *Judging Amy* and *LA Law*."

"*Kyria* Fotini," the detective says, ignoring the idiot in the room, "were you in Agria that morning?"

"Yes."

"Did you see the deceased?"

"Do not answer that!" Pavlos jumps out of his seat. "He is trying to trick you."

"I'm not a lawyer," Lemonis says. "I'm a policeman."

"Ha-ha. Very good joke."

"Wasn't a joke."

"If I had known I was coming to the circus," she says. "I would have brought peanuts."

But are they listening to her?

No.

They're too busy comparing metaphorical penises. Whose is bigger, she can't tell. But the crooked one definitely belongs to Pavlos. If he has a law degree, they gave it to him out of pity, just so he would go away and let the lawyers do law.

"The last time I saw my brother he was alive," she tells them. "That is all I know."

"*Po-po.*" Pavlos waves his arms in the air. "What did I say? Do not say anything."

Lemonis ignores him. "When was that?"

"Early this morning."

"And you haven't seen him since?"

"And you haven't seen him since?" Pavlos repeats it in a mocking, girlish tone.

"No," she says.

"You came all the way to Greece and you saw him how many times?"

"Two. The first was by accident."

"But this is family—the only family you have."

"My brother is—was—not family. He was blood, that is all. Blood does not make a person family. My granddaughter is the only family I have.

"Witnesses place you leaving the Dukakis house just before the earthquake."

Somewhere deep inside her, a door slams. One with bars of unforgiving steel. How will they make their plane now?

How will she keep her promise to Stelios?

They won't. She can't.

"I think I will wait for a real lawyer," she says slowly.

Pavlos launches a protest. "I am a real lawyer!"

"Maybe one who did not get his degree from a *Cracker Jack's* box."

"Cracker Jack?"

She gives him a look—one that doesn't end in a retainer.

❦ 102 ❧

Lucy

PAVLOS LEAVES IN A HUFF. HE DOESN'T KNOW WHAT A *Cracker Jack's* box is, but that's not where he got his law degree, he mutters on the way out.

Neat, she's going in sans lawyer. This can only end well. The detective leads her into one of those rooms with the two-way mirrors. She waves just in case someone's watching.

"I don't speak Greek, so it's pointless asking me anything."

"Good thing I speak English," Detective Lemonis says.

Huh. How about that. She can't throw a rock without hitting an English-speaking Greek between the eyes.

"Lucky."

No, not lucky at all. She was hoping for a fast escape on a technicality. Not that she did it, but she's seen all the TV shows. This cramped room with its metal chairs and table, and its depressing paint job, is a Venus flytrap. Drag some poor chump (like, uh, her) into this room and you're not coming out without cuffs, unless you live under some kind of lucky star.

"When was the last time you saw your uncle?"

"Great-uncle. The first and only time I saw him. We never actually met."

"When was that?"

"Last week. I don't remember which day. They kind of blur when you're on vacation."

He smiles but it's a lie, just like his easygoing manner. He's got a dead body and an empty cell. All he needs is someone to fill the barred room at his inn.

It's not going to be her and it's not going to be Grandma. Or Akili.

Loyalty, for Lucy, is a lifetime contract.

"So you were not on the mainland today?"

"In the afternoon, yeah. In the morning I was on Trikeri."

"And your grandmother?"

"She was out walking when I got up."

"So she was not there?"

"Not in our room."

"She was walking on the island?"

"As far as I know," she says, hoping he swallows it.

"Your grandmother told me she was in Agria."

Oh. Shit.

So she shrugs. "Long walk, I guess."

"How did she seem when she came back?"

"Like Grandma."

"Elucidate, please."

She cocks her head. "That's a big word. Did you eat a dictionary?"

✻ 103 ✻

Akili

AKILI WALKS INTO THE ROOM ALONE. ONLY ARMOR HE'S wearing is shorts and a T-shirt.

Detective Lemonis doesn't waste time. Which is funny, because here he is wasting time with Akili—again.

"Did you kill your father?"

"No."

"Did you want to?"

"Everyone who ever met him wanted to kill him. He was that kind of man."

"Did you want to?"

"A long time ago."

"Why?"

No weakness in him. Back straight, head up, body in the upright and relaxed position. "He was a terrible husband."

"A bad father?"

"To be a bad father you have to be a father first."

"How was he a terrible husband?"

"He beat my mother like it was his work."

"So, not a good man?"

He casts a stone at the deep pool that is his memory, watches the ripples. Looks for a variation in the theme. Nothing. Not one moment where his stepfather was a father of any value.

"The only good thing he ever did was die. The tragedy of it is that he didn't go before my mother."

Lemonis arches his back, yawns. "Tell me about your father's accident."

"Accident?"

"How did he end up disabled?"

"He fell."

"How did he fall? What were the circumstances?"

Akili shrugs. Tries staying casual, cool. The circumstances of the bastard's accident were his own fault. Self-inflicted.

Hit a woman often enough, don't be surprised if a fist comes out of the sky to strike you down. That's what happened. Akili wasn't the fist of God; his was the fist of a son finally big enough to change his mother's fortune.

Payday. The bastard came home with the same-old yellow envelope in his pocket. No checks back then; his company paid cash. He would carefully dish out enough money for the groceries, then the rest he'd tuck away for good times.

Good times meant going down to the *taverna* or *kafeneio*, playing *Pro-Po* and talking shit with the other men. No wife, no child.

A wife and child were not 'good times'.

That day, his mother asked for a little extra. Sixteen-year-old Akili had outgrown his sneakers.

"Maybe if he wasn't so fat he would not outgrow his shoes so fast, eh?"

That's what he said. Akili's mind sealed that one in shrink-wrap so he'd never forget.

Mama leaped to his defense with her usual battle cry, that Akili would lose the weight when he joined the army.

"I do not work hard so the boy can get fat on my drachma."

"I know," Mama had said, in that tone Akili hated. It was the sound of words with the soul punched out of them.

"Oh, you know do you? What do you know?"

"That you work hard," she said.

"What else do you know?"

A long pause, then: "I don't know."

Akili stood in the dim, narrow hallway, clinging to the wall like a cobweb. Usually he waited for the bastard to leave before sneaking in to comfort his mother. He had to creep in quietly, approach her the way one approaches a skittish horse. Otherwise she would turn her face away, claim she was fine.

But that day he was not waiting on the bastard to leave. Akili was waiting for his father to raise his hand, so he could cut it out of the sky.

"You know nothing," the bastard said. "Nothing!"

"I know."

"The boy is fat. But you keep feeding him and feeding him. Enough. He is old enough to leave school and get a job. If it was good enough for me, it is good enough for him."

"I want—"

"Oh, what do you want?"

Her voice tripped over itself and the words spilled out. "I want him to finish school, to be something more."

"Something more, eh? Something more than who? Me? Am I not good enough for you? You want a fancy man, works in an office and has soft hands and a fat belly? Okay, take your fat son and go look for a fancy man. A *gomenos* to put food on the table for the two of you. And for what? What will he get?

A fat boy and a woman who looks old and cannot satisfy him in bed. What a prize the two of you are."

"Stop it," she whispered. Not to him. Maybe to herself.

Akili believed it was a prayer for him to intervene.

"You want me to stop? *Make me*."

There's a silence that comes before a fist flies. A hitch in the fabric of time. A moment where the mind must process the trigger before it releases its hounds.

That silence, that hitch, that moment—Akili knew them intimately.

Like a cannon ball, he rushed into the kitchen, tackling the bastard on his way through. That chickenshit asshole folded, but Akili beat him flat with his fists. And when he got up, charged his stepson, Akili stepped aside, let him fly—then fall—through the open door. The concrete steps snapped him in two.

He recounts every gritty, sordid detail, lays every word on the metal table in neat, invisible rows. Lemonis soaks up his story, saying nothing, doing nothing.

"Now you know. The question is, what will you do with this knowledge?"

Nothing from the detective, at first. Just a long, uncomfortable pause during which he taps his pen on the table.

"What you said the other day is true. The law is not gray. There any many times I have wished it was. It is black and it is white, with nothing in between. Guilty or innocent. Convicted or acquitted."

"Virgin Mary, is this an interrogation room or an amphitheater? Enough of the philosophical soliloquy."

❧ 104 ❧

Lucy

THREE WISE MEN?

Nope.

Three Amigos?

Nope.

Three musketeers?

Nope.

"We're the three smart-asses," Lucy says.

Akili, of course, just looks at her, because he hasn't got clue one what she's babbling about. Good thing she's got Grandma here to fill him in. Which she does.

Akili laughs. He looks good in a cell, stretched out on his bed. If she can call it a bed. From here (which, granted, isn't far) it looks like a sack stretched over concrete. There's even a pillow that bears an uncanny resemblance to a bag of landscaping lava rocks.

Greece's austerity measures, folks.

What's for eats? Water mixed with gypsum? Yum, yum.

Bunks for her and Grandma. Double the concrete sacks, double the lava rocks. She's already called dibs on the top, mostly out of decency, but also because the view is better up here.

Yes, the view of Akili.

Hey, he's back to being the hot guy again, now that they're no longer clinging to the same family tree. And he is hot. Very sexy. He's tanned and fit and she can't tear her eyes away from the ink on his arms or the golden ropes that have twisted them into originals.

It's a two-way street between the bars, because he's having a hard time peeling his gaze off her, too.

That detective is an idiot. There's no way he or Grandma killed anybody. She definitely knows she didn't do it—unless someone else borrowed her body without her say-so, and that doesn't happen except in science fiction. Which begs the question: Who killed her great-uncle?

"Who do you think did it?"

"Give me a minute and I will call the psychic hotline," Grandma says. "Maybe that nice Dionne Warwick will answer."

"You do that," Lucy says. "Does Akili know?"

They exchange a few words. "He says he will call the psychic hotline and let you know."

Ha-ha. "Well I don't know. In case you were both wondering."

"That is too bad; we were relying on you to tell us."

"Professor Plum in the Library with the candlestick."

"Very logical. You should tell Detective Lemonis. Then maybe he will let us all go."

"Forget it," Lucy says. "I don't think any of us are really in here for murder. He's teaching us a lesson, that's all."

"And what is the lesson?"

"Don't be a smart-ass."

🕊 105 🕊

Fotini

SHE'S A DOUBLE ADAPTER, PASSING THE CURRENT TO TWO devices: Lucy and Akili.

That is okay though. The distraction they provide is a welcome one. It keeps her mind off other problems, like the airplane that's leaving tomorrow, minus two pilgrims.

Poor Stelios, what must he think of them now?

Although knowing that old goat and his penchant for romance, he will show up after midnight with a rope and a truck, intending to set them free.

❧ 106 ❧

Fotini

THERE'S A KERFUFFLE OUT IN THE HALLWAY. IT'S MOVING this way.

Keys rattle. The door flies open, ricocheting off the wall. It has no choice—it's being driven by a walking stick.

In walks Katerina Manatos, Iason's mother, the constable flitting around behind her. Poor bastard, he's following a tornado and he doesn't know it.

"Lucy, my love," the old woman says, "why are you in jail?"

"I tripped."

"On what?"

Lucy shrugs. "An asshole."

Fotini shoots her granddaughter a warning look. Not Iason's mother; she roars with laughter. "Did you hear that Lemonis?" she yells down the hallway. "You are an asshole."

His voice comes back filtered, thin. "So they say."

"He is an asshole, yes, but a small one."

"I heard that," Lemonis calls out.

"Very good hearing, that one. You would think he could put the right person in jail."

The constable steps around the old woman to shove his key in the lock. With a shudder and a long litany of complaints, the door slides open. "The girl and Akili can go. Detective Lemonis needs to you stay."

Worse than she hoped; better than she feared.

Lucy looks at her. "That wasn't an apology, was it?"

"Oh, Lucy. You and Akili can go. I have to stay." Her smile quivers. "But I will be out soon, I promise."

"You can't stay here!" She wheels around on the constable, on *Pro-Yiayia*. "She can't stay here. We're going home tomorrow."

"Lucy ..." Grandma says gently.

"No. You're coming, too. Or I'm not going anywhere."

To prove her point, Lucy wraps her arms around the bars in a big bear hug. "You stay, I stay."

"That's not how it works."

"If you ask me, Greece seems like a place where they make up the rules as they go along, so they can just ... just ... make a new one!"

She's got a death-grip on those bars. She's never letting go —ever. But the constable, he seems like he's used to resistance. Normally he's trying to persuade people into the cell, not out, but it's all the same muscle. One at a time, he unpicks Lucy's fingers.

"Ouch," she says. "The police are abusing me. Anyone got a phone? Film it! I'm putting it on *YouTube* so people know."

Grandma asks, "Know what, my love?"

"That Greeks hate Americans."

"Greeks don't hate Americans, Lucy." She crouches down, close to where the constable is working to break her free. He'd have an easier time shucking oysters with a bobby pin. "Hurt her," she tells the man, "and I will cut out your heart."

"With what?"

"My hands. Did you see the second *Indiana Jones* movie?"

"It was terrible."

"It was terrible, but the heart scene was good, no? That is how I will do it."

He lets Lucy go, crab-walks to the open door. "Lemonis? These people are crazy."

There's a pause, then: "Who has the gun, Constable?"

"I do."

"Then where is the problem?"

Great pep talk. Succinct. Now the constable is all puffed up and ready to shovel Lucy out of here. He thrusts his arms under her armpits, pulls.

"He touched my boob," Lucy hollers.

She's about to leap to her granddaughter's defense (verbally, because physically, last time she looked she was on the wrong side of these bars) when Iason's mother rains her walking stick on the groping cop.

"It was an accident," he cries.

"So is this," the old woman says, whacking him again. "For this I pay taxes, to employ molesters?"

Lemonis's voice wanders down the hall. "Are you beating my constable?"

"Only a little, and only because he deserves it," *Kyria* Manatou the elder calls out.

"Jesus Christ," he mutters. A moment later he appears in the open doorway. "Get her out of here." Not saying it to the women, to her blood, but to Akili.

Fotini's okay with that. If anyone can get Lucy out of here, it's Akili. That's a good thing. It's about time somebody other than the dead had influence over her.

Elbowing the constable out of his way, Akili touches

Lucy's shoulder. The effect is immediate: Lucy relaxes into a howling heap.

"Listen to me, Lucy," Fotini says. "Listen. You will be more useful to me out there than in here. Do you understand?"

Nodding. Lots of nodding. Good.

"Go," she tells Akili. "Take care of her. And tell that old goat Stelios that I miss his face.

❧ 107 ❧

Lucy

"Tonight we drink!" The priest speaks in broken English, raises his glass to God knows who.

Stelios winks at her. But does she appreciate way he's trying to keep things normal? Sort of. "Every night you drink, Father," he says.

"You would too if you were stuck on this island."

"You can leave anytime, my friend. The ferry passes every day."

"The church has trapped me here. Trikeri is a mousetrap." He fixes his attention on Lucy. "Do you want to know a secret?"

Lucy leans in closer. Does she want to know a secret? Hell yeah.

"There are no miracles," he says.

"No!" Stelios's eyes open wide. His mouth forms an O of

surprise—what she can see of it beneath the mustache. "That cannot be true."

"It is true, I swear on it." He crosses himself, kisses his own ring. "And I am a man of God, so you know my word is good."

Except for the whole thing where he lies to people about the miracles, his word is solid. Because priests are known for their integrity. Ask the Catholic Church. Ask that Haggard clown back home with the meth problem and the penchant for penis. Up until the *gotcha* moment, that guy was adamant gays were doomed to burn.

The priest does a palms up. "I do not want to lie about the miracles, but it is the only thing that brings money to Trikeri. The tourists come—"

"Almost none of them," Stelios says.

"—the festival comes—"

"Once a year," Stelios says.

"—people come from all over—"

"No," Stelios says, shaking his head. "Only local people and tourists come."

"—to pray for a miracle."

"If they come, they come to drink and eat. They don't know about any miracles."

The priest squints at Stelios. "Did you say something?"

"Who me? No. I am a very quiet man. Lucy?"

"Very quiet. Like a mouse."

"Hmm ... I thought I heard you say something."

"Ghosts," Stelios says. "They talk too much."

A boat docks, then Akili swaggers in wearing jeans and a tight T-shirt. His gaze glues itself to her face. He says something—God knows what. Does it matter?

Nope.

She leaps up, grabs his arm, pulls him out of the *taverna*.

"Later." She aims the word over her shoulder.

"Much later, I hope," Stelios says, big smile on his face.

"Remember, God is watching you," the priest calls out. "So keep your legs together."

———

AT NIGHT, TRIKERI IS A HONEYCOMB OF DARK AND SECRET places. The lights from the shore form a tiny constellation, but they're no match for the blazing pinpricks in the heavens. Who can look at the land when there's so much sky?

Somewhere between the lights and the monastery, Lucy stops dead.

This is the place. Here.

Sticks and stones won't break her bones, but she kicks them aside anyway. She's never been the kind of person anyone's accused of having a stick up her ass.

When the ground is clear—more or less—she lies flat on the ground, hands behind her head. Got herself a front row seat to watch the stars.

The air shifts as Akili drops down beside her, mirroring her move.

His hand finds hers. He says something too Greek for her to get.

"Don't talk," she whispers. "Just fuck me."

Not exactly romantic, but romance isn't what she needs right now.

His head turns. Yeah, it's dark, but she can see the question in his eyes.

"Want something done right," she mutters, "do it yourself."

In a flash, she's straddling him, hands either side of his head.

There's no way he's not reading this particular body language. She's as subtle as a klaxon. Maybe his head hasn't received the memo, but his cock knows. It's making all the right moves, heading north for the oncoming tsunami. He's harder than some of those stones she kicked away.

She tugs on her dress, drags it over her head. Casts it aside like a fishing net. Should be obvious by now what she's fishing for.

Ah, now he gets it. Either that or she's given the kind of consent he understands. Whatever. Now his hands are starting to roam. They're going places—and those places are all on her. He's traveling her plains with his hot, hot hands. Very nomadic. Very sexy. Trikeri's temperature is falling but hers is rising.

Don't stop, she thinks. Don't stop.

He doesn't stop. The man's just getting started.

THE STARS WATCH THEM SHINE.

Somewhere across the sea, a caged woman is hoping they're making freedom worthwhile.

They are.

❧ 108 ❧

Lucy

WHEN LUCY TALKS, IT'S TO THE NIGHT AS MUCH AS the man.

"I'm staying in Greece, at least until Grandma can go home with me. I won't leave her. I won't."

They're almost seamless, she and Akili. When he breathes, she breathes.

Is this how it always is? Her memory is shoddy.

There have been other guys, but this is the first time she can recall synchronicity. Too bad this is going nowhere. If they spoke the same language they'd have a shot at something. But relationships are tough enough without having to rely on sign language and *Pictionary*.

The thought, when it comes, is unwelcome. But that's how reality can be. Truth doesn't show up in soft, woolen coats; it prefers nudity, no matter that most of the time it really should throw some clothes on that mess.

Grandma could be in jail for a while. Not a few days, weeks, months.

Longer.

Years.

The word sticks in her throat, like a wad of warm gum.

Years.

And Lucy will be here in Greece with her life on pause, waiting on Grandma to come home.

Grandma won't want her to stay. She'll tell her to go—go back to America and live.

But right now, with Akili hot against her skin, it's occurring to her that the nice thing about life is that it can be lived anywhere. When it comes to location, life isn't picky. Here or there, it rolls on down that road, until it hits a wall.

There could be time to learn Greek, maybe teach Akili some English, too. Time to get to know Katerina and *Pro-Yiayia* and the rest of her family.

Obstacles? Yeah, there are obstacles, too.

Where is she going to live? She can't stay indefinitely at the hotel.

And what about work? Fresh air is wonderful, but it doesn't sate the appetite or keep the electricity running.

"What am I going to do for money?"

Akili rolls her over, pins her to the ground, shows her that all those under-endowed statues must have been modeled on very cold men.

Well she can't do *that* for money, but she can definitely do it for fun.

❧ 109 ❧

Fotini

AMAZING HOW MANY DIFFERENT WAYS THE DETECTIVE CAN ask the same questions.

She has another lawyer now, a better one, with bigger, sharper teeth and a law degree that wasn't the educational equivalent of pity sex. Her lawyer lunges across the table barking, whenever Lemonis steps across an invisible line.

Detective Lemonis is a man who crosses that line easily and repeatedly.

But in the end there is nothing she can say to convince him that hers were not the hands that elevated her brother to his dying place.

She thinks about the boy she knew, the teenager he became, the sour blood they shared. The murder he did with their father.

He had it in him, didn't he? The ability to deceive.

Out of (almost) nowhere she says, "Who said he was crippled?"

The detective jerks his head up from the file he's scratching in. "Excuse me?"

"Fotini, say nothing." Her lawyer moves into the protective position.

"No," she tells the lawyer. "Who was the doctor who said my brother was crippled?"

"*Kyria* Manatou, he had been in that chair for years. Everybody knew he could not walk."

"You didn't know him—not like I knew him. Our father ... he ... he did something to my brother. By the time I left Greece, he was capable of anything, even long-term deceit."

Lemonis looks alert, interested. "What are you saying?"

"I do not think he was crippled. Maybe he was at first, when the doctor diagnosed him. But if he was, I think he got better."

"What for? Why would a guy do that?"

"Because like our father, he was a manipulative asshole. He collected benefits, he had a wife to wait on him, and when she passed, he had a son who was too guilty to throw him out on the street with the rest of the garbage."

"Fotini—" the lawyer starts.

"Let me speak! I didn't kill him. All I did that day was talk to him. I told him was a piece of shit he was, what a waste of oxygen, how I couldn't be bothered hating him anymore because he wasn't worth hating. But I did not kill him or help him kill himself."

"So you say. But all of this—" Lemonis thumps a knuckle on the file. "—says he could not have done it alone unless he was an able-bodied man."

"Then he was able-bodied!"

"Not according to his doctors."

She swivels in her seat, faces her lawyer. "Can you believe this clown? Is he deaf?"

This, she thinks, is where Lucy gets it from: Her.

Her education, her training, her years counseling others on so many issues, including anger management, and this is what it comes down to: insulting a police detective.

But the man is a bonehead. He's turning down a solid lead for the easy catch. As little crime as this place sees, she figured he'd relish the chance to flex his police muscles.

❧ 110 ❧

The JFK-bound plane leaves without them.

❄ III ❄

Lucy

LUCY WANTS TO PUNCH GREECE IN THE FACE.

Well, its legal system. And a certain detective.

She considers crying, but Stelios doesn't need that. He's too good to her, with his endless cups of coffee and cheerful quotes, ripped directly, most likely, out of one romance novel or another.

"She will go on. You will see."

And: "The truth will set her free."

Hokey, but sweet. He's a good man—a good fit for Grandma. He tells her about his ex wife, and she tells him about the mother, father, and sister she lost.

Not easy conversations, but these aren't easy times.

Eventually he gets to the meat. "What are your plans, Lucy?"

There are no plans—only one plan.

"I'm staying. There's no way I'm leaving Grandma."

"You know what she would say."

"I know."

"But you think she is wrong."

"Of course she's wrong!"

He chuckles, but it's half-hearted. Like hers, one atrium, one ventricle are dented. "I think she is wrong, too. Stay, Lucy. Stay. Take whichever room you wish." He pokes a finger at the ceiling. "It's yours. No cost."

"That's very sweet of you, but—"

"Take it. You and Fotini, you are like family to me now. I would not know what to do with myself without you here."

There's something in her eyes. It's hot, wet, and it's tied to the hurting in her heart and this man's overwhelming generosity.

"Thank you," she says, reaching for his hands.

"Bah. It is nothing. I only wish I could do more."

"It means the world to me. And it will to Grandma, too."

❧ 112 ❧

Akili

Kyria Fotini's lawyer is well-seasoned in her solemn suit and her expensive briefcase. She waits patiently in the pizzeria until there's a lull.

But before that, he makes sure she has something to drink, something to eat.

"Fotini—*Kyria* Manatou—mentioned something interesting today. She questioned whether or not your father was in fact disabled."

Interesting. So interesting he drops the tin he's oiling. He's considered a million scenarios, but not this one.

"If he wasn't, why did the doctor say he was?"

"Perhaps he was in the beginning, but the injury later healed?"

"It's possible." He groans, picks up the tin and continues the oiling. "Now that I think about it, that would be just like him."

400

"Lemonis discounted the possibility immediately, of course. It sounds convenient and far-fetched. That man would fake such a severe disability for all these years, it's the kind of thing that happens in movies or books—not real life. *Kyria* Manatou suggested that your brother did, in fact, commit suicide on his own, with his whole and uninjured self as an accomplice."

"There's no way to verify now, is there?"

"I am not a doctor, but I suspect not. Still, it is interesting, yes?"

Yes.

***

DR PAPADOPOULOS (MEDICAL DOCTOR AND VETERINARIAN) laughs. "What a story you are telling me. Who does such a thing? Pretend to be crippled for more than ten years—bah!"

Akili's stepfather, that's who. The more he thinks about it, the more plausible it gets.

"So you would have known if he was lying?"

"Of course!"

"How?"

The doctor/veterinarian's brain blips, his eyes blink. He's formulating an excuse. "Uh ... I am sure I would have known. Who tells those lies?"

"A psychopath?"

"Your father was not a psychopath. He was a sick, old man who could not walk—and had not walked in over ten years. His muscle tone was poor, consistent with his condition. He did not respond to the usual tests."

"What tests?"

"I will show you."

The doctor grabs a blunt rubber tomahawk, slams it on Akili's knee.

His leg jerks up—hard. Nails the mustachioed doctor in the balls.

Now they're both tearing up, howling at the ceiling.

"That," the doctor says. "That is what your father did not do."

"Did you hit him that hard?"

"No, he was a patient. Patients are money. You are just a man with a ridiculous theory. You I hit hard."

Yeah, yeah. "And nothing?"

"Nothing. He was dead from the waist down."

"Did you check him again recently?"

"What for? That injury does not fix itself."

"What if it did?"

"I would want to know where he went to pray and how much money he paid for his candles."

CANDLES: THEY'RE OMNIPRESENT IN GREEK ORTHODOX churches. They're long, thin, and the color of teeth after too many years swilling coffee and sucking cigarettes. They're there when you enter the church, hanging about like a mute *Walmart* greeter, often piled in a wooden box. Beside them, you'll find a one-armed stand, holding up a shallow, flat-bottomed bowl that tends to come in two shapes: rectangular or round.

Pick one (or more) out of the box, touch its single strand of hair to one of the already-burning candles, then say a silent prayer as you push its bottom into the sandpit.

See that second box? The one with the narrow mouth and the padlocked lid? Go ahead, put your money in there. It's quite safe-ish.

NICE NOT BEING ON THE SUSPECT LIST. TOO BAD THEY'RE using *Kyria* Fotini as a placeholder for the real criminal.

Akili's got things to say, and the person he's got to say them to is Detective Lemonis.

He finds the detective in his office, shuffling paper from one side of the desk to the other. The world is computerized —Greece is computerized—but still it trusts only the written word.

"You're a *kolos*, Lemonis."

"*Kalimera* to you, too, Akili. What do you want?"

He leans against the open doorway, arms folded. "Figured I'd come see if you're doing your job."

"Does it look like I'm doing my job?"

"No. Looks to me like you're procrastinating. Meanwhile I've been out doing your job."

"What job is that?"

"The one you're not doing—talking to people."

"Who have you been talking to?"

"Nobody. The old man's doctor."

"Nobody," he mutters. "What did he say?"

"Nothing that can help *Kyria* Fotini."

"I think the only person who can help her is dead," Lemonis says, "that is what I think."

"Can you—"

He shakes his head, shifts another folder in the pile. "You know I can't."

"Won't."

"Can't. I report to people higher up. I cannot go to them with suspicions and conjecture."

"There is reasonable doubt."

"That is for juries and judges, not the police."

"You serve the people, but you are not serving them now. What good are you?"

"Sometimes I wonder," Lemonis mutters.

✺ 113 ✺

Lucy

LUCY CHOOSES THE ROOM CLOSEST TO THE SEA. IT'S slightly smaller than the other, but how much space does she need? All she has is a suitcase full of clothes and herself.

It's sweet of Stelios to let her stay. Whether he knows it or not, as soon as she finds work she's going to pay him for the room. After all, she is biting into his business. It's only fair, after all he's done for her.

The phone downstairs rings. A moment later, Stelios hollers her name.

"It's your grandmother," he says.

She flies down the stairs. It is Grandma—she sounds just like home.

"Can you come and see me?"

"Of course. I'm coming right over."

"Bring Stelios, too, okay?"

"Okay, sure. Anything else?"

"No, my love. I just want to see you."

They're halfway across the sea when the strangeness in Grandma's tone strikes her. She's heard it before, in the days before Lana died.

A icicle slides between her ribs, plunging its tip into her heart. She learns forward, over the boat's bow, willing the vessel to fly faster.

❧ 114 ❧

Fotini

THE LAWYER COMES WITH NEWS. NOT GOOD NEWS, BUT news. They are moving her to Volos tomorrow, where there is room for her to await her trial. If they find her guilty, she will go to the women's prison in Thiva, an hour north of Athens. Acquitted? Then she can go home.

"When is the trial?"

"I do not have a date yet."

"Can you guess?"

"Six months. Maybe more."

Six months.

Her brother, her father, they have won.

💥 115 💥

Lucy

THERE'S A ONE-WOMAN TRAFFIC JAM WHEN THEY REACH land in Agria. *Kyria* Dora rolls toward them, gathering speed as she goes.

"Lucy! Who is your friend?"

Oh God, seriously?

It's not that she doesn't like *Kyria* Dora—who can help liking her? Despite the black wardrobe she's one of Greece's most colorful creatures.

But her timing is *le* suck.

"I can't talk now, I'm sorry. We have to go."

"Is it your grandmother?"

"Yes."

"I will pray for her," *Kyria* Dora calls out.

Sweet, but what *Kyria* Dora is really praying for is a good story.

ONLY TWO DAYS, BUT GRANDMA HAS LOST WEIGHT.

"I want you to go home," she says, her voice titanium hard. "Go home and live your life."

Lucy looks at Stelios. "Didn't I tell you?"

"You told me."

"And what did I say?"

"No.

"Exactly." She reaches across the table for her grandmother's hands. "We've had this conversation, except we had it without you. I'm staying until we can go home together."

"No. I will not allow you to put your life on hold."

"Oh, you won't allow it?" Lucy asks. "Who is going to stop me? You?"

"This girl," Grandma says, muttering to Stelios.

❧ 116 ❧

Fotini

MORNING COMES. IT HAS A CRISP EDGE THAT SAYS SUMMER won't be a burden for too much longer. Even in this cell there's a hint of dying leaves and the sweetness of the grape, reaching its peak. This is plucking season. All Greek wine is birthed at this time of year.

She's contemplating her own eventual demise—probably in a cold, cramped Greek prison—when the constable flings the door open.

"You have a visitor."

"Who—"

The older *Kyria* Manatou. Her former mother-in-law. She's here with her eagle eyes and her sharp tongue, scanning the cell as if she expected to find herself someplace less institutional. Lady, Fotini thinks, this is jail, not the *Sheraton*.

"So you are still here? It is a good thing the bars are vertical. They make your *kolos* look smaller." The constable brings in a chair. She and her big, black handbag settle on its lap.

"You look like a piece of coal in all that black."

The old woman laughs. "That is Greek women for you. We start as diamonds, then with age we become coal."

"Did you come to gloat?"

"For what?" Genuine surprise. "You are not my enemy. There is a long list of people I want to see in jail before you."

Why be anything except blunt? *Kyria* Manatou is not a woman who needs the baseball bat wrapped in cotton wool. "What do you want?"

"I came to get you out of here."

"Forget it. I am not your business, old woman."

"I am not your business," she mimics. "Of course you are my business. You were my son's wife. You gave him a child and a grandchild. And you gave me a great-granddaughter. In return, I will give you freedom."

No.

Who is this woman that she can trust her? She is not just Greek, she is an adversary, one of the voices that stood against her marriage to Iason.

"What's the price?"

The old woman shrugs. "It does not look good for the family if you are in prison."

"So this is all about appearances." Funny. Too bad all she can manage is a laugh that sounds suspiciously like a dog getting ready to vomit.

"Some of it, but not all." She leans forward, dark, watery eyes fixed on Fotini's. "I want Lucy to stay in Greece."

Of course she does. Who would not want to keep Lucy?

"That is Lucy's choice. I cannot make her do anything."

This is a game, part strategy, part luck. The bastard offspring of poker and chess. Lucy has already made up her mind, but she doesn't tell the older woman that.

The old woman scoffs, slaps her knee with one gnarled hand. "You have more influence over her than anyone. It is time for her to know her Greek family, to learn the family business. I am old, Fotini. I joke about immortality, but we both know my end cannot be too far away. When I go, I want the girls in the family to run the business—Katerina and Lucy. The boys are not nearly as clever. They like the money, but not the hard work. There will be plenty of money for them, but my granddaughter and great-granddaughter will have the power."

Fotini isn't blind. If this opportunity is real, it is golden. Like *Kyria* Manatou, she won't be around forever. Here Lucy has people who are hers.

Here Lucy has a chance.

But does she have choices?

"What if she says no?"

"Then it is up to us to convince her to say yes."

"I cannot—will not—manipulate her. Manipulation is not love." Lucy is her heart.

What to do?

"Manipulation is life." *Kyria* Manatou taps her walking stick on the floor. "I am manipulating you right now. If you do as I wish, you win your freedom. And are you not manipulating me, trying to get something for nothing?"

Fotini does the math. She can't find an answer that adds up to one old woman holding enough power to sway the police.

"You're a family of farmers. You grow things and then sell those things. How can you possibly have enough influence to have them release me?"

The old woman smiles. It's the wide opening of genuine delight—a winner's smile. "Greece is starving, and money is a very big cake. The imprisonment of one woman who took

411

out the garbage is of less value than my ... Let us call it a donation."

"We are two old women, let us call it what it is: a bribe."

"I like you, Fotini." Her once-mother-in-law rocks back in the chair. "It is good to be honest with someone. Some people never meet a soul with whom they can be honest. We could all be a family." She reaches into the handbag on her lap, pulls out a sheet of paper, offers it to Fotini.

"What is it?"

"Is your vision that bad? *Po-po* ..."

The constable takes the paper, passes it through the bars.

Not paper—a photograph. Iason, exactly as she remembers him, leaning against one of the Manatos olive trees, smiling into the camera's unbiased eye.

"I did not think you had one," his mother says, a light mist in her voice. "Every woman should have a photo of a husband she loved."

"I still love him," she whispers.

"So do I, Fotini. So do I."

What a boy he was—a beautiful boy. He would have become a magnificent man. If only ...

It is agonizing, the decision to let yourself love another when your old love is lost. But then you realize there never was a decision; love comes, whether you grant it passage or not. It is a hurricane that cares nothing for your storm doors. There was Iason, and now Stelios is on his way into her heart. And yet, it takes nothing away from that first love.

Love does not shrink hearts.

She swallows, clearing away the tears. "I suppose you want me to speak with Lucy first?"

A knuckle strikes the metal door, a brief warning that it's about to swing open. When it does, Detective Lemonis is there, wearing an unhappy expression. This is what a man looks like when the world is twisting his arm.

"No, Fotini," Iason's mother says. "We must trust each other to do the right thing. To get you must give in this world. I am giving and I expect to get. But not today."

❧ 117 ❧

Fotini

FOTINI'S RETURN TO TRIKERI IS A QUIET ONE. DETECTIVE Lemonis does not speak. Who can blame him? He was bested by an old woman with deep pockets and higher ups with hungry wallets.

But he is not so sour that he cannot offer an old woman his hand when they arrive at the dock.

"Understand that I did not kill my brother."

"I believe you," he says, focused on some distant point beyond her shoulder. "But I wanted to prove it. And I would have, in time."

Time. That ancient bitch. "I am a patient woman, but the other *Kyria* Manatou has less time than either of us. So she changed the rules."

He nods, but he doesn't look at her. "When did Greece become a whore?"

414

"Every nation is someone's whore. Land is doomed to that fate the moment man steps on its face."

———

SO MANY TEARS.

"Stelios, I did not know you could cry."

"I cannot help it. I love a happy ending."

"This is not an ending."

"Of course it is. There must be an ending before there is a beginning. Tomorrow we will wake up and discover we have opened a new book."

"Where is Lucy?"

He points at the ceiling. "She is opening her own book. It is one of those new romances, where there is sex very early."

"Akili?"

"Akili."

"Good," she says. "This will make things easier."

A questioning look on his handsome face.

"My freedom is a gift, yes, but it has strings." She tells him of her former mother-in-law's visit, of her conditions. Of her trust.

When she's done, he says, "It could be worse."

"It could be worse," she agrees.

❧ 118 ❧

Lucy

LUCY WRITES HER NAME ON AKILI'S CHEST IN WIDE, decorative loops. Her ink is invisible but indelible.

No pillow talk for these two.

No pillows, either. They're all the way over there.

GRANDMA'S LAUGH CREEPS INTO HER LAZY, post-pleasure doze.

She stiffens.

So does Akili. Well, part of him.

Thanks, imaginary Grandma. Way to kill the buzz.

But it's not imaginary, is it? Because she's hearing her again, from somewhere beneath the bed.

In the *taverna*.

She jumps up. "Holy shit!"

It's a mad scramble for clothes. Rushing, she divvies them up into two separate piles, then hurls Akili's at him.

"Grandma." She stabs her finger at the floor. "She's here."

It's English, but Akili seems to get it. For a moment she stops, watches him dress. It's almost a crime to cover all that up. That broad, tan chest, that muscular V that points the way south, the scars she can't keep her hands off.

Then she's into her clothes and down the stairs at super-sonic speed.

"Grandma! You're here!"

Wait a minute.

Eyes narrowed to suspicious slits, hands on hips, she focuses on Stelios. "Did you break her out of jail?"

"Me?" He points at his chest. "No. But I wanted to."

"Then how?"

Grandma wraps her up in those familiar arms. "I made a deal with a minor demon."

"Grandma, what did you do?"

Her grandmother switches to Greek, that's how she knows Akili has followed her down the stairs.

Is she blushing? Her cheeks are hot so she must be. She's an adult, but it's still weird when Grandma knows she's been bonking.

There's a pause in the conversation as Grandma dishes out another hug, this one for Akili. Then she returns to Lucy.

"Lucy." She takes a deep breath, and the bottom falls out of Lucy's world. "We need to talk."

✾ 119 ✾

Fotini

THAT BOTTOM DOESN'T FALL FAR.

"Really? That's it?"

"Lucy, it's too much to ask of you."

They're sitting on the beach she's grown to love, on the island that could easily become home. Lucy's hand is in hers; even that short time in jail made her lonely for human contact.

"It's not so much. I planned to stay if you were going to —" Her voice hitches. "—to prison. This is the same plan, with you not in prison. That makes it totally bearable."

"Are you sure?"

"No," she says brightly. "Nothing is ever sure, is it? But I'm close to sure, and that's good enough."

SIX MONTHS LATER ...

✺ 120 ✺

Lucy

KATERINA IS A HARD TASKMASTER. EVERY DAY SHE HUNTS Lucy down, pushes her to study her Greek. And in return Lucy sharpens her cousin's English-speaking edge. Katerina is learning real English, not the stuff in textbooks. Melissa Tyler helps. The girl is a walking, talking, slang machine. She knows the language the way only a teenager can.

Hard work learning another language when you've left childhood behind in a cloud of glittery dust, but it can be done. Lucy's not that old a dog that she can't learn new tricks.

And she *is* learning new tricks.

Ask Akili.

✸ 121 ✸

Akili

KIKI ANDREOU IS ALSO A HARD TASKMASTER. NOBODY IN history has ever assigned more homework. But he's a good student, studies hard. Doesn't want to earn the wrath of Kiki, does he?

It's not often you get a second shot at friendship.

Or a first shot at love.

And he does love Lucy. He's working on the right words to keep her in his life, in his house.

Not his mother's house—but his.

A new house without ghosts.

Sometimes he still sees Stavros, but he keeps his distance. His old friend's ghost prefers to watch his wife work.

"I have to watch over her," Stavros says one day. "She's the only one keeping me here now. The rest of you have moved on."

122

Stelios - The Final Words

HE LOVED HIS FIRST WIFE, BUT NOT WITH THE PASSION HE has for Fotini. They are older, but that does not make their love more pale. If anything, it is richer, deeper, a love shared by two people who knows exactly who they are.

But of that old love he has memories—good and bad.

And he has Akili.

The boy is not his son, but he was *hers*. Sometimes he looks at Akili and he remembers the past, bitter and sweet.

What he did, he did for two loves, the old and the new.

ALSO BY ALEX A. KING

One and Only Sunday (Women of Greece #2)

Freedom the Impossible (Women of Greece #3)

Light is the Shadow (Women of Greece #4)

No Peace in Crazy (Women of Greece #5)

Summer of the Red Hotel (Women of Greece #6)

Women of Greece Box Set - 2-4

Paint: A Short Love Story

Disorganized Crime (Kat Makris #1)

Trueish Crime (Kat Makris #2)

Doing Crime (Kat Makris #3)

In Crime (Kat Makris #4)

Outta Crime (Kat Makris #5)

Reliquary (Reliquary, #1)

Lambs (as Alex King)

85528787R00257

Made in the USA
Middletown, DE
25 August 2018